"Have these children names?"

Willa's reversion to the formal, polite tone called Matthew back to his purpose in coming. "Yes, of course. This is Joshua—he's six years old and in first grade." He smiled down at his nephew. "And this is Sally." His niece pressed back against his legs. He placed his hands on her small, narrow shoulders and gave a reassuring squeeze. "She's five years old, and feeling a little overwhelmed at the moment."

The hem of the teacher's gown whispered over the wide plank floor as she came to stand in front of them. She looked down and gave the children a warm, welcoming smile he wished were aimed at him. "Hello, Joshua and Sally. I'm your teacher, Miss Wright. Welcome to Oak Street School."

Miss Wright. She was indeed. Matthew frowned and sucked in a breath, irritated by such whimsy. Miss Wright, with her narrow, aristocratic nose and small, square chin, was wreaking havoc with his normally sensible behavior. He was acting like a smitten schoolboy.

Books by Dorothy Clark

Love Inspired Historical

Family of the Heart
The Law and Miss Mary
Prairie Courtship
Gold Rush Baby
Frontier Father
*Wooing the Schoolmarm

Love Inspired

Hosea's Bride
Lessons from the Heart

Steeple Hill Single Title

Beauty for Ashes
Joy for Mourning

*Pinewood Weddings

DOROTHY CLARK

Critically acclaimed, award-winning author Dorothy Clark lives in rural New York, in a home she designed and helped her husband build (she swings a mean hammer!) with the able assistance of their three children. When she is not writing, she and her husband enjoy traveling throughout the United States doing research and gaining inspiration for future books. Dorothy believes in God, love, family and happy endings, which explains why she feels so at home writing stories for Love Inspired Books. Dorothy enjoys hearing from her readers and may be contacted at dorothyjclark@hotmail.com.

DOROTHY CLARK

Wooing the Schoolmarm

Love Inspired

If you purchased this book without a cover you should be aware that this book is stolen property. It was reported as "unsold and destroyed" to the publisher, and neither the author nor the publisher has received any payment for this "stripped book."

Recycling programs for this product may not exist in your area.

™ LOVE INSPIRED BOOKS

ISBN-13: 978-0-373-82923-1

WOOING THE SCHOOLMARM

Copyright © 2012 by Dorothy Clark

All rights reserved. Except for use in any review, the reproduction or utilization of this work in whole or in part in any form by any electronic, mechanical or other means, now known or hereafter invented, including xerography, photocopying and recording, or in any information storage or retrieval system, is forbidden without the written permission of the editorial office, Love Inspired Books, 233 Broadway, New York, NY 10279 U.S.A.

This is a work of fiction. Names, characters, places and incidents are either the product of the author's imagination or are used fictitiously, and any resemblance to actual persons, living or dead, business establishments, events or locales is entirely coincidental.

This edition published by arrangement with Love Inspired Books.

® and TM are trademarks of Love Inspired Books, used under license. Trademarks indicated with ® are registered in the United States Patent and Trademark Office, the Canadian Trade Marks Office and in other countries.

www.LoveInspiredBooks.com

Printed in U.S.A.

The Lord is nigh unto them that are of a broken heart; and saveth such as be of a contrite spirit.
—*Psalms* 34:18

Books with historical settings require a great deal of time-consuming research. This book is dedicated with deep appreciation to Rhonda Shaner Pollock of the Portville Historical & Preservation Society for her gracious and unfailing help in uncovering details of a schoolmarm's daily life in a rural village in 1840. Thank you, Rhonda.

"Commit thy works unto the Lord, and thy thoughts shall be established."

Your Word is truth. Thank You, Jesus. To You be the glory.

Chapter One

Pinewood Village, 1840

"Here we are. This is the schoolhouse." Matthew Calvert looked from the small, white, frame building to his deceased brother's children. Joshua had on his "brave" face, which meant he was really afraid, and Sally looked about to cry. *Please, Lord, don't let her cry. You know my heart turns to mush when she tears up.* "Everything is going to be fine. You'll make nice friends and have a good time learning new things."

He placed his hands on the children's backs and urged them up the steps to the small porch before they could resume their pleading to stay at home with him this first day in the new town. Their small bodies tensed, moved with reluctance.

He leaned forward and glanced in the open door. A slender woman was writing on a large slate at the far end of the room. The sunlight coming in a side window played upon the thick roll of chestnut-colored hair that coiled from one small ear across the nape of her neck to the other, and warmed the pale skin of a narrow wrist that was exposed by the movement of her sleeve cuff as she printed out a list of words. She looked neat and efficient. *Please, God, let her also be kindhearted.* He nudged his niece and nephew forward and stepped inside. "Excuse me."

The teacher turned. Her gaze met his over the top of the double rows of bench desks and his heart jolted. He stared into blue-green eyes rimmed with long, black lashes, rendered speechless by an attraction so immediate, so strong, every sensible thought in his head disappeared.

The teacher's gaze dropped to the children, then rose back to meet his. "Good morning, Reverend Calvert. Welcome to Pinewood."

The formal tone of the teacher's voice brought him to his senses. He broke off his stare and cleared his throat. "Thank you. I—" He focused his attention, gave her a questioning look. "How did you know who I am?"

Her mouth curved into a smile that made his pulse trip all over itself. She placed the book she held on her desk. "You are from the city, Reverend Calvert. You will soon learn in a village as small as Pinewood that one knows all the residents and everything that happens." She brushed her fingertips together and minuscule bits of chalk dust danced in the stream of sunlight. "I dare say I knew within ten minutes of the time you descended from your carriage and carried your bags into the parsonage that you had arrived." She gave him a wry look. "But, I confess, I did not know you were coming here this morning."

"I see." He lifted the left side of his mouth in the

crooked grin his mother had called his mischief escape. "So I have managed a 'coup' of sorts by bringing the children to school?"

She stared at him a moment, then looked away. "So it would seem. Have these children names?"

Her reversion to the formal, polite tone called him back to his purpose in coming. "Yes, of course. This is Joshua—he's six years old." He smiled down at his nephew. "And this is Sally." His niece pressed back against his legs. He placed his hands on her small, narrow shoulders and gave a reassuring squeeze. "She's five years old, and feeling a little overwhelmed at the moment."

The hem of the teacher's gown whispered over the wide plank floor as she came to stand in front of them. She looked down and gave the children a warm, welcoming smile he wished were aimed at him. "Hello, Joshua and Sally. I'm your teacher, Miss Wright. Welcome to Oak Street School."

Miss Wright. She was indeed. Matthew frowned at his burst of whimsy. Miss Wright, with her narrow, aristocratic nose and small square chin, was wreaking havoc with his normally sensible behavior. He was acting like a smitten schoolboy.

Children's voices floated in the door. Their light, quick footfalls sounded on the steps. The voices quieted as five children entered and bunched at the doorway to stare at them.

"Come in and take your seats, children. We have a lovely surprise this morning. You are going to have some new classmates." The teacher gave a graceful little gesture and the clustered children separated, casting surreptitious glances their way as they moved toward the bench desks.

Matthew drew in a breath and hid the pang of sympathy he felt for Joshua and Sally. "I'd best be going, Miss Wright." She looked up at him and that same odd jolt in his heart happened. He hurried on. "The children have slates and chalk. And also some bread and butter for dinner. I wasn't sure—"

She smiled. "That is fine."

His pulse thudded. He jerked his gaze from Miss Wright's captivating eyes and looked down at Joshua and Sally. "Be good, now—do as Miss Wright says. Joshua, you take Sally's hand and help her across the street when you come home. I'll be waiting for you." He tore his gaze from Sally's small, trembling mouth and, circling around three more children filing into the schoolroom, escaped out the open door. The children needed to adjust to their new situation. And so did he. What had happened to him in there?

"Miss Wright!"

Willa halted as Danny Brody skidded to a stop in front of her. "Miss Hall wants you." He pointed behind her, then raced off.

Willa turned, saw Ellen promenading toward her and fought to hold back a frown. She loved her lifelong friend, but sometimes the pretentious ways she had developed irritated her. Still, one couldn't blame Ellen for parading about. She was the prettiest girl in town now that Callie Conner had moved away—and one of the biggest gossips. If this was about Thomas again—

"Gracious, Willa, why were you walking at such

an unseemly pace? If Danny weren't handy I never would have caught you."

"I have to fix supper, then help Mother with the ironing." She shifted the paper-wrapped package of meat she held to her other hand for emphasis. "Was there something you wanted, Ellen?"

Excitement glinted in her friend's big, blue eyes. "I wanted to tell you the latest news. Father told me that the new pastor is a *young* man. And nice-looking."

"He is." Willa gave an inward sigh and relaxed. She should have guessed Ellen had stopped her to talk about Reverend Calvert. The new church and pastor were all anyone in the village talked about these days. *Thank goodness.* She disliked discussing anything pertaining to God, but at least the church topic had replaced the gossip about her abruptly cancelled wedding.

"You've *seen* him?" Ellen leaned close, gripped her arm. "What does he look like? I didn't dare ask Father for details."

She thought back to that morning. "Well, Reverend Calvert is quite tall…with blond hair and brown eyes." She cast back for her impression of the pastor and tempered her words so Ellen would not guess she had felt a momentary attraction to the man. *That* would elicit a hundred questions from her friend. "He has a strong appearance, with a square jaw. But his smile is charming." *And his lopsided grin disarming.* She ignored the image of that grin that snapped into her head and forged on. "As is his son's. His daughter's smile is more shy in nature."

Ellen jerked back. "He has *children?*"

"Yes. Joshua and Sally. He brought them to school this morning." She tilted her head to one side and grinned up at her friend. "How did that important detail escape you?"

"I've been helping Mother with my new gown all day." Ellen's lovely face darkened. "Father didn't mention that the reverend was *married.*"

"Oh." Willa gaped at her perturbed friend. "*Ellen Hall!* Surely you weren't thinking of— Why, you haven't even seen the man!"

"Well, gracious, a girl can hope, Willa. When I heard the pastor was young and handsome I thought, perhaps at last there was a man of distinction I could marry in this *place.* I should have known it was hopeless." Ellen sighed with a little shrug. "I must go home. Mother is waiting to hem my new dress for Sunday. I'll have to tell her there's no hurry now. I certainly don't care to impress a bunch of *loggers.* Bye, Willa."

"Bye, Ellen." Willa shook her head and cut across Main Street away from the block of huddled stores before anyone else could stop her to chat. Imagine Ellen being so eager to marry a "man of distinction" she would make plans toward that end before she even *saw* Pastor Calvert.

She frowned, hurried across the Stony Creek bridge and turned onto the beaten path along Brook Street. Perhaps she should have told Ellen the truth about Thomas and why their wedding had been canceled. Perhaps she should have cautioned her about trusting a man. *Any* man. Not that it mattered. Her friend was in no danger from the attractive Reverend Calvert, and neither was she. The man was married. And that was perfect as far as she was concerned. She'd had enough of handsome men with charming smiles.

Willa tossed the soapy dishwater out the lean-to door then eyed the neat piles of clean, folded clothing that covered the long table against the wall. The sight of the fruit of her mother's dawn-to-dusk labor over hot laundry tubs and a hot iron kindled the old resentment. How could her father have simply walked away knowing his wife and child would no longer be allowed to live in the cabin the company provided for its loggers? He'd known they had no other place to go. If the company owner hadn't accepted her mother's offer to do laundry for the unmarried loggers in exchange for staying in the cabin...

Willa set her jaw, rinsed the dishpan at the pump, then walked back into the kitchen. She had struggled to find an answer for her father's behavior since she was seven years old, and now she had—thanks to Thomas. Perhaps one day she would be grateful to him for teaching her that men were selfish and faithless and their words of love were not to be believed. But it had been only three months since he'd tossed her aside to go west and her hurt and anger left little room for gratitude.

She plunked the dishpan down onto the wide boards of the sink cupboard, yanked off her apron and jammed it on its hook. Thomas's desertion didn't bear thinking on, but she couldn't seem to stop. At least the gossip had died—thanks to the new pastor's arrival. She took a breath to calm herself and stepped into the living room.

"Why did you do the ironing, Mama? I told you I would do it tonight. You work too hard."

Her mother glanced up from the shirt she was mending and gave her a tired smile. "You've got your job, and I've got mine, Willa. I'll do the ironing. But it would be good if you're of a mind to help me with the mending. It's hard for me to keep up with it. Especially the socks."

She nodded, crossed the rag rug and seated herself opposite her mother at the small table beneath the window. "I have two new students—Joshua and Sally Calvert. The new pastor brought them to school today."

"I heard he had young children. But I haven't heard about his wife." Her mother adjusted the sides of the tear in the shirt and took another neat stitch. "Is she the friendly sort or city standoffish?"

"Mrs. Calvert wasn't with them." Willa pulled the basket of darning supplies close and lifted a sock off the pile. "The pastor is friendly. Of course, given his profession, he would be. But the children are very quiet." She eyed the sock's heel and sighed. It was a large hole. "Mr. Dibble was outside the livery hitching horses to a wagon when I passed on my way home. He always asks after you, Mama." She threaded a needle, then slipped the darning egg inside the sock. "He asked to be remembered to you."

"I don't care to be talking about David Dibble or any other man, Willa."

She nodded, frowned at the bitterness in her mother's voice. Not that she blamed her after the way her father had betrayed them by walking off to make a new life for himself. "I know how you feel, Mama. Every word Thomas spoke to me of love and marriage was a lie. But I will not let his deserting me three days before we were to be wed make me bitter."

She leaned closer to the evening light coming in the window, wove the needle through the sock fabric and stretched the darning floss across the hole, then repeated the maneuver in the other direction. "I learned my lesson well, Mama. I will never trust another man. Thomas's perfidy robbed me of any desire to fall in love or marry. But I refuse to let him rob me of anything more." Her voice broke. She blinked away the tears welling into her eyes and glared down at the sock in her hand. "I shall have a good, useful life teaching children. And I will be happy."

Silence followed her proclamation.

She glanced across the table from beneath her lowered lashes. Her mother was looking at her, a mixture of sadness and anger in her eyes, her hands idle in her lap. "You didn't deserve that sort of treatment, Willa. Thomas Hunter is a selfish man, and you're well rid of him."

She raised her head. "Like you were well rid of Papa?"

"That was different. We were married and had a child." Her mother cleared her throat, reached across the table and covered her hand. "I tried my best to make your father stay, Willa. I didn't want you hurt."

There was a mountain of love behind the quiet, strained words. She stared down at her mother's dry, work-roughened hand. How many times had its touch comforted her, taken away her childish hurts? But Thomas's treachery had pierced too deep. The wound he'd given her would remain. She took a breath and forced a smile. "Papa left thirteen years ago, Mama. The hurt is gone. All that's left is an empty spot in my heart. But it's only been three months since Thomas cast me aside. That part of my heart still hurts." She drew another deep breath and made another turn with the darning floss. "You were right about Thomas not being trustworthy, Mama. I should have listened to you."

"And I should have remembered ears do not hear when a heart is full." There was a fierceness in her mother's voice she'd never before heard. "Now, let's put this behind us and not speak of Thomas again. Time will heal the wound." Her mother drew her hand back, tied off her sewing thread, snipped it, set aside the finished shirt and picked up another off the mending pile. She laid it in her lap and looked off into the distance. "I'm so *thankful* you hadn't married Thomas and aren't doomed to spend your life alone, not knowing if you're married or a widow. One day you will find a man who truly loves you and you will be free to love him."

Willa jerked her head up and stared at her mother, stunned by her words, suddenly understanding her bitterness, her secluded lifestyle. She'd always thought of her father's leaving as a single event, as the moment he had said goodbye and walked out the door, and her wound from his leaving had scarred over with the passing years. But her mother lived with the consequences of her father's selfish act every day. Her father had stolen her mother's life.

She caught her breath, looked down and wove the needle over and under the threads she'd stretched across the hole in the sock, thankfulness rising to weave through the hurt of Thomas's desertion. At least her life was still her own. And it would remain so. She would let no man steal it from her. No man! Not ever.

Matthew gathered his courage and peeked in the bedroom door. If Sally spotted him, the crying and begging to sleep in Joshua's room would start again. He considered himself as brave and stalwart as the next man, but Sally's tears undid him.

Moonlight streamed in the windows, slanted across the bed. He huffed out a breath of relief. She was asleep, one small hand tucked beneath her chin, her long, blond curls splayed across her pillow. He stared at the spot of white fabric visible where the edge of the covers met her hand and a pang struck his heart. He didn't have to go closer to see what it was. He knew. She was clutching her mother's glove.

Lord, I don't know what to do. Will allowing Sally to have Judith's glove lessen her grief? Or does it prolong it? Should I take the glove away? I need wisdom, Lord. I need help!

He walked to the stairs and started down. He loved Joshua and Sally and willingly accepted their guardianship, but being thrust into the role of parent to two young, grieving children was daunting. He was faced with tasks and decisions he was ill-prepared to handle. That one child was a little girl made it even more difficult. And he had his own grief to contend with.

He shot a glance toward the ceiling of the small entrance hall. "I miss you, Robert. And I'm doing the best I can. But it would be a lot easier if you'd had two sons." The thought of Sally's little arms around his neck, of her small hand thrust so trustingly into his made his heart ache. "Not that I would want it different, big brother. I'll figure it out. But it would certainly help with the girl things if I had a wife."

He frowned and walked into his study to arrange his possessions that had come by freight wagon that afternoon. Why couldn't he find a woman to love and marry? He was tired of this emptiness, this yearning for someone to share his life with that he'd been carrying around the last few years. He wanted a wife and children. Having Joshua and Sally these last few weeks had only increased that desire.

He lifted a box of books to his desk, pulled out his pocketknife and cut the cord that bound it. Robert had known Judith was the one for him as soon as he met her. But he'd never felt that immediate draw to a woman, the certainty that she was the one. He'd been making it a matter of prayer for the last year or so. But God hadn't seen fit to answer those prayers. Unless…

He stared down at the book he'd pulled from the box, a vision of a lovely face with beautiful blue-green eyes framed by soft waves of chestnut-colored hair dancing against the leather cover. His pulse quickened. Was what had happened to him in the schoolhouse God's answer to his prayers? There was no denying his immediate attraction to Miss Wright. An attraction so strong that he'd lost his normal good sense and eyed her like a besotted schoolboy. That had never happened to him before. But was it the beginning of love? Or only an aberration caused by his loneliness and grief?

He slid the book onto the top shelf of the bookcase behind his desk and reached into the box for another. It had been a humbling moment when the church council had asked him to leave the pulpit of his well-established church in Albany for two years to come and establish a foundation for the church here in Pinewood. But he'd been inclined to turn them down because of his loneliness. If he couldn't find a woman to love and marry among his large congregation and abundant friends in the city, what chance had he to find one in a small, rural village nestled among the foothills of the Allegheny Mountains in western New York?

He scowled, put the book on the shelf and picked up another. Robert's death had made up his mind. He had accepted the offer, hoping that a change of scene might help the children over their grief. Two years out of his life was a price he was willing to pay for the children's healing. That was his plan.

He reached into the box for the last book, then paused. What if God had placed that yielding in his heart because *He* had a plan? One that helped the children, but also included the answer to his prayers? He blew out a breath, put the last book on the shelf and tossed the empty box to the floor. And what if he were simply letting his imagination run away with him? At least he knew the answer to that question. "Thy will be done, Lord. Thy will be done."

He picked up the box with his desk supplies, cut the cord and started putting things in the drawers.

Chapter Two

Willa spotted their gray-haired neighbor sweeping her walk next door and sighed. Mrs. Braynard was as plump as her mother was lean, and as cheerful as her mother was bitter. She was also kind and concerned and…nosy. She closed the door and walked down their short, plank walk to the leaf-strewn beaten path beside the street. "Good morning, Mrs. Braynard. How is Daniel today?"

"He's doing better. He was able to move his arm a little when I was getting him up and around. The Lord bless you for caring." Her neighbor cleared the leaves and dirt from the end of her walk, paused and looked at her over the broom handle. "I heard the new pastor brought his children to your school. His wife a pleasant woman, is she?"

Willa clenched her fingers on the handle of the small basket holding her lunch. She hated gossip. She'd been on the receiving end of too much of it. But Mrs. Braynard meant no harm. She was simply overcurious. Nonetheless, whatever she said would be all over town within an hour. She took a breath to hold her smile in place. "I haven't met Mrs. Calvert. The pastor was alone when he brought the children. I'm looking forward to meeting her at the welcome dinner after church this Sunday." She turned away, hoping…

"Are you getting on all right, Willa? I mean—"

"I know what you mean, Mrs. Braynard." The sympathy in her neighbor's voice grated on her nerves. She hated being the object of people's pity—even if it was well-meant. She smiled and gave the same answer she'd been giving since Thomas had abruptly left town. "I'm fine. Now, I'm afraid I must hurry off to school. Tell Daniel I'm pleased to hear he is mending."

"I'll tell him. And I'll keep praying for you, Willa."

As if prayer would help. She pressed her lips together, lifted her hand in farewell and hurried down the path to the corner, a choked-back reply driving her steps. Mrs. Braynard, of all people, should know God had no interest in her or her plight. The woman had been praying for her mother and her ever since the day her father had said goodbye and walked out on them, and not one thing had changed. Not one. Except that now Thomas had deserted her, as well. So much for prayer!

She wheeled right onto Main Street and onto the bridge over Stony Creek, the heels of her shoes announcing her irritation by their quick, staccato beats on the wide, thick planks. She avoided a wagon pulling into the Dibble Smithy, passed the harness shop and livery and lowered her gaze to avoid eye contact with anyone heading across the street to the row of shops that formed the village center. She was in no mood for any more friendly, but prying, questions.

She crossed Church Street, then reined in her pace and her thoughts. Her students did not deserve a sour-faced teacher. She took a long breath and lifted her gaze. *Oh, no!* Her steps faltered, came to a halt. A clergyman was the last person she wanted to see.

On the walkway ahead, Reverent Calvert was squatted on his heels, his hands clasping Sally's upper arms, while he talked to her. It seemed Sally was in disagreement with him if her stiff stance and bowed head was any indication. Joshua stood off to one side, the intent expression on his face a mirror of the pastor's. The boy certainly looked like his father. He also looked unhappy.

Something was wrong. Had it to do with school? Her self-involvement dissolved in a spate of concern. Joshua must have felt her attention for he raised his gaze and caught her looking at them. His lips moved. The pastor glanced in her direction, then surged to his feet. She put on a polite smile and moved forward. "Good morning, Reverend Calvert. I see Joshua and Sally are ready for school."

A look of chagrin flitted across the pastor's face. "We were discussing that."

So there *was* a problem. Joshua and Sally did not want to go to school. She glanced down at the little girl and her heart melted at the sight of her teary-eyed unhappiness. "Well, I hope you are through with your discussion and Joshua and Sally may come with me. I am running a bit late this morning and I…could use their help." Something flickered in the pastor's eyes. Puzzlement? Doubt? It was too quickly gone for her to judge.

"I'm certain they will be happy to help you, Miss Wright. What is it you want them to do?"

What indeed? The schoolroom had been set to rights last night before she left for home. She looked at the tears now flowing down Sally's cheeks and scrambled for an idea. "Well…I am going to begin a story about a cat today. But the cat…has no name."

Sally lifted her head and looked up at her. Joshua stepped closer. Ah, a spark of interest.

"I see. And how does that require the children's help?"

She glanced up at the pastor. A look of understanding flashed between them. So he had guessed she was making this up and was trying to help her. Now what? How could she involve Joshua and Sally? "Well…each student will have a chance to suggest a name for the cat—" she felt her way, forming the idea as she spoke.

"Ah, a contest." The proclamation bore the hint of a suggestion.

A contest. An excellent idea. "Yes. The class will choose which name they like best." She shot the pastor a grateful look. He inclined his head slightly and she glanced down. Sally had inched closer, and there was a definite glint in Joshua's eyes. So the boy liked to compete. "And the student who suggests the chosen name will…win a prize." What prize? She stopped, completely out of inspiration. That still did not require the children's help.

"And you need Joshua and Sally to help you with the prize?" Reverend Calvert's deep voice was soft, encouraging.

"Yes…" Now what? She took a breath and shoved

aside her dilemma. She would think of something by the time they reached the schoolhouse. She stared at the tree beside the reverend. Ah! A smile curved her lips, widened as the idea took hold. "The prize will be a basket of hickory nuts from the tree behind the school. And I need someone to gather the nuts for me." She shot the reverend a triumphant look, then glanced from Joshua to Sally. "Will you collect the nuts for me?"

The little girl looked at her brother, followed his lead and nodded.

"It sounds like an interesting day for the children, Miss Wright."

She glanced up. The reverend smiled and mouthed "Thank you." Her stomach fluttered. He really did have a charming smile. She gave him a polite nod and held her free hand out to Sally. "Come along, then. We must hurry so you children can gather the nuts before the other children come. The prize must be a *secret*." She halted, tipped her head to the side and gave them a solemn look. "You *can* keep a secret?"

They nodded again, their brown eyes serious, their blond curls bright in the sunlight.

"Lovely!" She smiled and moved forward, Sally's small hand in hers, Joshua on her other side, and the Reverend Calvert's gaze fastened on them. The awareness of it tingled between her shoulder blades until they turned the corner onto Oak Street. A frown wrinkled her brow. Twice now she had seen the pastor with his children. Where was their mother?

"It was a pleasure meeting you, gentlemen." Matthew shook hands with the church elders and watched them file out through the small storage room at the back of the church. They seemed to be men of strong faith, eager to do all they could to make the church flourish. He was looking forward to working with them.

He scanned the interior of the small church, admired the craftsmanship in the paneled pew boxes and the white plastered walls. He moved to the pulpit, the strike of his bootheels against the wood floor echoing in the silence. The wood was satin-smooth beneath his hands. He brushed his fingers across the leather cover of the Bible that rested there, closed his eyes and quieted his thoughts. A sense of waiting, of expectation hovered in the stillness.

"Almighty God, be with me, I pray. Lead and guide me to green pastures by the paths of Your choosing that I might feed Your flock according to Thy will. Amen."

He opened his eyes and pictured the church full of people. Would Miss Wright be one of them? He frowned and stepped out from behind the pulpit. He was becoming too concerned with Miss Wright; it was time to get acquainted with the village.

He stretched out his arms and touched the end of each pew as he walked down the center aisle, then crossed the small vestibule and stepped out onto the wide stoop. Warmth from the October sun chased the chill of the closed building from him. Did someone come early on Sunday morning to open the doors and let in the warmth?

Across the street stood an impressive, three-story building with the name Sheffield House carved into a sign attached to the fascia board of the porch roof. Passengers were alighting from a long, roofed wagon at the edge of the road that bore the legend Totten's Trolley.

He exchanged a friendly nod with the driver, then jogged diagonally across the street and trotted up three steps to a wide, wooden walkway that ran in front of a block of stores standing shoulder to shoulder, like an army at attention.

He doffed his hat to a woman coming out of a millinery store, skirted around two men debating the virtues of a pair of boots in a shoemaker's window next to Barley's Grocery and entered the Cargrave Mercantile.

Smells mingled on the air and tantalized his nose, leather, coffee and molasses prominent among them. He stepped out of the doorway and blinked his eyes to adjust to the dim indoors. The hum of conversation stopped, resumed in lower tones. He glanced left, skimmed his gaze over the long wood counter adorned with various wood and tin boxes, a coffee mill and at the far end a scale and cashbox.

He gave a polite nod in answer to the frankly curious gazes of the proprietor and the customers, then swept his gaze across the wood stove and the displays of tools along the back wall. On the right side of the store was the dry goods section and the object of his search. A glass-fronted nest of pigeonhole mailboxes constituted the post office. He stepped to the narrow, waist-high opening in the center of the boxes. A stout, gray-haired man, suspenders forming an X across the back of his white shirt, sat on a stool sorting through a pile of mail on a high table with a safe beneath it.

"Excuse me—"

The man turned, squinted at him through a pair of wire-rimmed glasses perched on the end of his nose, then slid off his stool and came to stand in front of the small shelf on the other side of the window. "What can I do for you, stranger?"

Matthew smiled. "I've come to introduce myself, and see about getting a mailbox. I'm Matthew Calvert, pastor of Pinewood Church." The conversations in the store stopped. There was a soft rustling sound as people turned to look at him.

The postmaster nodded. "Heard you'd arrived. Figured you'd be along. I'm pleased to make your acquaintance, Pastor Calvert."

"And I, yours, Mr...."

"Hubble. Zarius Hubble." The man stretched out his hand and tapped the glass of one of the small cubicles. "This is the church mailbox. Lest you have an objection, I'll put your mail in here. Save you having to rent a box."

"Thank you, Mr. Hubble. That will be fine."

The postmaster nodded, then fixed a stern gaze on him. "I can't do that for others with you who will be getting mail, mind you. Your missus or such will need their own box."

"That won't be necessary." Matthew turned and almost collided with a small group of people standing behind him. The short, thin man closest to him held out his hand.

"I'm Allan Cargrave. I own this establishment,

along with my brother Henry. You met him this morning. I've been looking forward to your coming, Pastor Calvert. We all have."

Matthew took his hand in a firm clasp. "Then our goal has been the same, Mr. Cargrave. I'm pleased to meet you." He smiled and turned to the others.

Willa glanced at her lunch basket, now half-full of hickory nuts, going out the door in Trudy Hoffman's hand and smiled. The impromptu contest had proved successful in a way she had not expected. Trudy and Sally Calvert had both suggested Puffy as a name for the cat in the story and friendship had budded between the girls when the name was chosen as the favorite by the class. The friendship was firmed when Sally told Trudy she could have the basket as they shared the prize.

Her smile faded. She was quite certain there was something more than shyness bothering Sally. She'd seen tears glistening in the little girl's eyes that afternoon. She walked to the door to watch Joshua and Sally cross the town park to the parsonage. Another smile formed. If the squirrels didn't get them, the park would soon be boasting a trail of hickory nut trees started by Sally's half of the prize falling from Joshua's pockets.

She pulled the door closed and watched the children. Why weren't they running and laughing on their way home? She studied their slow steps, the slump of their small shoulders. Something was amiss. They looked…sad. Perhaps they missed their friends in Albany. It was hard for children to leave a familiar home and move to a strange town where they knew no one. She would make certain the village children included Joshua and Sally in their games at the welcome dinner Sunday. And she would speak with Mrs. Calvert about the children. Perhaps there was something more she could do to help them adjust to their new life in Pinewood. Meanwhile, she had a new lunch basket to buy. She hurried down the stairs and headed for the mercantile.

Matthew blotted his notes, closed his Bible and pushed back from his desk. Moonlight drew a lacy shadow of the denuded branches of the maple in the side yard on the ground, silvered the fallen leaves beneath it. An owl hooted. His lips slanted into a grin. Miss Wright was correct. Pinewood was very different from Albany.

His pulse sped at the memory of her walking toward them, neat and trim in her dark red gown with a soft smile warming her lovely face. She had, again, stolen his breath when their gazes met. And the way she had solved Sally's rebellion against going to school today…

A chuckle rumbled deep in his chest. She had made up that business about a cat with no name and the contest with a prize right there on the spot.

It was obvious Miss Wright loved children. How did she feel about God?

He clenched his hands and set his jaw, shaken by a sudden awareness of the expectation in his heart of seeing her sitting in the congregation Sunday morning.

Chapter Three

"How could you be so wrong about those children? They are his *wards*."

Willa placed her platter of meat tarts on the plank table and looked up at Ellen. "Pastor Calvert brought them to school, they look like him and their last name is the same. I assumed he was their father, not their uncle. It was an understandable mistake." Tears stung her eyes. Those poor children. To lose both their mother and father at such a young age. No wonder they looked sad.

"Perhaps, but— Oh, *look* at this old gown." Ellen batted at the ruffles on her bodice. "If I had known Pastor Calvert was a bachelor I would have had Mother hem my new gown. She says the color makes my eyes look larger and bluer."

Willa squared her shoulders and gave Ellen a look permitted by their years of friendship. Her friend hadn't given a thought to the children—other than to be thankful the pastor was not their father. "You look beautiful in that gown, and you know it, Ellen. Now stop pouting. It's wasted on me. I've watched you looking in the mirror to practice protruding your lower lip, remember?"

The offending lip was pulled back into its normal position. "Very well. I suppose I understand your error. And I forgive you. But all the same, I *am* distressed. Had I known the truth of Matthew Calvert's marital state, I could have thought of a plan to catch his attention. Look!"

The hissed words tickled her ear. She glanced in the direction Ellen indicated. Matthew Calvert was coming across the church grounds toward the tables, his progress hindered by every young, unmarried lady in his congregation *and* their mothers. "So that's where all the women are. I wondered. Usually they are hovering over the food to— Billy Karcher, you put down those cookies! They're for after the meal."

The eight-year-old looked up from beneath the dark locks dangling on his forehead and gave her a gap-tooth grin. "I'm only makin' thure I get thome."

Willa fought back a smile at his lost-tooth lisp and gave him her teacher look. "Those cookies are to share. You put that handful back and I promise to save two of them for you."

The boy heaved a sigh, dropped the cookies back onto the plate and ran off to join the children playing tag in the park. She searched the group. Where were Joshua and Sally?

"Selfish little beast."

Willa jerked her gaze back to Ellen. "Billy is a *child,* not a beast."

"They seem one and the same to me." Ellen glanced toward the church and sucked in a breath.

"Pastor Calvert is coming this way. And he seems quite purposeful in his destination. I guess I caught his attention when Father introduced us after all." A smug smile curved Ellen's lovely, rosy lips. She turned her back, raised her hands and pinched her cheeks. "Are my curls in place, Willa?"

She looked at the cluster of blond curls peeking from beneath the back of Ellen's flower-bedecked hat and fought down a sudden, strong urge to yank one of them. "They're fine." She turned away from her friend's smug smile. Ellen's conceit had alienated most of their old friends, and it was putting a strain on their friendship. She sighed and moved the cookie plate to the back side of the table out of the reach of small, grasping hands. Ellen had been different before Callie Conner's family had moved away. Their raven-haired friend's astonishing beauty had kept Ellen's vanity subdued. And Callie's sweet nature—

"May I interrupt your work a moment, ladies?"

Matthew Calvert's deep voice, as warm and smooth as the maple syrup the villagers made every spring, caused a shiver to run up her spine. She frowned, snatched the stem of a bright red leaf that had fallen on a bowl of boiled potatoes and tossed it to the ground. With a voice like that, it was no wonder the man was a preacher of some renown.

Good manners dictated that she turn and smile— indignation rooted her in place. Joshua and Sally were nowhere in sight, yet Matthew Calvert had come seeking out Ellen to satisfy his own…*aims*. Well, she wanted nothing to do with a man who neglected the care of his young wards to satisfy his own selfishness.

She looked at the people spreading blankets on the ground in preparation for their picnic meal and silently urged them to hurry. Beside her, Ellen made a slow turn, smiled and looked up through her long lashes. *Another* ploy perfected before the mirror. One that made men stammer and stutter.

"May I help you, Reverend Calvert?"

Willa scowled at her friend's dulcet tone and moved a small crock of pickles closer to the potatoes, focused her attention on the green vine pattern circling the rim of the large bowl. She had no desire to hear the pastor's flirtatious response to Ellen's coyness. She wanted to go home—away from them both.

"Thank you, Miss Hall, you're most kind. But it's Miss Wright I seek."

Shock zinged all the way to her toes. What could Matthew Calvert possibly want with her? Ellen evidently thought the same if the hastily erased look of surprise on her friend's face was any indication. She turned. "You wished to speak with me?"

Something flashed in the pastor's eyes. Surprise? Puzzlement? Shock at her coolness? No doubt the handsome Matthew Calvert was unaccustomed to such treatment from women.

He dipped his head. "Yes. I've come to ask if you would be so kind as to keep watch on Joshua and Sally this afternoon, Miss Wright." He glanced at the tables and a frown furrowed his forehead. "I see that you are busy, and I hate to impose, but I am at a loss as to what else to do."

His gaze lifted to meet hers and she read apparent

concern in his eyes. Guilt tugged at her. Had she been wrong about him neglecting his wards?

"As this welcome dinner is in my honor, I must visit with my parishioners, and Joshua and Sally are uncomfortable among so many new people. I thought, perhaps, as the children know you and are comfortable with you…" He stopped, gave a little shrug. "I would consider it a great favor if you could help them. But, of course, I will understand if you must stay here at the tables."

So he wanted to be free of the children so he could get acquainted with his parishioners…like Ellen, no doubt. She forced a smile.

"Not at all. Ellen can help in my place." She ignored her friend's soft gasp. Let her flirt her way out of that! "Where are the children?"

"They're sitting on the front steps at the parsonage. I didn't want to force them to join us."

Of course not. That would hamper his…getting acquainted. She nodded, reached under the table and drew a plate from her basket, placed three meat tarts and three boiled eggs on it, then lifted the cookie plate in her other hand and started across the intervening ground. The pastor fell in beside her.

"Let me carry those for you, Miss Wright."

She halted, glanced up and shook her head. "I think it best if I go alone. You go and meet the *people* of Pinewood, Reverend Calvert." From the corner of her eye she saw Ellen shake out the ruffles on her long skirt and glide across the leaf-strewn ground toward them. She hurried on toward the children, but could not resist looking over her shoulder. It did not seem to bother the pastor that Ellen had left the table of food unattended. They were laughing together as they walked toward the blanket Mrs. Hall had spread on the ground. It seemed Reverend Calvert would partake of his first church dinner in Pinewood with the prettiest girl in the village by his side.

Willa glanced toward the church. People were beginning to gather their things together. She moved to the top of the gazebo steps. "Children, the game is over. Come and get your cookies, then go join your parents. It's time to go home."

"First one to touch wood wins!" Tommy Burke shouted the challenge, then turned and sprinted toward the gazebo. Children came running from every direction. Joshua put on a burst of speed surprising in one so young.

Willa smiled and gripped the post beside her, secretly rooting for him to outrun the older boys. Joshua needed something fun and exciting to think about. So did Sally.

She glanced over her shoulder, her heart aching for the little girl curled up on the bench along the railing. It was easy to get Joshua involved in games because he was very competitive. But Sally was different. The little girl had said her stomach hurt and stayed there on the bench while the other children played. Was it shyness or grief over her parents' deaths that made her so quiet and withdrawn?

She lifted the plate of cookies she'd saved from the bench and held them ready for the racing, laughing boys and girls. Billy Karcher stretched out his hand and touched the gazebo rail, Joshua right behind him.

"I win!" Billy tripped up the steps, snatched a cookie from the plate, grinned and took his promised second one. He lisped out, "Thee you tomorrow, Joth!" and jumped to the ground. Joshua waved at his new friend, turned and grabbed a cookie.

Willa resisted the temptation to smooth back the blond curls that had fallen over his brown eyes and contented herself with a smile. "A race well run, Joshua."

He grinned, a slow, lopsided grin that lifted the left side of his mouth, and flopped down on the bench beside his sister. "I'll *beat* him next time!"

He looked so different! So happy and carefree. The way a six-year-old should look. If only Sally would have joined in the games. She sighed and turned her attention back to the children grabbing cookies and saying goodbye.

"I find no words adequate to express my appreciation for your having come to my aid this afternoon, Miss Wright." Matthew smiled at Joshua busy kicking maple leaves into a pile while Sally leaned against the tree trunk and watched. "Or for engaging Joshua in the games."

"It was easy enough. Joshua is very competitive."

His gaze veered back to fasten on her. "I suppose I should correct him for bragging about that race, but I'm too happy to see that smile on his face. And, truth be told, I feel like bragging about it myself. I saw those boys, some of them had to be two or three years older than Joshua."

There was a definite glint of pride in the pastor's eyes. It seemed the competitive spirit ran in the Calvert family. "You're right, they are." She turned to look at Joshua, smiled and shook her head. "I've no doubt I will have my hands full at recess time tomorrow. Joshua declares he will beat Billy the next time they race, and I hear the ring of a challenge in those words."

"Do you want me to speak with him about it?"

The pastor's voice was controlled, but there was an underlying reluctance in it. She glanced his way. "No, I do not, Reverend Calvert. I am accustomed to handling the exuberance of young children. And I believe a few challenges, given and taken with his new schoolmates, is exactly what Joshua needs—under the circumstances."

She bent and picked up the plate she had left on the porch after her earlier, impromptu picnic with Joshua and Sally.

"I believe today proved that to be true, Miss Wright. This is the first time since Robert and Judith's deaths that Joshua has really played as a youngster should. I think he's going to be all right. I cannot tell you how grateful I am. But I'm concerned about Sally."

There was a heaviness in his voice. She turned. He was looking at the children, his face drawn with sorrow. She drew in her breath, told herself to keep quiet and leave. But she couldn't turn away from a hurting child. "I don't mean to pry, Reverend Calvert, but it's very difficult to engage Sally's interest in playing with the others. She is very quiet and withdrawn for a young child. And, though she tries very hard to hide them, I have seen tears in her eyes. I thought it was her shyness, but perhaps it is grief?"

"She misses her mother terribly. And it's hard for me to understand about girl things. Joshua is easier—I know about boys." He scrubbed his hand over his neck, turned and looked at her. "It's difficult dealing with their grief. It's only been six weeks since my brother and his wife died in the carriage accident. It was such a shock that I am still trying to handle my own grief. But I have talked to the children, tried to explain about God's mercy, and that they will see their mother and father again…" He took another breath and looked away.

She drew breath into her own lungs, forced them to expand against the tightness in her chest. "Forgive me, I did not mean to intrude on your privacy." She started down the path to the wood walkway.

"Wait! Please."

She paused, squared her shoulders and turned.

His lips lifted in a wry smile. "Once again I must appeal to you for help, Miss Wright. I am a pastor, not a cook, and the children and I are getting tired of eating eggs for every meal. I need a housekeeper, but it must be someone who understands children and will be careful of their grief. I thought, perhaps, as you are familiar with everyone in the village, you could suggest someone I could interview?"

She drew her gaze from the sadness in his eyes and gathered her thoughts. Who was available who would also understand the special needs of the Calvert children? "I believe Bertha Franklin might suit. She's a lovely, kind woman, an excellent cook…and no stranger to sorrow. And she definitely understands children. She has raised eight of her own. If you wish, I can stop and ask her to come by and see you tomorrow. Her home is on my way."

"I would appreciate that, Miss Wright." His gaze captured hers. "And thank you again for watching the children this afternoon. And for helping Joshua remember how to play."

His soft words brought tears to her eyes. She nodded, spun about and hurried down the wood walkway toward town.

Willa dipped her fingers in the small crock, rubbed them together, then spread the cream on her face and neck. A faint fragrance of honeysuckle hovered. She replaced the lid, tied the ribbons at the neck of her cotton nightgown and reached up to free her hair from its confining roll. The chestnut-colored mass tumbled onto her shoulders and down her back. She brushed it free of snarls, gathered it at the nape of her neck with a ribbon and stepped back from the mirror.

The touch of her bare feet against the plank floor sent a shiver prickling along her flesh. She hopped back onto the small, rag rug in front of the commode stand and rubbed her upper arms. The nights were turning colder, the air taking on the bite that announced winter was on its way. Thank goodness the company loggers kept her mother well supplied with firewood. And the parents of her students provided wood for the stove at school. There was already a large pile outside the back door.

She sighed, stepped off the rug and hurried to the window to push the curtain hems against the crack along the sill to block the cold air seeping in around the frame. Tomorrow morning she would start her winter schedule. She would rise early and go to school and light a fire in the stove to chase away the night chill. And then she would make a list of boys to help her keep the woodbox full throughout the winter.

She stepped to her nightstand, cupped her hand around the chimney globe, blew out the flame then climbed into bed. Two boys working together in weeklong rotations should be sufficient. Joshua and Billy would be the first team. She gave a soft laugh, tugged the covers close and snuggled down against her pillow. Those two boys would probably race to see who could carry in the most wood in the shortest time.

An image of Joshua's happy, lopsided grin formed against the darkness. He certainly looked like his uncle. And so did Sally, in a small, feminine way. Tears burned at the back of her eyes. Those poor children, losing both of their parents so unexpectedly. She had been devastated when her father left, and she'd had her mother to comfort her. Of course, Joshua and Sally had their uncle. He had looked concerned for the children when he talked with her. But that didn't mean his concern was real. Her father had seemed concerned for her before he turned his back and walked away never to return. But why would Matthew Calvert bother to put on an act for her? The children were not her concern.

Once again I must appeal to you for help, Miss Wright.

Oh, of course. Her facial muscles drew taut. She was a teacher. The pastor must have reasoned that she cared about children and played on her emotions to enlist her aid. And it had worked. She had been so gullible. Because of the children? Or because she wanted to believe there was truth behind Matthew Calvert's quiet strength and disarming grin?

She jerked onto her side, opened the small wood box on the nightstand with her free hand and fingered through the familiar contents, felt paper and withdrew the note Thomas had left on her desk the day he deserted her. There was no need to light the lamp and read it, the words were seared into her mind. *Willa, I'm sorry I haven't time to wait and talk to you, but I must hasten to meet Jack. He sent word he has funds for us to head west, and I am going after my dream. Wish me well, dearest Willa.*

Her chest tightened, restricted her breath. Three days before their wedding and Thomas had forsaken her without so much as a word of apology or regret. A man's concern for others was conditional on his own needs.

She clenched her hand around the small, folded piece of paper, drew a long, slow breath and closed her eyes. When her father abandoned her he'd left behind nothing but a painful memory and a void in her heart. Thomas had left her tangible proof of a man's perfidy. She had only to look at the note to remind herself a man was not to be trusted. Not even a man of the cloth with a stomach-fluttering grin.

Chapter Four

"Thank you for coming by, Reverend Calvert."

"Not at all, Mrs. Karcher." Matthew inclined his head in a small, polite bow. "I find making personal calls is the best way to get acquainted with my parishioners. And it is beneficial to do so as quickly as possible." He included the Karcher daughter, who'd had the misfortune of inheriting her father's long-jawed, hawk-nosed looks, in his goodbye smile.

"Well, Agnes and I are honored to be your first call." A look of smug satisfaction settled on the woman's face, one of her plump elbows dug into her daughter's side. "Aren't we, Agnes?"

"Yes, Ma." Agnes tittered and looked up at him, her avid expression bringing an uneasy twinge to his stomach. "I'm pleased you liked my berry pie, Reverend Calvert. I'll make an apple pie the next time you come." Her bony elbow returned her mother's nudge.

The *next* time? The expectation in Agnes's tone set warning bells clanging in his head. "Indeed?" A lame reply, but there was no good answer he could make to her presumption. He looked down at his hat and brushed a bit of lint from the felt brim, then stepped closer to the door. Perhaps he could get away before—

"Agnes's pies are the best of any young woman in Pinewood. And she's a wonderful cook."

—and perhaps he couldn't. He braced himself for what he sensed was coming.

"Mayhap you can come for dinner Saturday night, Reverend? I'm thinking those wards of yours would be thankful for some of Agnes's good cooking."

And there went his chance for an uneventful leave-taking. Mrs. Karcher's invitation could not be ignored. He looked up, noted the eager, hopeful gleam in both women's eyes and held back the frown that tugged at his own features. Both mother and daughter seemed to have forgotten his visit included Mr. Karcher and decided he had come because of Agnes. He cleared his throat and set himself to the task of disabusing them of that notion without hurting their feelings and damaging the pastor-and-congregant relationship. "I appreciate your kind invitation, Mrs. Karcher, but I'm afraid I must decline. My Saturdays are spent in prayer and preparation for Sunday. As for the children, I have hired Mrs. Franklin as housekeeper and cook. She feeds us well."

Surprise flitted across their faces. They had apparently not yet heard that piece of news. He hurried on before Mrs. Karcher recovered and extended another, amended, invitation. "Please convey my regards to Mr. Karcher. I regret that I had so little time to spend visiting with him. I shall make another call on *him* when he is less busy at the grist mill."

His slight emphasis on the word *him* dulled the hopeful gleam in the women's eyes. They had understood. He dipped his head in farewell, stepped outside and blew the air from his lungs in a long, low whistle. He was accustomed to the fact that young ladies and their mothers found bachelor pastors attractive as potential husband material, but he'd never before been subjected to anything quite so…blatant.

He ran his fingers through his hair, slapped on his hat and trotted to his carriage. Thunder grumbled in the distance. He glanced up and frowned at the sight of black clouds roiling across the sky. They were coming fast. The other visit he'd planned for this afternoon would have to wait.

"Time to head for home, girl." He patted his bay mare on her shoulder, climbed to the seat and picked up the reins. Lightning flashed. Thunder crashed. The mare jerked, danced in the traces. "Whoa, Clover. It's all right. Everything's all right."

The bay tossed her head and turned her ears toward his voice, calmed. "Good girl. Let's go now." He clicked his tongue and flicked the reins, glancing up as lightning glinted along the edge of the tumbling clouds. The black, foaming mass was almost overhead now. He would never make it back to town before the storm hit, and the children…

His chest tightened. Joshua would be all right. But Sally— "Lord, please be with Sally. Please comfort her, Lord, until I can get home." He reined the mare onto the Butternut Hill Road, stole another look at the sky and eased his grip on the lines to let her stretch her stride as he headed back toward the village.

* * *

"The…hen…is on the…b-*box*."

Willa smiled and nodded encouragement as Micah Lester shot her a questioning look. "Box is correct. Continue, please."

The boy lowered his gaze to the English Reader book in his hands and took a deep breath. "The rat ran…fr-*from*…the box."

She nodded as he again glanced her way. "And the last sentence, please."

"C-can the…hen…run?"

"Very good, Micah. You may take your seat." She stepped to his side and held out her hand for the book. Thunder grumbled. Her students straightened on their benches and looked up at her. She placed the book on her desk and went to the window. Black clouds were rolling across the sky out of the west. She turned back, looked at the expectant expressions on the children's faces and laughed. "Yes, school is over for today. A storm is coming, but if you hurry, there is time for you to reach home before it arrives. Gather your things. And remember…you're to go straight home."

She moved to the door, stepped out onto the small porch and held the door open against a rising wind. The children scurried past her and ran down the stairs still donning their coats and hats, calling out their goodbyes as they scattered in every direction. "Hurry home now, or you'll be caught out in the open and get a good drenching!"

She glanced up at the dark sky. Lightning glinted against the black storm clouds. Thunder crashed. She stared at the gray curtain falling to earth from beneath the approaching clouds and frowned. She was in for a soaking. By the time she snuffed the oil lamp, adjusted the drafts on the heating stove and gathered her things it would be impossible for her to reach home before the storm hit. Those clouds were moving fast. Should she wait it out? No. If she waited it could get worse. There was no promise of clearing behind that black wall of froth. She sighed, stepped inside and closed the door.

"C'mon, Sally. We got to get home. Miss Wright said so!"

Joshua. She turned and peered through the dim light in the direction of the boy's voice. He was tugging at his sister who was huddled into a ball in the corner. "Joshua, what's wrong with Sally?" Her skirt hems skimmed her shoe tops and swirled around her ankles as she hurried toward them.

The boy jerked to his feet and spun around to look up at her. "I'm sorry, Miss Wright. I know we're supposed to go home, but Sally's scared. She won't get up."

His face was pale, his voice teetered on the edge of tears. "It's all right, Joshua." She gave him a reassuring touch on the shoulder, then knelt down. "Sally—"

White light flickered through the dark room. Thunder cracked. The little girl screamed and launched herself upright and straight into her arms with such force that she almost tumbled backward. She caught her balance and wrapped her arms around Sally's small, trembling body.

Rain pelted the roof. Lightning streaked against the darkness outside the window and lit the room with a sulfurous yellow glow. Thunder crashed and rumbled.

Sally sobbed and burrowed her face hard into the curve of her neck. She placed her hand on top of the little girl's soft, blond curls and looked up at Joshua. The boy's eyes were watery with held-back tears, his lips trembling.

"Joshua, what is—" The door jerked open. She started and glanced up.

Matthew Calvert stepped into the schoolroom and swiveled his head left and right, peering into the dim interior. *"Josh? Sally?"*

"Uncle Matt!" Joshua lunged at his uncle. Sally slipped out of her arms and ran after him.

She rose, shook out her skirts then lifted her hands to smooth her hair.

Matthew Calvert dropped to his knees and drew the children close. "I was out on a call. I came as quickly as I could." The pastor tipped his head and kissed Sally's cheek, loosed his hold on Joshua and reached up to tousle the boy's hair. "You all right, Josh?"

Joshua straightened his small, narrow shoulders and nodded. "Yes, sir. But Sally's scared."

"I know. Thanks for taking care of her for me."

She noted Joshua's brave pose and the adoration in his eyes as he looked at his uncle, Sally clinging so trustingly, and turned away from the sight before she gave in to the impulse to tear the children out of his arms. She well remembered how loved and safe she had felt when her father had held her—and how devastating it had been to learn that the love and security had been a lie.

She swallowed to ease a sudden tightness in her throat and stepped to the open door. *Those children have no one else. Please don't let Joshua or Sally be hurt by their uncle.* Her face tightened. Who was she talking to? Certainly not God. He didn't care about such things.

Lightning crackled and snapped, turned the room brilliant with its brief flash of light. Thunder growled. A gust of wind spattered the rain sluicing off the porch roof against her and banged the door against the porch railing. She shivered, grabbed the door and tugged it shut. Murky darkness descended, too deep for the single overhead oil lamp she had lit.

"Forgive me, Miss Wright, I forgot about the door."

She turned and met Matthew Calvert's gaze, found something compelling there and looked away. "It's of no matter." She rubbed the drops of moisture from her hands and moved toward the heating stove, then paused. She would have to walk by him to reach it, and she did not want to get close to Matthew Calvert. Something about him stirred emotions from the past she wanted dead and buried. She busied herself brushing at the small, wet blotches on her sleeves.

"Joshua, get your coat and hat on. Sally, you must get yours on, too. It's time to go home."

She watched from under her lowered lashes as he gently loosed Sally's arms from around his neck and urged the little girl after her brother.

"Miss Wright…"

His deep voice was quiet, warm against the drumming of the rain on the roof. She lifted her head and again met his gaze. It was as quiet and warm as his voice. And dangerous. It made her want to believe him—as she had believed her father and Thomas. She clenched her hands. "Yes?"

"I need to speak with you…alone." His gaze flicked toward Joshua and Sally, then came back to rest on hers. "Would you please stop at the parsonage on your way home? I need to explain—" Another sizzling streak of lightning and sharp crack of thunder brought Sally flying back to him. Joshua was close behind her.

She swallowed back the refusal that was on her lips. She wanted no part of Matthew Calvert. The man had already used her once to free himself from his responsibility to the children so he could spend time with Ellen at the church dinner. But she was a teacher, and his wards were her students. She needed to learn whatever she could that might help the sad, frightened children. Especially if their uncle continued that sort of behavior. She well knew the pain a man's selfishness could bring others. She gave a stiff little nod and went to adjust the drafts on the stove.

"Thank you for coming, Miss Wright. Let me help you out of that wet cloak." Matthew stepped behind her, waited until she had pushed back the hood and unfastened the buttons, then lifted the garment from her shoulders.

"Thank you." She took a quick step forward, squared her shoulders and clasped her hands in front of her.

He stifled an unreasonable sense of disappointment. Willa Wright's expression, her pose, every inch of her proclaimed she was a schoolmarm here on business.

Well, what had he expected? No...*hoped*. That she would come as a friend?

He hung her damp cloak on one of the pegs beside the door and gestured to the doorway on his left. "Please come into the sitting room. We can talk freely there. Sally has calmed, now that the lightning and thunder have stopped, and she and Josh are playing checkers in his room." He urged her forward, led her to the pair of padded chairs that flanked the fireplace. "We'll sit here by the fire. The rain has brought a decided chill to the air."

"Yes, and it shows no sign of abating." She cast a sidelong glance up at him. "You had best be prepared for cold weather, Mr. Calvert. It will soon be snowstorms coming our way."

Would they be colder than her voice or frostier than her demeanor? Clearly, she was perturbed over his asking her to come. "I'm no stranger to winter cold, Miss Wright. We have snowstorms in Albany." He offered her a smile of placation. Perhaps he could soothe away some of her starchiness. "In truth, I enjoy them. There's nothing as invigorating as a toboggan run down a steep hill with your friends, or as enjoyable as a ride on a moonlit night with the sleigh bells jingling and the snow falling."

"A sleigh ride with...friends?"

"Yes, with friends."

She nodded, smoothed her skirts and took a seat. "A very romantic view of winter in the city, Mr. Calvert. I'm afraid there are harsher realities to snowstorms here in the country." She folded her hands in her lap and looked up at him. "You wanted to speak with me. I assume it is about the children?"

He looked down at her, so prim and proper and... and *disapproving*. He glanced at the rain coursing down the window panes. Small wonder the woman was irritated with him. He turned and pushed a length of firewood closer to another log with the toe of his boot. What did it matter if she was upset with him? This was not about him or his confusing feelings for the aloof teacher. "Yes, it's about the children."

He looked into the entrance hall, toward the stairs that climbed to their bedrooms, then sat on the edge of the chair opposite her. "Miss Wright, as I have previously explained, I had parenthood thrust upon me a little over seven weeks ago under extremely stressful circumstances, and I—well, I'm at a loss. As I mentioned, there is much I don't understand. Especially with Sally. However, I did not go into detail."

He stole another look toward the stairs and leaned forward. "I asked to speak with you because I believe you are due an explanation of Sally's behavior during a storm. You see, the day my brother and his wife died—" The pain of loss he carried swelled, constricted his throat. He looked down at the floor, gripped his hands and waited for the wave of grief to ease.

The fire crackled and hissed in the silence. The rain tapped on the windows—just as it had that day. He lifted his head. The firelight played across Willa Wright's face, outlined each lovely feature. He looked into her eyes, no longer cool, but warm with sympathy, and let the memories pour out. "I was teaching Joshua to play chess, and that day Robert and Judith brought him to spend the afternoon with me while they went to visit friends. Sally went with them."

He pushed to his feet, shoved his hands in his pockets and stood in front of the fire. "When it grew close to the time when Robert said they would return for Josh, a severe thunderstorm, much like the one today, blew in. We were finishing our game when a bolt of lightning struck so close to the house that it rattled the windows and vibrated my chest. A horse squealed in panic out front. I jumped to my feet and hurried to the window. Josh followed me."

He stared down at the flames, but saw only the carnage of a memory he prayed to forget. "There were two overturned, broken carriages in the street. One of them was Robert's. His horse was down and thrashing, caught in the tangled harness. I told Josh to stay in the house and ran outside, but there was nothing I could do. Robert and Judith were…gone."

He hunched his shoulders, shoved his hands deeper in his pockets and cleared the lump from his throat. "Sally was standing beside her mother, tugging on her hand and begging her to get up. She was scraped and bleeding, but, thankfully, not seriously injured." His ragged breath filled the silence. That, and the sound of Sally's sobs and Joshua's running feet and sharp cry that lived in his head.

"I'm so sorry for you and the children, Reverend Calvert. I can't imagine suffering through such a terrible occurrence. And for Sally to—" there was a sharply indrawn breath "—it's no wonder she is terrified of thunderstorms."

The warm, compassionate understanding in Willa Wright's voice flowed like balm over his hurt and concern. The pressure in his chest eased. "Yes."

"And it's why Josh tries so hard to protect her and take care of her, even though he hates thunderstorms, too." He looked down into her tear-filmed eyes. "He recognized his father's rig and followed me outside. He…saw…his mother and father." He shook off the despair that threatened to overwhelm him when he thought of the children standing there in the storm looking shocked and lost and made his voice matter-of-fact. "I thought you should know—so you could understand their behavior. I'm sure you have rules about such things."

She nodded and rose to her feet. "There are rules, yes. It is the custom in Pinewood to close the schools and send the village children home when a storm threatens, lest they be caught out in it." Her voice steadied. She lifted her head and met his gaze. "I'm thankful you called me here and told me what happened, Reverend Calvert. Now that I understand, should there be another thunderstorm, I will keep Sally and Joshua with me until you come for them, or should the hour grow late, I will bring them home and stay with them until your return."

"That is far beyond your duty as their teacher, Miss Wright." A frown tugged at his brows. "I appreciate your kindness, as will the children, but I assure you, I meant only to explain, not to impose upon you."

She went still, stared up at him. "Nor did you, Reverend Calvert. You did not ask—I offered." A look he could only describe as disgust flashed into her eyes.

She tore her gaze from his and turned toward the door. "I must get home."

He held himself from stopping her, from demanding that she tell him what he had done to bring about that look. "Yes, of course. I did not mean to take so much of your time."

They walked out into the entrance hall and he lifted her cloak off the hook. The sound of rain drumming on the porch roof was clear in the small room. "You cannot walk home in that downpour, Miss Wright." He settled the still-damp garment on her shoulders. "If you will wait here, I will get the buggy and drive you home."

"That is not necessary, Reverend Calvert." She raised her hands and tugged the hood in place. "I'm accustomed to walking home in all sorts of weather. The children need you here."

Why must the woman be so *prickly* when he was trying to do her a kindness? The stubborn side of his nature stirred. "I insist, Miss Wright. The lightning has stopped. The children will be fine with Mrs. Franklin. Wait here." He snatched his coat off its hook and hurried out the door before she could voice the refusal he read in her eyes.

The buggy moved along the muddy road, each rhythmic thud of the horse's hooves a step closer to her home, yet the way had never seemed so long. She had done it again! She'd allowed the man to reach her heart in spite of her resolve. Willa stared down at her hands and willed her gaze not to drift to the handsome profile of Reverend Matthew Calvert. The sense of intimacy created by the curtain of rain around the buggy did not help.

The horse's hooves struck against the planks of Stony Creek bridge and the carriage lurched slightly as the wheels rolled onto the hard surface. She grabbed for the hold strap to keep from brushing against him and held herself rigid as the buggy rumbled across the span, splashed back onto the mud of Main Street, then swayed around the corner onto her road.

"Miss Wright, may I ask your opinion about something that troubles me with Sally?" Matthew Calvert turned his head and looked at her.

She lifted her hand and adjusted her hood to avoid meeting his gaze. She was too easily swayed by the look of sincerity in his brown eyes. And she knew better, although her actions didn't reflect it. Hadn't the man just manipulated her into offering to watch his children if he was delayed, perhaps deliberately, in coming for them during a thunderstorm? What did he want of her now?

"To be fair, I must tell you it is a personal situation and has nothing to do with school. I simply don't know what to do for the best. And I thought a woman would have a better understanding of a little girl's needs than I."

If it did not pertain to school, why involve her? She opened her mouth to suggest he ask Bertha Franklin, then closed it again at the remembered feel of Sally clinging to her. "What is it?" She fixed her mind on her father's and Thomas's selfishness and brought a "no" ready to her lips.

"Sally misses her mother terribly. It seems especially difficult for her at bedtime. That first evening, when I put them to bed in the parsonage, she wanted to sleep in Joshua's bedroom. She cried so hard, I moved a trundle bed in for her." He glanced her way again. "Perhaps I should not have done so, but it…troubles… me when she cries."

She steeled her heart against the image of the grieving little girl and boy, and kept her eyes firmly fixed on the rain splashing off the horse's rump. Sympathy came too easily when she looked into Matthew Calvert's eyes.

"When we moved here, I decided permitting Sally to sleep in Joshua's room was not for the best, and, in spite of her tears, I put her in a bedroom by herself. When I went to check on her later that night, I found her asleep—with one of Judith's gloves clutched in her hand."

The poor, hurting child! Tears stung her eyes. She blinked them away and, under the cover of her cloak, rubbed at the growing tightness in her chest. "That is my cabin ahead."

The reverend nodded and drew back on the reins. The horse stopped. The drum of the rain on the buggy roof grew louder.

"Miss Wright, Sally takes comfort from Judith's glove, but it seems she is becoming more dependent on it. It was the first thing she wanted when we came home earlier." He turned on the seat to face her. "I don't know what to do, Miss Wright. And, though I feel it is unfair of me to ask for your advice, I feel so inadequate to the situation that I find myself unable to refrain from doing so." The sincerity in his voice tugged her gaze to meet his. "In your opinion, should I let Sally keep the glove? Or should I take it away?"

She couldn't answer—couldn't *think* clearly. Her memories were too strong, her emotions too stirred. This man and his wards were a danger to her. She squared her shoulders and shook her head. "I'm afraid I have no answer for you, Reverend Calvert. However, I will consider the problem, and if a suggestion should occur to me, I will tell you." She pulled her hood farther forward and prepared to alight.

He drooped the reins over the dashboard, climbed down and hurried around to offer her his hand. She did not want his help, did not want to touch him, but there was no way around it. She placed her hand on his wet, uplifted palm and felt the warm strength of his fingers close over hers as she stepped down. The gesture was meant to steady her, but the effect was the opposite. She withdrew her hand, clasped the edges of her cloak against the driving rain and looked up at him. "Thank you for your kindness in bringing me home, Reverend Calvert."

"Not at all, Miss Wright. It was the least I could do. Watch that puddle."

His hand clasped her elbow. He guided her around the muddy water onto the wet planks that led to the stoop. Water from the soaked yard squished around his boots as he walked her to her door, released his hold and gave a polite bow of his head.

"Thank you for allowing me to unburden myself of my concerns over Sally and Joshua, Miss Wright. It was good of you to listen. Good afternoon."

She nodded, opened the door and stepped inside,

but could not resist a glance over her shoulder. He was running to his buggy.

"I expected you home when the storm started, Willa. Was there something wrong? I heard a buggy. Are you all right?"

She closed the door, turned and shoved the wet hood off her head. "I'm fine, Mama. Reverend Calvert's ward, Sally, is frightened of thunderstorms and it took a bit to calm her. The reverend drove me home because of the rain."

"You were scared of thunder and lightning when you were little. Remember?"

"Yes, I remember." *Too many things. The memories keep rearing up and betraying me.* "You used to hold me and tell me stories."

Her mother smiled and nodded. "I hope the reverend's little girl gets over her fright. It's a terrible thing when a child is afraid." She narrowed her eyes, peered closely at her. "Are you certain you're all right, Willa? You look…odd."

"Well, I can't imagine why. I'm perfectly fine." She *was.* Or at least she would be, as soon as the tingly warmth of Matthew Calvert's touch left her hand.

Chapter Five

Willa wrapped her bread and butter with a napkin, placed the bundle in the small wicker basket, added an apple and slammed the lid closed. Why couldn't she stop thinking about yesterday? About the way her heart had sped at Matthew Calvert's nearness when he removed her cloak? About that carriage ride, and the way her breath had caught when he took her hand in his? Those things were mere courtesies. Yet here she was mooning about them. It was disgusting. Why wasn't she thinking about the way he had again manipulated her into offering to help with the children to free his time? Where was her self-control?

She dropped the dirty knife in the dishpan, swirled her cloak about her shoulders, grabbed her lunch basket and strode to the kitchen doorway. "I'm ready to go, Mama."

Her mother nodded, poured the iron kettle of steaming water she held into the washtub, then turned and stepped to the pump to refill it. "I figured you'd be going early to stoke up the stove. It turned right cold last night."

She pressed her lips together and nodded. She hated the tiredness that lived in her mother's voice. Hated that her mother worked from dawn to dusk every day but Sunday to keep the small cabin they called home. Most of all she hated her father for walking away and leaving her mother to find a way for them to survive without him.

She lifted the hem of her long skirt and stepped down into the lean-to wash shed.

Her mother raised her head and gave her a wry smile. "One thing about scrubbing clothes for a living—you're never cold." Her green eyes narrowed, peered at her. "What are you riled about?"

"Nothing. Except that you work too hard. Let me get that!" Willa plopped her basket on the corner of the wash bench and grabbed hold of the kettle handle. "You need to eat, Mama. I made a piece of bread and honey for you. It's on the kitchen table."

Her mother straightened and brushed a lock of curly hair off her sweat-beaded forehead. "Don't you know it's the mother who's supposed to take care of the child, Willa?" There was sorrow and regret in the soft words.

"You've been doing that all my life, Mama." She grabbed a towel and pulled the iron crane toward her, lifted the newly filled kettle onto a hook beside the one already heating and slowly pushed the crane back. The flames devouring the chunks of wood rose and licked at the large pot. The beads of water sliding down the iron sides hissed in protest. "I hope that someday I will be able to take care of you, and you will never have to do laundry again."

Her mother smiled, dumped the first pile of dirty

clothes into the washtub, set the washboard in place and reached for the bar of soap. "You're a wonderful daughter to want to take care of me, Willa. But your future husband might have something to say about that."

She snatched the soap out of her mother's reach. "I told you there's not going to be a future husband for me, Mama. I am never going to marry. Thomas cured me of that desire." *And Papa.* "Now please, go and eat your bread while the rinse water is heating. I have to go."

She put the soap back in its place, hung the towel back on its nail and picked up her basket. "Please leave the ironing, Mama. I will do it tonight. And I'll stop at Brody's on my way home and get some pork chops for supper. Danny told me they were butchering pigs at their farm yesterday. Now, I've got to leave or I'll never get the schoolroom warm before my students come."

She kissed her mother's warm, moist cheek, opened the door of the lean-to and stepped out into breaking dawn of the brisk October morning. Dim, gray light guided her around the cabin to the road and filtered through the overhanging branches of trees along the path as she hurried on her way.

The stove was cold to the touch. Willa grabbed the handle of the grate, gave it a vigorous shake to get rid of the ashes that covered the live embers, then opened the drafts. The remaining coals glowed, turned red. She added a handful of kindling, stood shivering until it caught fire, then fed in a few chunks of firewood, lit a spill and closed the firebox door.

The flame on the spill fluttered. She cupped her free hand around it, stepped to the wall and unwound the narrow chain to lower the oil-lamp chandelier. The glass chimneys fogged from her warm breath as she lifted them one by one, lit the wicks, set the flame to a smokeless, steady burn and settled them back in place. Heat smarted her fingertips. She lit the oil lamp on her desk and blew out the shortened sliver of wood.

Everything was in readiness. Almost. She grabbed the oak bucket off the short bench and headed for the back door to fetch fresh drinking water from the well.

The door latch chilled her fingers. She stared at her hand gripping the metal and a horrible, hollow feeling settled in her stomach. This would be the sum of her life. She turned and surveyed the readied classroom, then looked down at the bucket dangling from her hand. She would spend her years teaching the children of others—until her mother's strength gave out and she had to take over doing the loggers' laundry to keep their home. Her back stiffened. "Well, at least I won't have to live with a broken heart." She hurled the defiant words into the emptiness, squared her shoulders and opened the door. If she hurried there was still time for her to write her letter before the children came.

Dearest Callie,
I was so pleased to receive your latest letter. And I thank you for your kind invitation to visit, perhaps I shall, later when school closes. I do apologize for being so tardy in answering, but you

know helping Mama with her work leaves me little time for pleasurable activities.

I must tell you about Reverend Calvert and his wards. I am certain your aunt Sophia has written you about him as there is little talk of anything else in Pinewood since his arrival. And, truly, I am grateful for that as talk of Thomas's hasty departure has ceased.

Willa frowned, tapped her lips with her fingertip and stared at the letter, then dipped her pen in the ink-well and made her confession.

You, and Sadie, and Mama are the only ones who know the truth of Thomas's desertion of me. My pride demands that others believe I told him to follow his dream and go west without me, that the choice to remain behind was mine. I could not bear to face the pity of the entire village! Sadie knows well what I mean.

Oh, Callie, the *folly* of believing a man's words of love. But I know you are aware of that danger. How my heart aches for you, my dear friend. I am so sorry your parents persist in their desire to find a wealthy husband for you, no matter his character. You write that you are praying and trusting God to undertake and bring you a man of strong faith and high morals in spite of their efforts, but I do not believe God troubles Himself with the difficulties and despairs of mere mortals. He certainly has never bestirred Himself on Mama's behalf. Or mine.

Reverend Calvert is tall, and well-proportioned, and exceedingly handsome. He possesses an abundant charm, and a very persuasive manner. A dangerous combination, as you might imagine. One must stay on one's guard around him lest

Light footfalls raced across the porch. The door opened. Willa wiped the nib of her pen, stoppered her inkwell and blotted the unfinished letter.

"Good morning, Mith Wright." Billy Karcher shucked his jacket and hat, hung them on a peg on the wall and gave her a grin. "I'm getting a new tooth. Wanna thee?"

"Good morning, Billy. I certainly do." She folded the letter and tucked it into her lunch basket to finish later.

The second grader tipped his head up and skimmed his lips back to expose the white edge of a new front tooth.

"Thank you for the prompt service, Mr. Dibble." Matthew watched the fluid stride of his bay mare as the blacksmith led her in a tight circle. She was no longer favoring her left rear leg. "She seems fine now. What was the problem?"

"Nail was set wrong. Irritated the quick enough it got sore." The blacksmith shook his head and led the horse over to him. "It's a good thing you brought her in. Shoddy work like that can maim a horse." He handed over the halter lead. "I checked the other shoes. They're all good."

"That's good to know." He stroked the bay's neck, got a soft nicker and head bump in return. "What do I owe you?"

"Fourteen cents will take care of it."

He counted out the coins, smiled and handed them over. "Thank you again, Mr. Dibble. It's been a pleasure meeting you. I'll look forward to seeing you in church Sunday."

The man's gray eyes clouded, his hard, callused hand dropped the coins in the pocket of the leather apron that protected him. "I don't go to church, Reverend. I figure all that praying and such is a waste of time. God's never done anything for—" The livery owner's straight, dark brown brows pulled down into a frown. "I'll leave it there. Details don't matter."

"They do to the Lord. But He already knows them."

"He don't pay them no mind."

"Perhaps you've misunderstood, Mr. Dibble." He smiled to take any challenge from his words, stroked his mare's neck and framed a careful reply to the man's acrimony. "God doesn't always answer our prayers as we hope or expect He will. Or perhaps God hasn't had time—"

"I understand all right. There ain't no way to not understand. And He's had time aplenty." David Dibble gave a curt nod and strode off toward his livery stables.

He watched him disappear into the shadowed interior. "I don't know what is causing Mr. Dibble's anger and bitterness, Lord, but I pray You will answer his prayers according to Your will. And that You will save his soul. Amen." He took a firm grip on Clover's halter and started for the road.

A buggy swept into the graveled yard, rumbled to a halt beside him. He glanced up, tugged on the halter and stopped his horse. "Good afternoon, Mr. Hall." He lifted his free hand and removed his hat, dipped his head in the passenger's direction. "Miss Hall."

"Good afternoon, Reverend Calvert." Ellen Hall's full, red lips curved upward. "How fortunate that we have chanced to meet. Isn't it, Father?"

The words were almost purred. Ellen Hall looked straight into his eyes, then swept her long, dark lashes down, tipped her head and fussed with a button on her glove. A practiced maneuver if he'd ever seen one—and he'd seen plenty back in Albany. He ignored her flirting and shifted his gaze back to Conrad Hall.

"Fortuitous indeed." The man's blue eyes peered at him from beneath dark, bushy brows. "Mrs. Hall and I would like to extend you a dinner invitation, Reverend. Tomorrow night. Our home is the second house on Oak Street, opposite the village park. We eat promptly at six o'clock."

The man's tone left no room for refusal. And it was certainly impolitic to turn down an invitation to dine with one of the founders of the church, but he had no choice. He chose his words carefully. "That's very kind of you and Mrs. Hall, sir, but I'm afraid I must decline. I'm not yet fully settled in and my children—"

"Will be welcome, Reverend. We shall see you at six tomorrow night." The man glanced at his daughter, then flicked the reins and drove off.

Ellen gave him a sidelong look from beneath her lashes, lifted her gloved hand in a small wave and smiled. He dipped his head in response, then replaced his hat and tugged the bay into motion.

"Did you see that, Clover?" His growled words were punctuated by the thud of the bay's hooves as he led her across the wood walk into the road. "If I ever see you flirting with a stallion like that, I'll trade you to Mr. Totten and you can spend the rest of your days pulling his trolley."

The horse snorted and tossed her head as he turned her toward home.

"What are you *doing* in here, Willa? The children are gone. And I've been waiting..." Ellen closed the door and swept down the aisle between the bench desks.

Willa snuffed the flame of the last lamp, raised the chandelier and turned to face her friend. "I was finishing a letter to Callie. I want to post it on my way home. You wanted something?"

"I have news."

She looked at Ellen's smug expression and shook her head. "Obviously, it pleases you."

"Oh, it does."

She nodded and stepped to the stove and twisted the handles to close the drafts for a slow burn that would preserve the fire for morning.

"Don't you want to hear my news?"

"Of course." She turned and grinned up at her friend. "And you will tell me as soon as you have your little dramatic moment." She stepped to her desk and picked up her basket.

"Oh, very well." Ellen hurried up beside her and

gripped her forearm. "Reverend Calvert is coming for dinner tomorrow night!"

It took her aback. There was no denying it. And there was absolutely no reason why it should. She nodded and smiled. "That's quite a 'coup,' Ellen. Every young woman in the village has been hoping to have the reverend for dinner." She started for the door. "Was the dinner your father's idea, or—"

"He thinks it was." Ellen laughed and tugged the velvet collar on her coat higher as they went out the door. "I planned it, of course—with Mother's help."

Of course. "I'm surprised he accepted." *Really?* "I know he's turned down other invitations because of the children." *But those young women don't possess Ellen's beauty.* She stifled a spurt of disgust and hurried down the porch steps and turned toward town.

"Yes, I'd heard, so I planned for that. I had father tell him the children were welcome."

She stopped and stared up at Ellen. The smug look on her friend's face made her want to shake her. "And are they welcome?"

"Of course, as long as they don't get in the way. And they won't. I've made certain of that. They will have their own meal in the breakfast room. And Isobel has been instructed to keep them there until my performance is finished." Ellen smiled and patted her curls with a gloved hand. "I'm going to recite a Psalm. I want the reverend to see my spiritual side."

"I'm certain he will be duly impressed."

"He will be when he sees my new gown." Ellen laughed and moved ahead. "Bye, Willa." She waved a gloved hand and turned onto the stone walkway to her house.

Willa released the white-knuckled grip she had on the basket handle and marched down the sidewalk. Her disgust carried her all the way to Brody's meat market. She took a deep breath, pasted a smile on her face and went inside to buy pork chops for their supper. A supper that would have *included* children at the table—if she had had any.

Chapter Six

"What's wrong with you, Willa? You've not been yourself for a couple of days now." Her mother lifted an undershirt out of the last basket of clothes she'd taken off the line, gave it a sharp snap through the air and folded it. "What's got you so nettled?"

"Nothing, Mama." Willa pressed the hot iron along the sleeve of the shirt she'd laid flat on the table, lifted it, then slammed it down on the other sleeve and shoved it along the length to remove the wrinkles.

"Well, you're certainly acting riled. If you don't calm yourself, you're gonna break that table. You have a student giving you trouble?"

She glanced up and met her mother's assessing gaze, sighed and placed the iron in its trivet, then swiped the end of the towel draped over her shoulder across her moist, heat-flushed face. "No. It's Ellen. She told me yesterday the Halls were having Reverend Calvert and his children to supper tonight. And Ellen—well, she's being *Ellen*."

She snatched the pressed shirt off the table, folded

it, then unrolled another dampened one and smoothed it out on the table with her hands.

"Flirting with the pastor, you mean?" Her mother stilled, fixed a look on her. "That bother you, does it?"

"Certainly not! I don't care about Reverend Calvert. He can flirt with whomever he pleases. But the children…" She plucked the iron off its trivet and swept it over the body of the shirt. "I've told you how they are grieving, and Ellen made plans to feed them *alone* in the breakfast room. And she has ordered Isobel to keep them there until her entertainment is over." She took another swipe at the shirt with the iron, then cast a look at her mother. "She intends to recite a Psalm for the reverend. She wants him to see her *spiritual* side." She huffed out a breath, frowned down at the shirt on the table. It was still wrinkled.

"Your iron's cold."

There was something in her mother's voice. Was she *amused?* She glanced at her, but could not see her face. She looked down and tapped the iron with her fingertip. "So it is." She marched to the fireplace, set an iron trivet over a pile of hot coals and plunked the cold iron down on it, snatched up a hot one and went back to her work. "I feel sorry for Joshua and Sally being stuck in a room by themselves in a strange house all evening, that's all."

"Hmm."

There it was again. She jerked her head up, caught the remnant of a hastily erased smile on her mother's face. "Well, isn't it right that I should be concerned about the children? They *are* my students."

"Oh, yes indeed." Her mother nodded, ducked her head and began to fold the socks in the basket.

She stared at her mother's bowed head for a long moment, then carefully lowered the iron and pressed a sleeve, concentrating on removing every wrinkle to keep from thinking about Ellen wearing her new gown for Matthew Calvert's benefit.

He shouldn't have done it. He shouldn't have walked out like that. It certainly wasn't wisdom to anger Conrad Hall or his daughter. But when their maid had rushed in apologizing because the children had *escaped* her… Matthew glanced down at Sally kneeling beside her bed while she said her prayers and his face tightened. He would do it again.

"…and bless Josh and Uncle Matt and please don't ever, ever take them away. Amen." Sally rose from her knees and climbed into bed, her mother's glove clutched in her hand.

He swallowed hard and sucked in air. He couldn't bear the fear in Sally's voice when she uttered those words to close her nightly prayers. He'd tried so hard to reassure her that he and Joshua would be all right, but that tragic carriage accident had taught her that people she loved could be taken from her life in an instant. *Please comfort Sally, Lord. Please ease her grief and take away her fear.*

He looked down into her brown eyes, bright with tears, tucked the covers close beneath her little chin and leaned down to kiss her silky, soft cheek. Her small arms slid around his neck and squeezed.

"I didn't mean to be bad, Uncle Matt." Her little

voice wobbled, broke on a sob. "I was scared 'cause I couldn't find you."

"I know, Sally." He pulled her into his arms and hugged her close. "And you're not bad. You're a very good girl."

"The lady thought I was bad." She leaned back and looked up at him. "She was mad."

Yes, Ellen had been angry when Josh had brought Sally to him, although she had tried to hide it behind a pretended concern for the children. He cleared the lump from his throat, straightened and smiled down at her. "Miss Hall didn't understand you were afraid." He wiped away her tears and covered her little hands with his. His fingers brushed against Judith's glove. "Sometimes people get angry when they don't understand. Now you go to sleep. I'll see you in the morning."

"Bertha said she'd make me and Josh pancakes. Will you eat pancakes with us?"

"I sure will." The reassurance seemed to comfort her. She sighed and closed her eyes. "Good night, Sally." He rubbed her cheek with the back of his finger, glanced at the fire to make sure it didn't need tending and walked out the door.

What was he to do about the glove? He had to decide soon. He frowned and made his way along the hall and stepped into Joshua's bedroom. "All settled in, Joshua?"

"Yes, sir." His nephew peered up at him from beneath his covers. "I brushed my teeth and said my prayers."

An ache swelled in his heart. Joshua looked so much

like Robert. He acted like him, too, always trying to do the right thing. "Good man." He smiled, ruffled Joshua's blond curls, noted the unhappy look in the boy's brown eyes and sat down on the side of the bed. "Is something bothering you, Joshua?"

The boy stared up at him a moment, then nodded. "Do we have to go and have supper at that house again? Sally was crying. She didn't like being away from you."

And neither did you. He looked down into Joshua's brown eyes, clouded with concerns and fears no little boy should have to carry, and shook his head. "Perhaps someday. But I promise you we will not go to the Halls' for supper again anytime soon." *Even if we are invited, which is doubtful after the way I walked out of there.* He leaned down close and lowered his voice. "Want to know a secret?"

Joshua's eyes widened, his curls bobbed as he nodded.

"I didn't like eating my supper away from you and Sally, either."

"You didn't?"

He gave a solemn shake of his head. "Nope."

The boy blinked, swallowed hard. "'Cause we're a family now, even if we haven't got a mama, right?"

The words squeezed his heart and constricted his throat. "Right." He pushed the word out and pulled Joshua into a close hug, fought back tears as his nephew threw his arms around his neck and buried his head against his shoulder and held on tight.

"I miss Mama and Papa."

The tears surged, smarted his eyes. Joshua tried so

hard to be brave, but he was only a scared little boy. He tightened his hold and pressed his cheek against his nephew's soft, blond curls and cleared his throat. "I know you do, Josh…I know. But I promise you it will get better." *God, please help me make it better for Josh and Sally.*

Matthew poured coffee into his cup, set the pot on the cool surface at the back of the stove and crossed the kitchen to look out the window. His breath steamed the cold glass. He wiped away the fog with his palm and stared at the touch of frost on the curled edges of the dried leaves on the path to the stables.

What a failure of an evening. He frowned, leaned his shoulder against the window frame and took a swallow of the hot coffee. He never would have agreed to the dinner date had he known Ellen intended to shunt Joshua and Sally aside to spend the evening in a room by themselves. He had thought they were being entertained, until Sally had panicked and Joshua had brought her to find him.

He circled the cup in the air, watched the dark, hot brew swirl around, then took another swallow. Ellen had pretended compassion at Sally's sobs, and he'd almost believed her.

I know you have only recently become the guardian of your dear wards, Reverend Calvert, so a bit of advice from an experienced father might be in order. Father always says children need discipline, that you must keep a firm hand with them. I'm sure you agree.

His fingers tightened around his cup. Ellen's voice had been silky, her smile a sweet one meant to win his accord, but she knew Joshua and Sally had recently been orphaned, and her words had chilled him. He considered her comments insensitive and inappropriate. However, he had to admit she was right in one thing—he was inexperienced at being a father. Was he wrong in his treatment of the children? Was his sympathy for their grief only making it worse? Should he simply take Judith's glove from Sally and be done with it?

He scowled down at his cup. The coffee had lost its appeal. He crossed to the sink cupboard, tossed the rest of the brew into the bucket on the shelf below, put the cup in the dishpan and headed for his study. He needed some answers and he knew only one place to find them. He had some praying to do.

Shivers prickled her flesh. Willa brushed her hair, grabbed a ribbon off the commode stand and ran across the plank floor and climbed into bed.

Another shiver shook her. She gathered her long hair at the nape of her neck, tied it with the ribbon, then snuffed the lamp and slid beneath the covers. The air sneaking through the cracks around the window by the side of the bed touched her exposed cheek. She tugged the quilt higher, turned on her side and curled into a ball. The bed warmed. Her shivering stopped. She sighed, relaxed her taut muscles and closed her eyes.

Callie's letter. It was still in her lunch basket. She'd forgotten to mail it yesterday. She frowned and stretched out, wiggled her feet to warm their new place. That's what she got for allowing herself to be so irritated by Ellen's plans. She would mail the letter tomorrow, although the way the temperature was plummeting she didn't even want to think about morning. At least she didn't have to get up early and make that cold walk in the dark to school. Tomorrow was Saturday. She yawned, snuggled deeper beneath the covers and waited for the pleasant, drifting sensation of approaching sleep.

Had Matthew Calvert been awed by Ellen's beauty tonight? Had he enjoyed himself flirting with Ellen while his children were hidden away in the breakfast room?

She scowled, snapped her eyes open and stared into the darkness, all somnolence set to flight by her demanding thoughts. Why was she lying there thinking about the reverend and Ellen? It was the children she cared about…only the children. She yanked the quilt tighter against her back and again closed her eyes. But try as she would to concentrate on Joshua and Sally, it was images of Matthew Calvert flirting with Ellen that filled her head before sleep swept her into oblivion.

Chapter Seven

Willa smiled at the wagon shop owner who had opened the door to Cargrave Mercantile and stepped back to let her pass. "Good morning, Mr. Turner." She lifted the hem of her long skirt and stepped over the threshold.

"Nippy out this morning."

"Yes, it is." She looked toward the back of the store and smiled at the elderly men seated on chairs and leaning toward the checker board on top of the large keg in front of the stove. "You're frowning, Mr. Fabrizio. Are you losing to Mr. Grant...*again?*"

The man straightened at her teasing. His bald head gleamed in the lamplight and his bushy gray eyebrows cast shadows over the dark eyes twinkling up at her. He raised one weathered hand to cover his heart, murmured something in his native Italian, winked and flashed her a grin she was sure had captured many a young woman's heart in his youth.

She had learned enough Italian to know that whatever else he had said, he'd called her beautiful. She pushed her hood off to hang down her back and shook her head. "I should know better than to tease you, Mr. Fabrizio. You are an incorrigible flirt."

She joined in the men's laughter, pulled Callie's letter from her basket and stepped to the open window in the wall of pigeonhole mailboxes. "Good morning, Mr. Hubble."

"Morning, Willa." The postmaster paused in his task of sliding mail into the small cubicles and squinted at her through his wire-rimmed glasses. "Who's the letter for this time—Callie or Sadie?"

"Callie." She placed the letter on the small shelf on the other side of the open window, watched as he wrote down the rate on the top right corner, then handed him the coins.

The door behind her opened. The attached bells announced a new customer. She glanced over her shoulder, smiled as a strikingly lovely older woman entered. "Good morning, Mrs. Sheffield."

The older woman's eyes warmed, her lips curved into an affectionate smile. "*Willa,* how lovely to see you." She peered at her from beneath the brim of her fur-trimmed coal scuttle bonnet. "I have to place an order for supplies and then I am going home. Would you have time to come and join me for a cup of tea? It's been too long since we've had a real visit."

"I would enjoy that, Mrs. Sheffield. I have to purchase some things for Mama, but then I can come along."

"Lovely. I shall see you then." The woman patted her arm, moved to the counter, laid down a list in front of Allan Cargrave, who was measuring coffee beans into a small burlap bag for another customer, then lifted her hand in farewell. The bells tinkled her departure.

Willa selected the darning supplies she'd come after and dropped them into her basket. She moved along the shelves, admired a packet of fancy pearl buttons, then ran her fingers over the end of a new bolt of bottle-green velvet. What would it be like to wear a dress of such soft, beautiful fabric trimmed with such lovely buttons? Surely such a gown would catch Matthew Calvert's eye.

She stiffened and withdrew her hand. No doubt Ellen would soon find out. Mrs. Hall was certain to purchase the new fabric and buttons for her dressmaker's shop, and Ellen was as certain to cajole her mother into making her a dress out of them. She would look beautiful in the velvet.

A twinge of envy shot through her. She frowned and headed for the counter. What was wrong with her? She had never before been envious of any of her friends' good fortune.

The scent of coffee lingered in the air. She set her opened basket on the counter, took a sniff and smiled. "That coffee smells good, Mr. Cargrave. I'll take a bag of 'Old Java.' And I need indigo and baking soda for Mama, please."

Willa followed the path that led around the Sheffield house and climbed the back stairs to the porch that stretched the length of the large building.

She crossed to the settle benches standing guard at both sides of the kitchen door and paused, overcome by a sudden rush of sentiment. How many times had she visited this house with Callie through the years? Sophia Sheffield had always welcomed her niece's friends. Memories flowed, tugged her lips into a grin.

She glanced at the far end of the porch, then hurried to peer over the railing at the vertical boards that enclosed the space beneath. The third board from the corner had been loose and she and Callie used to crawl inside and share their childhood hurts and dreams. It was their secret place. Theirs and Sadie's. Sadie had been invited in, but no one else. Callie had been firm about that, and because it was her aunt's house, she had the say. They had all been unhappy at excluding their friend Ellen, but she had liked to gossip even then, and Callie warned that Ellen would tell. They had all stuck to their rule.

Her grin widened. Gracious, she hadn't thought about their hiding place in years. She would have to mention it the next time she wrote Callie. Was the board still loose? She looked closely but couldn't tell. Still, it was not likely. It must have been discovered and repaired by now. Her smile faded. She had shed a lot of tears under this porch after her father deserted her and her mother. And said a lot of prayers, as well. God had chosen not to answer them—if He had bothered to listen.

She turned and walked back to the kitchen door and rapped lightly.

"Come in!"

The door creaked as it always had. The delicious aroma of meat roasting on a spit in the fireplace scented the air. She turned and placed her basket on the table where she had shared many a cookie with

Callie, pushed back her hood and removed her cloak. Warmth from the cooking fire chased the chill from her face and hands as she hung it on a peg beside the door. "It always smells wonderful in here."

"I guess that's because, with a hotel full of guests, we're always cooking or baking something."

She turned and looked down the length of the large kitchen. "Mrs. Sheffield! Where is Rose?"

Sophia Sheffield laid the spoon she was using to baste the meat back into the pan on the hearth that was catching the juices and straightened. "The poor woman has badly strained her back. She's in her room resting."

She nodded and eyed the puffy brown rounds cooling on the long work table that occupied the center of the space between the huge stone fireplace and the iron cook stove on the opposite wall. "Are those molasses cookies? They were Sadie's favorites."

"Callie's, too." Sophia nodded, lifted the steaming teakettle from the stove and poured hot water into the china teapot sitting on a tray beside the cookies. "You favored the 'white ones.'"

Hearing her childhood name for sugar cookies tugged her lips into another grin. "I still do." She stepped forward and carried the tea tray to the small table while Sophia put the kettle back on the stove. There were two cups and saucers on the table—china ones with blue vines circling the rims. It used to be three tin cups of milk. She sighed and took her seat. "Wouldn't it be lovely if Callie and Sadie were here, Mrs. Sheffield?"

"It would indeed, Willa. You pour, dear." The older woman set a plate of cookies on the table and sat down opposite her. "After what Sadie endured at Payne Aylward's hands, I doubt she will ever return to Pinewood, but I'm hoping Callie will come for a visit soon. It's been almost a year since I've seen her. And I'm quite sure she is unhappy in Buffalo. It doesn't seem possible it's been four years since Barbara and Michael moved away." A frown creased her high forehead. "Has Callie written you about coming home?"

"Nothing certain." She poured tea into their cups, set the teapot back on the tray and reached for the cream. *I hate my life here in the city, Willa. Don't tell Aunt Sophie because she will be concerned for me, but Mother and Father parade me in front of the wealthy, elite men of this place in hope of arranging a "favorable" marriage that will increase their wealth and improve their social status. I so wish we had never moved from Pinewood.*

"I saw Ellen the other day. She told me they were having the new preacher and his wards for supper. Ellen seems quite taken with the man."

Sophia's voice drew her thoughts from Callie, replaced them with an image of Ellen wearing her new gown and reciting a Psalm for Matthew Calvert. "Yes, she does." It came out much sharper than she intended. She glanced at Sophia's raised eyebrows, the questioning look in her violet-blue eyes and hastened to change the subject. "The pastor's wards are my students. They are lovely, well-behaved children. It's so sad that they lost their parents so tragically."

The door leading to the Sheffield House dining room opened and one of Sophia's maids stepped in.

"Excuse me, Mrs. Sheffield, but there's a man come to stay. He's waiting in your office."

"Thank you, Katie." Sophia sighed and rose. "I'll only be a minute, Willa. And then we'll continue our visit." A smile creased her lovely face. "Meanwhile, have a cookie—even if they aren't 'white ones.'"

The sun had burned through the overcast sky while she was visiting with Sophia. Willa walked down the porch steps and pushed her hood off her head to let the warmth of the golden rays touch her face. The ripple of water brushing against weed-covered banks drew her gaze toward the river that flowed behind the stable. It was tame now, but in the spring the Allegheny would overflow its banks and flood the surrounding field. That area had been forbidden them as children, but they had often played in the stable.

She turned onto the path, caught movement out of the corner of her eye and turned back. A yellow kitten, chased by a small, black-and-white, barking dog, darted beneath a denuded bush growing at the corner of the stable.

"Shoo! Leave that kitten alone!" She set her basket on the steps and hurried down the path, waving her arms to distract the young dog from its prey. It barked, then turned tail and ran into the stable. The kitten crouched into a ball and stared up at her.

"Well, hello." She reached behind the bush. The kitten darted toward the open stable door. She quickly shifted her position so her long skirts blocked its way. She scooped it up, lifted it level with her face and smiled at its frightened mews.

"You have nothing to be afraid of. The puppy is gone and I'll not hurt you." She cuddled the trembling kitten close, stroked between its tiny ears and looked around for its mother, or more of the litter. There were no others in sight. She looked at the kitten, its tiny front paws now pushing against her cloak, its mouth searching for a source of sustenance, and frowned. It seemed awfully thin. She lifted it up to examine it more closely. "Are you an orphan?"

Sally. The name popped into her head, jolted her. Sally… Perhaps… She stared at the kitten, then again cuddled it close and hurried back down the path to talk with Sophia.

"Excuse me for interrupting your work, Reverend, but Willa—I mean Miss Wright—is outside. Says she'd like to talk with you."

Willa Wright wanted to see him? Matthew frowned and squelched the spurt of pleasure that shot through him. Of one thing he was certain—her call was not prompted by a desire to be in his company. "Please show her into the sitting room, Bertha. I'll be right along." He wiped the nib of his pen and blotted his notes for tomorrow's sermon.

"She doesn't want to come in. She asked particular that you come outside."

He stared at his housekeeper, then grabbed his suit jacket off the back of the chair and shrugged it on as he followed her to the kitchen.

"She's out there." Bertha Franklin nodded toward the door that led to the side porch and turned to the stove.

He straightened his cravat, smoothed the sides of his hair with the heels of his hands and stepped outside. She was standing at the end of the porch. Their gazes met. His heart lurched. "You wanted to speak with me, Miss Wright?"

"Yes. Thank you for coming outside." Her cool tone settled his pulse back to its normal beat. She stepped toward him. "I realize it's a most unusual request, but I didn't want the children to know I'm here. In case you don't—" She stopped, drew a breath. "Let me explain."

He nodded, forced himself to concentrate on her words instead of her.

"The other night during the carriage ride—" She paused, gave him a questioning look. "You do remember taking me home the night of the storm?"

"Quite well, yes." He should, it had cost him an hour or so of tossing and turning before he got to sleep. She evidently didn't like his answer for her chin raised and her shoulders squared beneath her cloak.

"Then you will recall telling me about Sally sleeping with her mother's glove, and asking for my advice."

Her voice softened when she spoke of Sally, her gaze turned warm and earnest. He lost his focus.

"I had no answer for you then, but I promised if one occurred to me I would tell you. I've come today because I believe I may have found one. If it meets with your approval of course. A kitten."

It was a moment before it sank in. "A *kitten*." What sort of an answer was that? He must have missed something. He frowned, mustered his senses.

She nodded and rushed into speech. "I know it seems odd, Reverend Calvert. I thought so, too. But then I realized— The only thing I have seen Sally truly interested in was the kitten story and contest. So, when I saw the kitten, I thought if Sally had a kitten to love and care for, it would take her mind off of her grief, at least part of the time. And—"

"Whoa. Wait a moment, Miss Wright."

She shot him a look of consternation.

He smiled and shook his head. "I'm not disagreeing, I simply need to catch up. What kitten?"

"I went to visit Sophia Sheffield earlier and discovered, quite by accident, that one of the stable cats had kittens. You see, a dog was chasing the kitten and—"

"Mrs. Sheffield's dog."

"No." She shook her head. "The dog—well, little more than a puppy really—is a stray hanging around her stable. Anyway, the dog was chasing the kitten and that's why I discovered it. And then I thought of Sally, and of how loving and caring for a kitten might help her over her grief."

"Yes, I see…" He gazed down into her incredible blue-green eyes, warm with compassion, earnest in her hope for Sally's healing. "And Mrs. Sheffield is willing to let Sally have the kitten?"

"*A* kitten, yes. She gets to choose. Unless you want Sally to have all three of them."

"Three?" Her eyes flashed with amusement. Her lips twitched, curved in a smile that made his pulse race. "I believe one will be sufficient." He turned toward the door. "I'll get Sally and Joshua, and you can take us to the kittens."

"There's one more thing."

She sounded hesitant. He turned back. "And that is?"

"I thought, perhaps, if you would allow Sally to take the kitten into her bed at night so she could cuddle it." She took a breath. "She can't do that while she is holding her mother's glove."

"Stop that barking! Get out of here!"

A stone came flying from the depths of the stable and hit the dog in the doorway. It yelped and ran off, crawled behind a clump of brush.

The stable hand stepped into view. "Way's clear now." He looked in the direction the dog ran, then walked back inside, muttering. "I'm gonna have to do somethin' about that cur. Can't have him barkin' at Mrs. Sheffield's guests when they come to the stable. Spookin' the horses all day…"

"Why did that man pitch a stone at the dog, Uncle Matt?"

He looked down at Joshua's face, noted the offended look in his eyes and squatted down to his level. "Mrs. Sheffield runs a hotel. She has a lot of guests and some of them keep their horses here in her stable. They have to be able to come in and out. And some of their horses are frightened by the dog's barking. It makes them restive. Do you understand?"

"Yes, sir. The dog shouldn't be round the stable."

He squeezed Joshua's shoulder, rose and took Sally's hand. "Lead on, Miss Wright."

She nodded and moved ahead. "This way."

"Why are we going in the barn, Uncle Matt?"

"You'll see, Sally."

Sunlight slanted in through the open door, lit their

way across the plank floor strewn with bits of hay and seed. A ball of orange-and-yellow fur darted out of the shadowed area behind a grain box in the corner and attacked another ball of black-and-white fur that was swatting at a string dangling from a burlap bag draped over the wall of a stall.

"Kitties!" Sally pulled her hand free and ran forward. The black-and-white kitten darted between two boards in the stall and disappeared. The orange-and-yellow one ducked back behind the grain box. Sally wedged the toe of her boot into a crack in the wall and scrambled on top of the chest, peered behind it. He'd never seen her so lively. "I can't reach them, Joshua!"

There was no answer. No brother running to Sally's rescue. He gave a quick glance around. Where did Joshua go? He frowned, stepped to the grain chest. "I'll get them, Sally." He reached for the orange-and-yellow kitten, got scratched for his effort. "A fighter, are you?" He captured the kitten, pulled it up and handed it to Sally. It jumped free of her grasp and ran into the stall.

"The kitty doesn't like me."

Sally's eyes teared up. Her little lower lip trembled. He vowed to stay there until he had caught one of the elusive felines and headed for the stall door.

"Look what I've found."

He turned back, watched Willa Wright reach behind a barrel, then straighten with a mewing, yellow kitten in her hands. She cooed to it, stroked it between its tiny pointed ears and carried it over to Sally. He couldn't take his gaze from Willa's face, the softness in her eyes, the gentle look of her mouth.

"Hold it gently and speak softly, Sally. It's only a baby and is frightened. If you hold it close, it will feel safe."

Sally nodded and cuddled the kitten against her velvet cloak. "Don't be afraid, kitty. I like you." The kitten stretched up and licked her chin. She giggled and looked up at it, her brown eyes shining with happiness. "The kitty likes me."

He nodded and cleared his throat, saw Willa Wright turn her back and raise her hand to wipe her cheeks. She moved in the direction of the door. He gritted his teeth and stayed rooted in place. He had no right to go to her—to keep her close.

"Can I have the kitty, Uncle Matt?"

He drew his thoughts back from the path they had started down and squatted in front of Sally. "A baby kitten needs a lot of love and care, Sally. You would have to give it food to eat and milk to drink every day. And take it outside and play with it after school. Can you do that?"

She gave a solemn nod.

"All right, then. You may have the kitten." He leaned forward and kissed her cheek, then glanced around. "You stay right here, Sally. I have to find Joshua."

"He's outside."

Willa Wright sounded odd—a little choked. He rose and hurried to her side. "Where?"

She glanced up at him, then looked away. "Beside the brush pile."

He looked where she had indicated. Joshua was on

his back on the ground, laughing and squirming as the dog on his chest licked his face.

He sucked in a breath and looked down at her, fixed his face in a mock scowl to cover his feelings. "A stray dog, Miss Wright?" Her gaze skittered away from his, but not before he'd caught the flash of satisfaction in her teary eyes.

"*Was* a stray dog, Reverend Calvert. I believe that puppy has found his owner." She lifted her chin and stepped over the log sill onto the gravel wagon way.

He stared after her. So prim and proper. So beautiful and loving toward the children. *Glory,* but he wanted that woman in his arms!

Chapter Eight

Willa skimmed her gaze from the deep, rich lace on the gown's round neck that left Ellen's shoulders bare, down the fitted bodice, to the long, full skirt that cascaded from the pointed waist in a series of folds caught up at intervals with satin knots. "It's a beautiful dress, Ellen. And you look especially beautiful in it."

Ellen laughed and did a slow pirouette. "Reverend Calvert thought so. He kept stealing glances at me during dinner."

"I'm sure he did." A twinge of irritation trickled through her. She should have made an excuse and continued on home when Ellen asked her to come see her new dress. She was losing patience with Ellen's vanity.

"Do you like my headdress, Willa? Mother copied it from a picture in *Godey's Lady's Book*." Ellen leaned over her dresser and looked in her mirror, touched one of the flowers that adorned the broad ribbon encircling her blond curls.

"It's lovely. Your mother makes wonderful flowers. I've always admired her skill." She stared at the deep lace that had fallen back to expose Ellen's wrist when she lifted her hand to the headdress. How many times had Ellen used that ploy to draw Matthew Calvert's attention to her beauty? She looked down at her own high-necked, dark blue wool dress, its only adornment a narrow blue ribbon at her small waist. It was not a garment to draw a man's eye—not that she wanted to. She'd learned her lesson when Thomas deserted her. All those proclamations of undying love…

She thrust away thoughts of Thomas, caught Ellen's gaze in the mirror and smiled. "Your mother was right. The blue of that Turkish satin does make your eyes look larger and more blue than usual—especially with the matching ribbon."

She turned away from Ellen's prideful smile and noticed her friend's Bible on the bedside table. "How was your recitation of the Psalm? Was the reverend suitably impressed?"

"He was, until those *wards* of his escaped Isobel."

"Escaped?" She glanced over her shoulder. Ellen was still admiring herself in the mirror. "That's an odd word to use."

"Oh, I assure you the word is appropriate. I told you Isobel was to keep them in the morning room until I had finished my entertainment." Ellen spun from the mirror to face her. "That girl started crying because Isobel told her she couldn't go to Matthew, and the naughty thing ran from the room! The boy stepped in front of Isobel when she tried to grab the girl, then ran to his sister and brought her, whining and crying, into the living room right in the middle of my recitation! They quite stole Reverend Calvert's attention from me.

I was furious—until it occurred to me that I could turn the situation to my profit."

"In what way?" What did it matter? It shouldn't matter. So why was she holding her breath?

"Why, to increase the reverend's interest in me as his future bride. His glances told me he finds me attractive, but of course, a man in his position must consider his wards, so I acted concerned for them. And then I suggested that he, being a new guardian, might profit by following Father's admonition that children must be disciplined with a firm hand." Ellen's lips curled.

She stared at her friend's smug smile. Ellen hadn't always been so callous and self-serving. Perhaps she didn't truly understand the situation. "Those children have suffered a great loss, Ellen. And they are in a new town, among people who are strangers to them. How could you suggest they needed discipline for wanting to be with their uncle?"

Ellen's gaze sharpened. "It so happened the reverend agreed with me, Willa. He took his wards off that very moment to put them abed." The smug smile returned. "I believe he was quite impressed by my maternal skills."

A heavy, sick feeling hit the pit of her stomach. Matthew Calvert had punished Sally and Joshua for interrupting his evening of flirtation with Ellen after the loss they had suffered? How could that be after the way he had so readily embraced her idea this morning and allowed them to have the kitten and the dog? Of course, if the pets helped the children heal from their grief and they were no longer so dependent on him, he would have more time for his other…pursuits. Anger chilled her. No wonder Matthew Calvert had appealed to her sympathy and asked for her advice.

"And, of course, Mother told him I had planned the entire evening—that I had chosen the menu, arranged for his wards to have their meal apart from the adults, and planned my recitation for his entertainment, so he is also aware of my homemaking and hostessing abilities. It's very important a pastor's wife possess such talents."

"Wife?" She snapped her gaping mouth closed. "You barely know Reverend Calvert, Ellen. What are you thinking? What of love?"

"Oh, I love him, Willa. Why would I not? He is exceedingly handsome and charming, and, most important, he holds a position of respect in the community. He is the perfect husband for me." Ellen smiled and did another slow pirouette in front of the mirror. "I've already told Father to accept when Matthew asks permission to court me."

Matthew? Ellen was calling him by his first name? He must have been *very* attentive last night. She closed her mind to the unwelcome images the thought conjured. "And what about Joshua and Sally?"

"Joshua and— Oh, his wards." Ellen shrugged her bare shoulders. "They won't be a problem. I'll manage them, just as I did last night. Only, when Matthew and I are married, they will soon learn they will be punished if they disobey."

"I see." She turned toward the door to hide her face. There was no telling what her expression would betray. "I must be going, Ellen. Mama is waiting for her indigo."

"Very well, Willa. I shall see you in church tomorrow."

The satin of Ellen's dress rustled. She glanced back over her shoulder and clenched her hands on the basket handle. She needn't have worried about betraying her anger. Ellen was already back before her mirror practicing her coquettish smiles.

Willa scowled at the toes of her boots rapidly flashing into view, one after the other, from beneath her skirt hems. How could she have let herself be deceived by that—that *manipulator?* How could she have believed for one instant that Matthew Calvert's requests for her help were based in an unselfish concern for Joshua and Sally's well-being? He had shown his true colors last night at the Halls', punishing those children for their need to feel cared about and safe. Well, he needn't think that she—

"Oh!" She bumped against a hard body. Strong hands clasped her shoulders, held firm when she tried to step back from the close contact. "Unhand me, sir!" She raised her free hand and shoved against the plaid jacket covering the man's chest.

"You don't mean that, Willa."

Thomas! Shock froze her. She lifted her head, gazed into the twinkling blue eyes that had so mesmerized her and came roaring back to life. "Let go of me, Thomas."

"Never, Willa. I came back to claim you for my own, and—"

"I'm not interested in your *lies,* Thomas. *Let me go!*" She dropped her basket and pushed at his arms.

Footsteps thudded against the ground, large, callused hands flashed into her view, clamped on Thomas's shoulders and pulled him away from her. David Dibble stepped in front of her, blocked Thomas from her with his body. "Be on your way, Hunter. Miss Willa doesn't want to talk to you."

Willa caught her breath at the menace in David Dibble's voice. She stared at the blue shirt stretched across his broad shoulders, at the hint of curl in the gray-brown hair that covered his nape and brushed his collar. She could swear it was bristling. Surely he wouldn't fight Thomas on her account? Tears sprang to her eyes.

"I'll go, but I'm not giving up. I'll see you again, Willa."

She drew a breath of relief, closed her eyes and listened to Thomas's retreating footsteps. Boots scuffed against the ground. She opened her eyes and looked up at David Dibble. There was anger in his gray eyes…and concern. Genuine concern. For her?

"You all right, Miss Willa?"

The concern was in his voice, too. She blinked away the tears and nodded.

He crouched down onto his heels, picked up the packet of buttons and bag of coffee off the ground, put them back in her basket, rose and held it out to her. "If Hunter bothers you again, you let me know. I'll put a stop to it."

Tears clogged her throat. She swallowed hard

and took hold of the basket handle. "Thank you, Mr. Dibble."

The anger in his eyes softened. He gave a curt nod and touched the rolled brim of his knitted hat. "Remember me to your mama."

"I shall." She watched him stride back to his livery, then hurried to the bridge, rushed across and turned onto Brook Street.

She scanned the area for any sign of Thomas, and finding none, hastened down the beaten path to their cabin. The door hinges creaked their welcome. She dashed inside, closed the door and leaned back against it to catch her breath.

"What took you so long, Willa? I've been waiting for— What's wrong? What's happened?" Her mother threw down the towel she held and started toward her.

She straightened and shook her head. "I hurried and ran out of breath."

Her mother stopped, fixed a look on her. "You might as well tell me the rest of it, Willa Jean. I'll hear soon enough anyway."

Her bravado crumpled. Her desire to spare her mother the stressful news was swept away by a strong, almost overwhelming need to be comforted. "Oh, Mama, Thomas is back. He stopped me by the bridge and wouldn't let me go. I tried to push him away, but—" The tears she'd been fighting back spilled over. She went into her mother's open arms and laid her head on her thin shoulder. So many times she had cried away her hurts and her confusion in her mother's arms. "Mr. Dibble saw my struggle and came and pulled Thomas away from me. He made him leave.

And he told me if Thomas bothered me again I was to come and tell him. That he would make him stop."

She sniffed and drew back. Her mother's eyes were bright with unshed tears. "Why would he do that, Mama?"

"Because that's the kind of man David Dibble is, Willa. He's a fine, fine man. Now, you go wash your face and rest a bit lest your head start to pain you. I have work to do."

Her mother touched her cheek, took the basket from her and walked into the kitchen. She stared after her. There had been something in her mother's voice when she spoke of David Dibble. It had been quickly covered, but it had been there. And it was something she'd never heard before.

A fine, fine man. She shook her head and headed for her room. There was no such thing in her experience.

Matthew started up the stairs, heard muffled giggles, smiled and went back to his study. The bedtime prayers could wait, he would give them a few more minutes to play with their pets. He shot a glance toward the ceiling. Did Robert and Judith know? Did they hear their children laughing?

He strolled over to his desk. What a blessing to hear the children's clandestine laughter instead of the dreaded, bedtime silence filled with their quiet sobs. "Thank You, Lord. Thank You that Joshua and Sally are laughing again."

What a debt he owed to Willa Wright for her suggestion about the kitten and puppy. There had been mild mayhem around the parsonage all afternoon and evening, what with Joshua and Sally darting in and out of rooms chasing after their exploring pets, and then laughing and racing around the yard trying to catch them when they took them outside.

He glanced down at his Bible and chuckled. An odd thing to be thankful for…mayhem. And Mrs. Franklin. Another blessing brought into their lives by Willa Wright. The housekeeper was stern in appearance, but she had a heart for the children—and they knew it. They hadn't even hesitated about running to the kitchen and showing her their pets and begging dishes of food and milk for them.

A log burned through, broke into pieces and sent a shower of sparks up the chimney. He walked over and added another chunk of wood to the fire. The housekeeper was a blessing all right. She'd glanced his way, caught his nod and complied, but she'd told Joshua and Sally they would be responsible for keeping their pets' dishes clean, that she had enough work to do. And then she'd told them the kitten and puppy would need a place to stay while they were in school and she'd put an old towel on the floor behind the stove where it was always warm. "Lord, I pray You will bless Mrs. Franklin for her kind heart."

He glanced up at the wall clock. He could wait no longer to settle the children and hear their prayers or they would be tired for church tomorrow. He left his study and climbed the stairs into the silence, paused. There was something different. The quiet felt… peaceful.

He tiptoed down the hall and quietly opened Joshua's bedroom door. The boy was sound asleep, a smile on his face, one skinny arm draped over the puppy sprawled across his small chest. So much for the dog bed they'd made out of a blanket and placed on the floor in the corner. He grinned, crossed to the nightstand and snuffed the lamp, tiptoed back out into the hall, closed the door and walked to Sally's room.

"Please, Lord…" He held his breath and opened the door. Sally was curled up on her side, her eyes closed, her small, pink lips slighted parted in sleep. One of her long curls was caught in the tiny paws of the kitten cuddled beneath her chin. He expelled the breath to ease the sudden pressure in his chest and crossed to the night table. Judith's glove was lying at the base of the lamp. The pressure swelled, his throat tightened. *Thank You, Lord. Thank You.* He snuffed the lamp, crept from the room and quietly closed the door.

Light from the lamp on the wall sconce threw a golden circle on the floor. He stood there staring at the pattern in the carpet runner for a long moment, then cleared the lump from his throat, shook his head and started down the stairs. Whoever would have thought he would rejoice that his niece and nephew had fallen asleep without saying their nightly prayers?

Willa stared into the darkness willing sleep to come, but the uncomfortable, tight feel of her body defeated her. She stretched and turned onto her side and tried to restrain her tumbling thoughts. They refused to obey her bidding.

Why had Thomas come back? What had happened to his dream of going west? *Something* had happened.

She didn't, for one moment, believe he had come home because he loved her.

I came back to claim you for my own.

Hah! She huffed a breath and flopped onto her other side. As if she would believe that lie! A man who loves you and wants you for his own doesn't walk out on you three days before you're to be wed.

What was she to do? The news of Thomas's return would have spread through the village like the flood waters of the Allegheny River in the spring—even faster. And tomorrow was Sunday. She couldn't even stay home and hide for a day while she thought about what to do. Everyone would be waiting and watching to see what she—

Oh, no! She bolted upright, her heart pounding. Everyone thought Thomas had left with her blessing. They would expect her to joyously welcome him back.

A pang of guilt struck. So did the cold, damp night air.

She shivered, flopped back onto her pillow and tugged the quilt up to her chin. Talk about being hoist by your own petard. She should have told the truth and faced the shame of Thomas's desertion. Still… Thomas would never cast himself in a bad light. He would not tell anyone about his foul treatment of her. She had only to wait a few days and then simply refuse his suit. There would be no stigma raised if she changed her mind. Everything would work out fine.

She yawned, turned on her side and closed her eyes. Everything would turn out fine....

Chapter Nine

"It's only until church is over, pup." Matthew scratched behind the whining dog's ears, opened the lid of the kitten's basket he'd set on top of the grain chest, closed the stable door and walked back to the house. Childish chatter and the calm responses of the housekeeper floated out of the kitchen. His heart swelled with thankfulness. Those pets had changed the entire atmosphere of the house. He picked up his sermon notes from his study and strode to the kitchen doorway. "I'm going to the church now, Mrs. Franklin."

The older woman nodded, put another piece of jam-slathered bread in front of Joshua. "We'll be coming as soon as these poke-alongs finish their breakfast and I get them fit out in their Sunday best."

Joshua shoved a spoonful of oatmeal into his mouth and lifted his head. "I'm not a poke-along, Uncle Matt. I'm just hungry."

He grinned at his tousle-haired nephew. "If you lick that elderberry jam off your cheek it should help ease that hunger problem."

Sally giggled.

"You, too, princess." He tapped a spot above the corner of his mouth, winked at her and stepped back into the entrance hall to check his own appearance.

The face that stared back at him from the mirror was nice-looking enough in a woman's eyes, he supposed. At least there were no major flaws he could see. He frowned and smoothed the hair at his temples *again,* straightened the folds on his cravat *again,* looked himself in the eye and shook his head. He'd never before had this hunger for a woman's approval. This gnawing eagerness, this *need* to have one look on him with favor. Willa Wright, and her cool demeanor, had changed all of that.

He turned from the mirror, walked to the door and stepped out into the cold morning air. The mere thought of seeing the woman had his stomach taut with anticipation. Willa Wright was not as distant as she acted, and he couldn't wait to look into her beautiful blue-green eyes and watch the warmth come into them as he shared with her the amazing change in the children her suggestion regarding the pets had wrought.

A cloud of warm breath formed in front of his face as he trotted down the steps to the frost-covered ground and strode toward the church. Why did she affect such a cool remoteness? He had never before experienced the sense of shared purpose, of *oneness* he'd felt when he talked with her about the children the other day. And he wanted to see that warmth in her eyes because of *him.* He wanted Willa Wright to look on him with—more than favor.

He puffed out another cloud and entered the church through the back room. The chill was gone. He laid his notes on the altar, moved to the stove and added more wood to the fire he'd started earlier. A wisp of concern he didn't want to acknowledge drifted into his mind. Where did Willa stand in her relationship with God? It was something he'd wondered about. She came to church, but people attended church for many different reasons, and he'd been a preacher long enough to know that some of those reasons had nothing to do with the Lord.

A small twist adjusted the stove dampers for a slower burn. He leaned against the nearest box pew and cast back through his memory. He couldn't recall any conversation in which Willa had mentioned her faith or spoken of the Lord. His calling, *and* his heart, required that the woman he married be possessed of a strong faith. Before his...regard...for Willa Wright grew any deeper, he had to know the answer to that question.

He shook off his sense of unease, set aside his personal concerns, and went and knelt before the altar to pray for God's blessing on the church and on the message he was about to share.

Thank goodness the wool hood hid her face. Willa tugged it farther forward and hurried up the steps. Her nose was probably as red as a beet—her cheeks, too. For sure they felt frozen. Well, what did she expect, sneaking across town and hiding in the unheated schoolhouse, like a craven coward, watching for Thomas while waiting for church to begin? But she'd had no choice. She did not want to be taken off-guard again. Thomas's unexpected appearance yesterday still had her unsettled and shaken.

It wasn't that she lacked fortitude. It was simply that she wanted to speak with him privately lest he make his claim of her in front of everyone. His *claim*. It made her sound like a piece of property. Well, she had no intention of becoming his possession. His desertion had broken their betrothal and released her from any responsibility of fidelity. Of course, the townspeople didn't know that. That's why she had to speak to him. Oh, why hadn't she simply swallowed her pride and been honest?

The door opened with a soft whisper. She slipped inside and eased the door closed. Henry Cargrave was offering the opening prayer. She stepped to the open pew on the left, spotted Sophia Sheffield motioning her to come and tiptoed down the aisle and joined her in her private box. Thankfully, the door was well oiled. She acknowledged her kindness with a nod and a smile and bowed her head. The aggravating thing was her plan to speak with Thomas alone had failed. He had not appeared. All her shivering and shaking had been in vain. And now, she had to worry about him waiting for her after the service. He knew she would be here. In Pinewood, teachers were expected to attend church.

"I take my text this morning from the book of Revelations…"

Matthew Calvert's deep, rich voice drew her from her thoughts. She pushed her hood back slightly, lifted her head and looked forward. His gaze shifted, met hers, lingered. Her fingers fumbled, froze. His gaze moved on. She let out a breath and lowered her hands to her lap.

Sophia leaned her way. She pushed her hood away from her ear and inclined her head.

"Matthew Calvert is too handsome for words. And a much better catch than Thomas Hunter."

Sophia's whispered words tickled her ear and stiffened her body. She cast a quick glance at those closest to them to make sure they hadn't overheard, then looked at the older woman. Why had she made such an outrageous statement? The answer lay in the violet-colored eyes twinkling at her from beneath the feather-trimmed brim of Sophia's green velvet bonnet. The woman had heard Thomas was back and was teasing her.

She settled back against the pew and cast another covert glance around. No one was paying them any mind. Thank goodness no one had overheard! There would be gossip enough sweeping through the village over Thomas's return—she didn't need another rumor, about her refusing his hand and setting her cap for the preacher. She would tell Sophia of Ellen's feelings for Matthew Calvert directly after church and that would be the end of it.

"Thank you for your kind invitation, Mrs. Townsend. I accept." Matthew smiled at the plump, elderly woman and shook her husband's hand. "I'll see you at tea Tuesday afternoon, Manning." He watched the tall, gray-haired man take hold of his wife's elbow and start down the steps, then turned to the next person in line.

"Excellent sermon, Reverend Calvert. Made a lot

of sense. I'll be thinking on it this week while I'm milking an' caring for the cows an' such."

He met the dairy farmer's strong grip and nodded. "I'm pleased to hear that, sir."

"My heart, also, was stirred to response, Reverend. I intend to make a stronger effort to draw closer to the Lord, to know Him as my personal Savior in the way you described."

His heart swelled with thanksgiving. He flexed his squeezed hand and smiled at the farmer's wife. "Nothing would please the Lord more. He longs for fellowship with His children, and—"

"'Behold, I stand, at the door, and knock: If any man hear my voice, and open the door, I will come in to him, and will sup with him, and he with me.'"

Ellen Hall. He held back the frown that started at her interruption.

The farmer glanced over his shoulder. "Hello, Mrs. Hall…Mr. Hall. You quote Scripture very well, Ellen." The man's gaze came back to rest on him. "We'll move on. Goodbye, Reverend Calvert." He took hold of his wife's arm and started down the porch steps.

He made a mental note to pay a visit to the man's farm during the coming week, and turned to bid farewell to the Halls.

"You preached a wonderful message today, Reverend Calvert."

He ignored Ellen's flattering tone and inclined his head. "I see you remembered the Scripture I took as my text, Miss Hall."

The feather trim on her blue velvet bonnet quivered as she tilted her head. She looked up through her long eyelashes and gave him a small smile. "It brings to my mind our dining together the other night."

"Indeed?" Must the woman turn everything—even the quotation of Holy Scripture—into an occasion for flirting? He shifted his gaze to her parents. "And that reminds me that I must thank you again for the lovely dinner, and again, apologize for my hasty leave-taking."

"We were sorry you left us early, Reverend." Conrad Hall shook his offered hand. "Ellen's recitation of Psalm eighty-four was excellent."

"I'm sure it was, sir."

"Father, please, Reverend Calvert was simply following your admonition to strong discipline for children. My small entertainment was of little importance compared to that."

His gaze was drawn by the movement of Ellen's hand. She tucked the collar of her velvet cape closer around her chin and protruded her bottom lip in a small pout. "I'm certain your adorable, young wards profited from your firmness, Reverend." The pout morphed into another smile.

He held his silence, dipped his head in response. How often did she practice those coy through-her-lashes looks? He couldn't imagine Willa Wright doing such a thing. But he did, there and then. And the image conjured of the prim-and-proper schoolmarm indulging in such an activity made his lips curve into a smile and his hunger to see her grow.

He skimmed his gaze over the people climbing into carriages, strolling home on the walkway or visiting with each other in the yard, but did not see her neat, trim figure among them. He'd missed her. She must have left before he reached the door. His smile died.

From the corner of his eye he saw Simon Pritchard step through the church door, pause and lean heavily on his cane. He made the Halls a polite bow. "Excuse me, please."

He stepped to the elderly man's side. "Mr. Pritchard, it's good to see you well again, sir. May I help you down the steps?"

The silk of Ellen Hall's long skirt rustled. He cast a sidelong glance her way. The young woman *was* pretty, very pretty, as the admiring glances of the men gazing up at her from the yard testified.

"Thank you, Reverend, but John's brung the carriage. He'll fetch me."

"Very well, Mr. Pritchard." He smiled and placed his hand on the elderly man's bony shoulder. "Perhaps one of these Sundays John will come inside."

"I ain't 'spectin' that to happen anytime soon." The old man snorted, shook his head and shuffled toward the steps.

He turned and went inside and swept his glance over the empty pews. "Thank You, Lord, for the privilege of ministering to Your people. Settle Your message of truth in their hearts and spirits that it may bear fruit for Thee, I pray. Amen."

He picked up his notes from the pulpit, closed the Bible and headed for the back door, his footsteps echoing in the empty church, the disappointment of not seeing Willa after the service, of not being able to share with her the news of the change in the children clouding his otherwise satisfying morning.

* * *

"Have you given your kitten a name?" Willa stood at the base of the steps of the side porch, reached toward the kitten curled up in Sally's lap and stroked between its small pointed ears with her fingertip. It was the only spot available. The rest of the purring ball of fur was covered by Sally's little hands.

Sally's nod set her blond curls bouncing. "I named him Tickles, 'cause his fur tickles my face when he sleeps under my chin."

"I see." She stared at Sally's beaming face and blinked back the tears that smarted her eyes. She could hardly believe the change in the little girl. "I think that's a wonderful name, and an excellent reason for choosing it." Perhaps Matthew Calvert had allowed Sally to have the kitten in her bed? And if so, had she given up her mother's glove?

"I could have named him Scratchy, 'cause that's how his tongue feels when he kisses me."

Sally giggled, a sound so joyous that it brought her own laughter bubbling up.

"Watch this, Miss Wright!"

She turned and looked at Joshua. He drew back his arm and threw a small piece of branch.

"Fetch it, boy! Fetch the stick!"

The puppy beside him barked, ran around in circles, then raced back to plant his front paws against Joshua's knees. The boy leaned down and petted his dog, looked up and gave her a sheepish grin. "I guess he hasn't learned the trick yet, but he will. He's a real smart dog." His brown eyes were alight with pride and love for his dog.

Her heart swelled. "I'm sure he is, Joshua." She squatted, drew her cloak over her long skirts that ballooned around her, and rubbed behind the dog's ears before she gave in to the urge to hug the young boy. "Does this fellow have a name yet?"

"Yes, ma'am. I call him Happy, because that's how he makes me feel."

Oh dear. She blinked. Blinked again.

"Well! What's going on here?"

She jerked her head up and looked straight into Matthew Calvert's brown eyes. Her breath caught in her throat, warmth flowed across her cheeks. She yanked her gaze away from his, let go of the dog and started to rise.

"Allow me."

She stared at his outstretched hand, remembered the tingling warmth of his touch when he'd helped her from his buggy and wished she had never yielded to the children's pleas for her to come see their pets. Irritation spurted through her. What was he doing home so soon anyway? The way he had been smiling at Ellen, she'd assumed she would have plenty of time to see the pets and leave.

She placed her hand on his palm, ignored the strength, the feel of his hand holding hers and rose.

The kitchen door squeaked open. "Joshua and Sally, you catch up those animals and come inside now. Dinner's ready." Bertha Franklin stepped to the edge of the porch and squinted down at her. "Why, Willa, I didn't know you were here. Did you want—" The older woman's gaze dropped, her eyes widened.

She jerked her hand from Matthew Calvert's grasp.

"The children asked me to come and see their pets. They— You see, I found them, the pets I mean, and—" she took a breath, pulled herself together "—and I have a proprietary interest in them." Bertha was staring at her. Were her cheeks red? They felt on fire. She leaned down and picked up the kitten's basket.

"Bye, Miss Wright!"

"Goodbye, children."

She fussed with the lid of the basket. Joshua and the puppy scrambled up the steps and followed Sally and her kitten inside. Bertha's footsteps crossed the porch.

"Remember me to your mama, Willa."

"I will, Bertha."

The door closed. She heaved a sigh, placed the basket on the porch and turned. Matthew Calvert had a definite, amused glint in his eyes, and something more. Something that brought that heat back to her cheeks. She looked down.

"I'm glad you came when the children asked, Miss Wright. I wanted to speak with you, and I thought I had missed you after church."

When you were talking with Ellen? The thought steadied her, fortified her against the oh-so-charming reverend. She stiffened her spine.

"I wanted to tell you that your suggestion about the kitten worked. Sally cuddled it all night. Her mother's glove stayed on her nightstand."

Tears welled. She took a breath to control them. "I'm so pleased for Sally's sake." She brushed at a bit of dried leaf clinging to her cloak, groped for the resistance his soft words had undermined. Think of how he behaves apart from the children. She lifted her chin and met his gaze full on. "Thank you for telling me, Reverend Calvert. Good afternoon."

He didn't move out of her path. She stumbled to a stop. So did her heart. Mindless things, hearts. She took a step back.

"I also wanted to tell you that I have discussed plans with the church elders to begin a Sunday school class for the young children." He smiled.

She stared at that oh-so-warm and sincere smile and her racing pulse slowed. Thomas smiled like that. Suspicion reared.

"They decided to have the class meet in the schoolhouse as it is close by and will be convenient for those who live outside the village and must drive to church. Of course, we need someone to teach the children."

Of course. He'd wanted to talk to her because he needed yet another favor. Would she never learn?

"The elders suggested I ask you. And I wholeheartedly agreed. You are wonderful with children, Miss Wright." His gaze captured hers. "Will you accept?"

His smile and his compliment left her cold. She shook her head, drew breath to explain that she could not teach children about a God she did not believe in, then clamped her lips shut. If the elders found out about her lack of faith, they would dismiss her and hire another to teach in her place. She was trapped into accepting. Unless…

She drew back her shoulders and lifted her chin. "Please thank the elders for considering me for the position, Reverend Calvert, but I feel there is someone better suited than I to teach the Sunday school class. A person with whom you share a mutual belief in 'firm discipline' for children. I suggest you ask Miss Hall to teach the class. I'm quite certain she will be eager to do so. Good day."

She swept by him and hurried down the stone walk toward the road. *Thomas.* She jerked to a halt. Thomas smiled and came toward her. She glanced back over her shoulder. Reverend Calvert was still standing by the porch steps watching her. Trapped again. She took a deep breath and moved forward.

Chapter Ten

Everyone they walked past stared and smiled. Willa threw a sidelong look at Thomas waving and calling out greetings, and tugged her hood forward. She forced yet another smile and waved at another couple, the carriage rumbling by.

"Must you be so…exuberant, Thomas?" She breathed a sigh of relief as they stepped off the Stony Creek bridge and turned onto Brook Street. It wasn't far now.

"How can I be otherwise when I have my promised bride walking at my side, Willa?"

"I am not your promised bride." She gave him a cool look. "We have been discussing how you walked out on our wedding, remember?"

"Tom!"

She glanced across the road at the hail.

Thomas turned slightly and waved to the man slouching against the hitching post in front of Nate Turner's Wagon Shop. "Good afternoon, Arnie."

"For sure it is you, Tom!" The wheelwright grinned and waggled his eyebrows. "Meet me later. I'll be at

Jack's." The young man straightened, swept off his hat and made her a deep bow. "Good afternoon, Miss Wright."

Mocker! He knew she did not appreciate his flirtatious teasing. Arnold Dixon had a very unsavory reputation. She lifted her chin, turned her head away and quickened her pace. Tom? Arnie? She hadn't known Thomas was friends with Arnold Dixon. And had Mr. Dixon been speaking of Johnny Taylor, another man of low repute, when he asked Thomas to join him?

"Whoa, slow down, Willa, honey. I want—"

"Do not call me 'Willa honey,' Thomas." She put a chill in her voice. "Nor 'your bride' nor any other such—" the word *endearment* stuck in her throat "—such…*thing*. You have no right. You forfeited that privilege when you de— When you left. I am Miss Wright to you."

He smiled and took hold of her elbow. "Now, Willa—"

"*Miss Wright*. And don't speak to me in that condescending tone." She pulled her elbow from his grasp and slipped her arm inside her cape where he could not reach it.

His features tightened.

"I know you're angry about my leaving the way I did, but I don't think you want to be acting that way, Willa. After all, you said everyone thinks you told me to go west after my dream. That being the way of it, they will all expect us to take up our plans to be wed again now that I'm back. You can tell that from their smiles."

"Then they shall be sorely disappointed." She caught her breath at her slip of tongue and started back down the path. Hopefully, he hadn't noticed.

"Is that what you're going to tell that nosy neighbor of yours? And suppose you tell *me* what that means." He gave her a speculative glance. "You agreed to accept my suit again."

She stopped and lifted her head. Mrs. Braynard was on her stoop, looking their way. She looked up at Thomas, took a breath and told him the truth. "It means I agreed to again accept your court, but I do not care for your presumption that my willingness to do so means our relationship is as before." She lifted her chin and confessed her plan. "I shall, of course, honor my word—for a few days—but then I shall tell Mrs. Braynard, and everyone else, that I have discovered I do not esteem you highly enough to marry you."

He rubbed his chin, then slowly nodded. "I see. Well, I guess I understand that." He narrowed his eyes, focused on hers.

She wanted to turn away, to avoid the intensity of his gaze, but held her ground.

"You don't want everyone to know I up and left you like I did."

She sucked in a breath at his bald statement, fought back tears at the cruelty of his words.

His expression changed into one she was quite certain was meant to show contrition, but it fell short of the mark.

"I made a bad mistake, Willa. I admit that. But what I did isn't the same as your pa deserting you and your ma."

She stiffened, clenched her hands. How dare he bring up her father! She never should have told him about him.

"Now don't get riled." He smiled down at her. "All I want is another chance to prove how much I love you, Willa, honey. I guess a few days is long enough to do that, then we'll go ahead with that wedding we had planned."

"No, Thomas. I—"

"Will most likely change your mind." His hand pressed against the small of her back, urged her forward on the path. "How is your mama, Willa?"

She glanced up at his abrupt change of topic, stared at the hard edge on his smile, at the dark glint in his eyes. What had happened to his charming ways? She didn't know this man. Unease settled like a stone in her stomach.

"Hello, Willa, dear." Mrs. Braynard beamed at them. "How nice to see you back, Mr. Hunter."

"Thank you, Mrs. Braynard. It's good to be back." Thomas made the elderly woman an exaggerated bow. "May I say you put this lovely October day to shame?"

"Well, aren't you silver-tongued, young man. As if you had eyes for any except your betrothed." Mrs. Braynard laughed. Her pudgy hands smoothed her full skirt over her thick girth.

Silver-tongued? Or a glib liar? Either way, she had been duped by Thomas into thinking he was something he was not. She wanted nothing more to do with him. She paused on the stoop of her cabin and turned toward him, drew breath to speak.

"Careful, Willa. The old busybody is still watching."

Thomas grabbed her hand, held it firm and bowed. "I'll see you tomorrow. Give my regards to your mama."

There it was again, that slight change in his voice when he mentioned her mother. She kept silent, stared at him, her unease growing.

He smiled, opened the door for her and walked back to the path, whistling.

There was something unsettling about him. How could she ever have thought herself in love with such a man? She took a deep breath and glanced next door. She would tell Mrs. Braynard the truth right now and face the shame. At least she would be done with Thomas.

"Willa?"

She spun around.

Her mother wiped her hands on her apron and smoothed back a lock of hair. "Why are you standing there with the door open? The house will cool down. Come and eat your dinner. I fixed chicken."

She looked into her mother's eyes and read the love there. *How is your mama, Willa?* Nausea swirled. So that was why Thomas was so certain she would overlook his desertion and marry him.

Her fierce, protective love for her mother rose. Her hands clenched in helpless fury. She could not subject her mother to the furor of resurrected gossip about her father's abandonment that would flood the village if the truth about Thomas's desertion of her became known. She couldn't put her mother through that again. Her stomach churned. She stepped inside and pushed against the door until it clicked shut.

"I'm coming, Mama." She unfastened her cloak and

hung it on a peg, forced a cheerful tone into her voice. "I was hoping you'd fix chicken."

"I know. It's your favorite." Her mother smiled and stepped back into the kitchen.

She took a deep breath, pressed her hand to her roiling stomach and followed. She'd find some way to swallow the food.

A game of chess could not compete with a puppy. Matthew looked at the abandoned game board on the table beside the window in the sitting room and smiled. He picked up a captured knight and absently fingered it. Who was that man? Did Willa Wright have a brother? He'd not heard of one. Of course, he'd been here only a few weeks. Still, Willa was right when she'd told him a small village has few secrets. News here traveled at a head-swirling pace. There was nothing malicious about it, though. It was simply how the villagers kept up with news of one another. Anyway, it seemed as though if she had a brother, he would have heard by now.

He set the knight back on the table and jammed his hands in his pockets. Whoever the man was, she knew him. She'd paused for a moment, glanced back at him, then walked on to meet the man. What had that quick glance at him meant? Probably nothing. To assign a motive to it would be pure conjecture, not to mention wishful thinking.

The man was a good-looking fellow. Fit, too. Looked to be a logger or a sawmill worker, judging by his clothes. Probably a sawyer. He plopped down onto the settee, leaned his head against the padded curved back and stretched out his legs. He'd been told loggers worked out of their camps in the hills and seldom showed up in town this time of year. He frowned down at his toes. Of course, the man might be a jobber. The foremen of the various camps lived in cabins in town and sometimes came home at weeks' end. That could explain why he hadn't seen him before.

Shouts and laughter from outside pulled him off the settee to see what was going on. He stepped to the window and looked out. The dog was chasing Joshua and Sally around the base of the huge maple tree that dominated the front yard. Sally tripped and fell headlong to the leaf-strewn ground.

He tensed, spun to go outside, heard her laughter and turned back. The puppy was licking her face and wagging his tail so furiously that he almost tipped himself over.

He grinned, leaned his shoulder against the frame and watched. Sally giggled and tried to push the puppy away, but she was no match for the wiggling, squirming dog who obviously enjoyed the game. He evaded her small hands, barked and attacked with new vigor, his tongue licking as fast as his tail wagged. Sally giggled harder and covered her face with her small arms.

"Joshua, help me!"

Her call to her brother came, muted but distinct, through the window.

Joshua jumped from behind the tree. "C'mon, Happy, c'mon, boy!" He slapped his small hands against his thighs, turned and ran. The dog left off his licking and raced after his master, barking and quickly gaining ground. Sally scrambled to her feet and ran after them.

His heart swelled so much it hurt. "Are you watching, Robert? Do you see your children laughing and playing, Judith? I sure hope so. I believe you do. Somehow, someway, I think you two know Josh and Sally are going to be all right. And that we have Willa Wright to thank for it."

Willa. He liked the name. It was sort of strong, yet soft. And it fit her. That little chin of hers raised like a flag of warning when she was feeling…what? Threatened in some way? But the truth of her nature was found in the softness and warmth of her eyes when her emotions overcame her… He frowned. The word that came to mind was…defenses.

He went back and collapsed onto the settee, stretched out his legs, clasped his hands behind the back of his neck and stared up at the plaster ceiling. Why would Willa feel threatened and defensive around him? He cast around in his memory for a reason but came up empty. He'd figure it out, though. Willa Wright was an enigma…a challenge. And he never backed away from—

"Uncle Matt! Uncle Matt!" The front door slammed against the wall.

He bolted upright and ran to the doorway, almost lost his balance and toppled backward when Sally hurled herself against his legs.

"C'mon!" She grabbed his hand and tugged him toward the open front door. "Happy chased Tickles up the tree and she's crying and she won't come down and it's getting dark and she's scared and—" She stopped tugging on his hand and looked up at him. Her little lip trembled, her eyes overflowed with tears. "I w-want my k-kitty. I don't want m-my kitty to be g-gone."

"Shh, Sally, don't cry." He bent, scooped her into his arms and wiped the tears from her soft little cheeks. "Tickles isn't going anywhere. I'll get him out of the tree."

She leaned back and looked into his eyes. "P-promise?"

He gave an emphatic nod and closed the door behind them. "I promise."

Willa shifted the bowl of potato peelings and chicken scraps from her mother's preparation of their dinner, leaned over the fence and dumped it into the trough for the Braynards' pigs. Most of the food from her plate was included in the slop. She hadn't been able to force it down after all.

The two sows lunged upright, snorting and grunting, and stuck their snouts into the wood basin. "Enjoy your meal, pigs. I couldn't eat mine."

"You ailing, Willa?"

"Oh!" The bowl slipped from her hands. She spun around, her hand pressed to her chest. "Daniel! It's good to see you out and around again…I think." She blew out a breath. "You startled me."

"I can tell." He grinned with the ease of a lifelong friend, stepped to her side, leaned over the fence and smacked the largest sow on the shoulder with his good hand. "Give over now!" He snatched her bowl out of the pigpen, squatted and wiped it on the grass.

"You're using your arm. Oh, Daniel, I'm so glad you're getting better." She smiled down at him.

"I've a ways to go, but I should be going back to camp soon. I'll help out with the cooking and stuff until I can get back to logging."

Her smile faded. "Do you think you should? Go back to logging, I mean. You were badly injured, Daniel." Would Thomas go to work logging? Hope stirred. That would give her time to think of what to do.

"You sound like Ma." Daniel rose and handed her the bowl. "If I don't go back we'd have to give up the cabin. I'd get along, but Ma wouldn't have a place to live."

Yes. She knew about that. So did Thomas. *But what I did isn't the same as your pa deserting you and your ma.* Had he always been so cruel? Why had she not noticed?

"Besides, that accident never should have happened—wouldn't have if that new hick on the crew had called out a warning like he should have." Daniel frowned and shook his head. "By the time I heard the snapping and cracking of that tree falling it was too late to get out of the way." He rubbed at his left shoulder. "I'm hoping the jobber might let me work as a teamster from now on. I've always been good with horses."

A teamster. Is that how Thomas earned his living? How could she not know? It seemed that in the rush of his courtship she'd made a lot of assumptions. "That would be wonderful. I'm sure your mother would be relieved."

He nodded, squinted down at her. "So what's ailing you?"

She shook her head. "Nothing serious. My stomach is…upset."

"That all?" He leaned back against the fence and studied her face. "You look kind of…unsettled, 'special when I came up on you."

She noted the concern in his eyes, sighed and leaned against the fence beside him. "Thomas is back."

"I heard. And that you didn't want to talk with him." He frowned. "He bothering you, is he? I thought David Dibble warned him off."

Her stomach knotted afresh. News spread so quickly. People must be wondering about her actions. "He did, but Thomas came and walked home with me after church." She looked down at the bowl she held against her apron so he couldn't read the turmoil in her eyes. "He says he wants to—" She caught her breath. She couldn't tell him *that,* he would know Thomas had deserted her. "He wants us to get married."

"That what you want? 'Cause if it's not, and he pesters you, I'll take care of it."

Tears threatened. If only she could tell him the truth. She blinked, looked over at Daniel and forced a teasing note into her voice. "With your bad arm?"

His jaw jutted. "I'd manage."

And hurt your arm again in the doing. No, my friend, this is my problem. "Thank you, Daniel. I'm certain you would, but it's not necessary. I simply have to decide what I want to do."

She pushed away from the fence. "I have to get back to the house. I have the lamps to clean." She took a few steps, slowed and glanced over her shoulder at him. "Don't leave for the camp without saying goodbye."

"I won't."

She nodded and picked up her pace.

"Willa?"

She stopped and turned. "Yes?"

"It's all right if you tell Thomas no. You won't be the first woman to change your mind about marrying a man. And it wouldn't be as if you didn't have a good reason."

Her breath snagged. What did that mean? Was he talking about Thomas's leaving? Did he know he had deserted her? No. There was no way anyone could know that. If they did, it would have been all over town when he left. She nodded and forced a smile. "Thank you, Daniel. I'll keep that in mind."

"Ain't you kind of old to be shinnyin' up and down trees?" Bertha ducked her head and washed another dish.

"I saw that smile, Mrs. Franklin." Matthew poured a cup of coffee and set the pot on a back stove plate to keep warm. "But to answer your question, yes, I suppose I am. Still, I did quite well until that dead limb broke." He sat at the table and took a swallow of the dark brew.

Bertha snorted and pulled her hands out of the sudsy water. "I suppose you did all right for a city-raised man. For sure no country-raised boy would grab hold of a dead branch while he's climbing—lest it was to break it out his way."

She dried her hands on her apron and came to stand in front of him. "Let me see that wound."

It was like being a ten-year-old boy again. He gave

her a sheepish grin and pulled up his shirt sleeve. A deep, ragged gouge ran from a few inches above his wrist over the back of his hand to the base of his fingers.

The housekeeper peered at it from all angles. "Looks like it bled well."

"I'll say. It ruined my shirt. Well, that and the tear."

She squinted down at him. "You wash it out good?"

"Yes." He had the sudden dread of a young boy that she was going to start scrubbing away at the gouge. A chuckle started in his gut and climbed into his throat. He took another swallow of his coffee and drowned the laughter before it broke free. There was no point in fueling a fire.

Bertha nodded, pulled his shirt sleeve down and straightened. "It needs salve and a bandage. You go to Cargrave's and tell Allan I said you need some of that green Indian salve and a bandage roll. He'll open the store and get you some." She moved back to the cupboard, rubbed the soap over the washrag and lifted another dish out from the water. "You ought to have salve and bandages in the house anyway with these youngsters running around willy-nilly. You never know when one of them will get banged up."

"That's true." He took another swallow.

Bertha turned and looked at him.

He put his cup down and jumped to his feet. "I'll leave as soon as I get my coat."

She nodded and went back to washing the dish. "I'll bandage that up when you get back."

The bells on the door of the mercantile tinkled clear and crisp on the cool air. Matthew stepped out of the store and looked up at the rim of pink and gold outlining the banks of clouds above the dark hills that surrounded Pinewood. Days were growing shorter. Winter would soon be upon them.

There was a click as the door was locked. He turned and held out his hand. "Thank you again for opening the store for me, Mr. Cargrave. I surely appreciate it."

The man shoved the skeleton key in his waistcoat pocket, gave him a wry smile and shook his offered hand. "I wouldn't dare defy Bertha Franklin, Reverend. Good evening."

He watched the storekeeper cross the wide wood walkway, walk down the three steps to the road and turn toward his home. He glanced down at the items in his hand and smiled. There were definite benefits to living in a small village. And to having Bertha Franklin for his housekeeper.

He moved to leave the small alcove that protected the doorway, heard footsteps coming and stepped back to wait for the people to pass.

"...marry her?"

"...gotta...somewhere...live. An'...'nough money... stake me..."

The thud of bootheels on the planks of the walkway blocked out stretches of the slurred, indistinct speech. Even so, he didn't care to hear more of the men's drunken conversation. He stepped out into the deepening dusk and turned for home.

"But...marry..."

"No one...gonna...where...I'm goin'. I'm...not tellin' ladies...for sure."

The two men in the darker area between storefronts

laughed uproariously, came closer. The one nearest to him lifted his hat and made a small bow in his direction as they passed.

"Good evening…sir."

His companion grabbed him as he toppled forward and yanked him erect. They laughed and thumped toward the steps.

He turned and stared after them. Was that… The men stumbled down the three steps into the open roadway and he got a better look. His brows knit in a deep frown. It was. That was the man who had come for Willa.

Chapter Eleven

"I'm *talking* to you, Willa."

Ellen's petulant tone penetrated her troubling thoughts. Willa stopped walking and looked over at her friend. "I'm sorry, Ellen. You were saying…" She let her voice trail off in invitation.

Ellen tossed her head, pulled her hems away from some thorny weeds and moved toward the slight rise ahead. "You asked me to come along with you, and I have. The least you can do is pay attention to me." She cast a pouty glance at her from beneath the quilted brim of her Neapolitan bonnet. "What's wrong with you anyway, Willa? You've been acting as vague as fog over the river all week long."

Oh dear. If Ellen had noticed her distraction, it was certain others had. She would have to do better. "There's nothing wrong with me. I've merely been preoccupied with a problem." She snagged her lower lip with her teeth. That bit of truth should not have been spoken. If Ellen connected that with Thomas— She took a breath and added a bit of obfuscation. "Teachers sometimes have problems, you know."

"Yes, problems called *children*." Ellen tossed another glance her way. "That is part of what I was trying to tell you before, Willa. I shall soon be a teacher."

She stopped dead in her tracks. "A teacher! *You*, Ellen?" She hurried to walk alongside her again.

"I know it's surprising, given the way I feel about the noisy, unkempt little beasts, but I have a reason."

She nodded and stepped round a pile of deer droppings. "You always do."

"Hi, Miss Wright…Miss Hall." Danny Brody raced by, backpedaled, waved, then turned and charged up the slope. "Hey, Billy, Tommy, wait for me!"

She lifted her hand to return the boy's wave, then instead smiled and waved at his older sister and her friends, who were hurrying by at a slower pace. Danny had already forgotten them.

"As I was *saying*…"

She turned her attention back to Ellen. "Yes?"

"Reverend Calvert is forming a Sunday school class for the young children of church members, and he has asked *me* to be the instructor."

Memory flashed. With her trouble with Thomas, she had forgotten about that. "And you accepted?"

"Of course. I'm certain he chose me because he was impressed by my handling of his wards the night Mother and Father invited him to dinner." A smug smile curved Ellen's lips. "I *knew* that inviting his wards would make him see me in a favorable light as a future mate."

Something inside her went still. "Why do you say

that? Has Reverend Calvert asked permission to court you?"

"Not yet, but he will. That's why I accepted the position." Ellen laughed and started climbing the sloped ground. "I think of questions about teaching the 'dear, little children' and use them to engage him in conversation whenever we 'chance' to meet about town, which has been several times this week." Ellen gave another little laugh. "Living close to the church and parsonage has made it easy for me to see when he goes out, and it's a simple thing to have chores to do in the same stores." Ellen's delicate brows lifted in an arched, satisfied look. "He has already warmed considerably in his…response…to me."

"Been widening those big blue eyes and looking at the reverend through your long lashes, have you?"

Daniel. Willa squelched a smile.

Ellen gasped and whirled about. "How dare you sneak up on us and listen to our private conversation, Daniel Braynard!"

Their childhood friend spread his hands in a gesture of innocence. "I can't help it if the ground is soft and the grass doesn't make noise when it's stepped on."

Ellen's eyes glinted. "You could have warned us you were there."

Willa lowered her head and bit down on her lower lip to stop her urge to laugh. The way Ellen spat out the words reminded her of Sally's kitten. But then, Ellen and Daniel had always scrapped like a cat and a dog whenever they were together. He loved to tease, and Ellen always took his bait.

"Now that would have been downright rude. Mama

always taught me not to interrupt when other people were speaking." Daniel grinned.

"And you think *eavesdropping* is good manners?" Ellen gave a disdainful snort—definitely a throwback response from their childhood—spun back around and flounced off up the hill.

She shook her head and hurried to catch Ellen, then looked back at Daniel. He dipped his head, but he was too late. She had seen his eyes. She froze on the spot, shock rooting her feet to the ground. "Daniel…"

He lifted his head at her whisper, met her gaze and his long legs ate up the short distance between them. "Don't tell her, Willa."

She stared at him, uncertain and tentative. They had shared secrets and confidences since early childhood, but it seemed there was one very important secret Daniel hadn't shared with her. "When?"

He didn't even try to pretend he misunderstood her. "Remember that day when we were walking across that log over Stony Creek and she fell in and I had to pull her out?"

She nodded, the image of twelve-year-old Daniel diving off the log into the swollen, swift-running flood waters beneath clear in her head.

"That was it for me." He shoved his hands in his jacket pockets and gave her a rueful grin that broke her heart. "You all thought I was shivering from that icy water. I wasn't." He turned his head and looked after Ellen stalking up the hill with anger in every line of her body. "I was shaking because when I pulled Ellen out of that water, looking so still and white, I realized she could have died and, right then, I knew I didn't want to live my life without her in it."

"But…" She stared at him, at his compressed lips, his square jaw, his hazel eyes dark with emotion, a Daniel she didn't recognize. She looked down at the ground and began climbing the hill after Ellen.

He fell into step beside her. "But what, Willa?"

She blinked, swallowed hard and shook her head.

He leaned close and nudged her with the elbow of his good arm. "You might as well ask before it worries you to the point you can't stand it anymore." He grinned down at her. "I don't want you coming knocking on my window in the middle of the night because you can't sleep."

This was the Daniel she knew. But now she knew it was a Daniel who hid a hurting heart behind teasing and laugher. She blinked again and forced a laugh. "That happened only once."

"And I had to find that baby bird, climb that tree and put it back in its nest while you held the lantern safe below. I thought that mama bird was going to peck my eyes out." He fell silent.

She stopped, placed her hand on his arm and looked full into his eyes. "You saved Ellen ten years ago, Daniel. Why haven't you told her?"

He stared down at her hand. She could hear the hum of people talking amidst bursts of laughter beyond the rise. She wished he would speak and ease the ache in her heart for him.

"Well, at first we were too young." His voice was full of memories. "And then—" His shoulders hunched, his voice hardened. "You see what's under your hand, Willa?"

She looked down, glanced back up. "Your coat?"

He nodded.

"I don't understand, Daniel."

His face tightened. "That's a plain old plaid wool jacket, Willa. The same as every other logger and teamster and sawmill worker wears. Ellen's got her sights set on something far above that. She wants the arm she rests her hand on to be wearing a fancy suit. And she wants all that goes along with that suit. She wants an easy life and prestige. I might be fool enough to love her, but I'm not fool enough to let her know." He looked up. "Sometimes, when a man loses his heart, all he's got left is his pride, Willa. He's got to protect that."

She gazed into his eyes and wished she hadn't asked, wished more that he hadn't answered.

"Are you *coming,* Willa?"

She raised her head and looked at Ellen standing on the crest of the rise. She drew breath. Daniel's good arm looped over her shoulders, and she lost it again.

"She's coming, Ellen." He moved forward, the strength of his arm carrying her along with him. "We were talking about that day you fell in Stony Creek and I pulled you out looking like a drowned muskrat." He chuckled and shook his head as they came up to her. "You sure were a sorry sight. You look some better today."

"Oh!" It was more huffed-out breath than a word.

Daniel laughed, then touched the rolled-up brim of his knit hat to them both. "Enjoy yourself, ladies. I see some of my crew over across the way, and I want to talk with them."

He strolled off, leaving her with an ache in her heart, a lump in her throat and an intense desire to grab Ellen Hall by the shoulders and give her a good shake.

"Here comes Reverend Calvert, Willa. I *told* you he was becoming interested in me."

"So you did." And why you're interested in him. Daniel was right. Willa looked the direction of Ellen's gaze. Matthew Calvert was indeed wending his way through the assembled people and heading in their general direction. Where were Joshua and Sally?

"Don't stare, Willa. And stop frowning!"

She drew her gaze back, watched Ellen pinch color into her cheeks and fluff the bow of her wide satin bonnet strings. Hurt for Daniel squeezed her heart. She looked across the field to where he stood with his logger crewmates beside the towering pile of stumps farmers and land owners had grubbed from their fields. They were lighting the fire. He was looking their way.

"Good afternoon, Miss Hall…Miss Wright."

She glanced over her shoulder. Matthew Calvert stood beside Ellen, his charming smile on his face. He was so handsome standing there in his *suit* that she could have slapped him.

"Good afternoon, Reverend. I see you've come out to enjoy the stump burning."

Ellen's purring tone made her feel like retching. She looked again toward Daniel. He had turned his back.

She clenched her hands and dug her fingernails into her palms to keep the tears from her eyes.

"I'm sure I shall, Miss Hall. It will be a new experience for me. Good afternoon, Miss Wright."

She turned to face him. "Good afternoon, Reverend Calvert." She gave a quick glance around the area, pretended surprise. "Where are your children, Reverend?" She ignored the irritated look Ellen sent her way. "Did they not want to attend the stump burning?" Her cool tone didn't seem to put him off. He turned that charming smile on her.

"Oh, indeed they did. But I'm afraid they've deserted me." He gestured toward the children scattered over the field, playing games and running races. "They are somewhere in that melee, playing with their friends."

The gaze he had fastened on hers warmed, his smile turned into a lopsided grin. Her heart faltered, then bounded along like a deer leaping logs, much to her fury. Where was her loyalty? Her common sense? What sort of spineless fool was she to let his charm so easily sway her?

"How delightful, Reverend. You shall not have to hurry off."

That purr again! She jerked her gaze to Ellen, watched her widen her big blue eyes and look at Matthew Calvert through her long lashes. Her fingers twitched to yank the Neapolitan bonnet down over her friend's face.

She darted another glance across the field toward Daniel, but the fire had caught hold and billowing smoke hid him from her view. A small flash beneath the trees at the edge of the clearing drew her attention. Thomas, Arnold Dixon and Johnny Taylor stood in the shadows, light from the flames of the soaring fire glinting off the flask they passed to one another. Her stomach knotted. So they *were* friends. *Drinking* friends. What else did she not know about Thomas? What if he saw her and came over?

The knots twisted tighter. She bowed her head, pressed her hand against her stomach and turned her back.

"You're very pale. Are you feeling ill, Miss Wright?"

She raised her head and looked straight into Matthew Calvert's brown eyes. Concern darkened them. She took a deep breath. "No, I— Excuse me." She whipped around. "I have to go, Ellen."

"You do look peaked, Willa. I'll come—"

"No, I'll be fine. You stay. Agnes will be looking for us." She pulled her hood forward, hurried to the top of the rise and started down the other side, her steps keeping pace with her rushing thoughts. What had she gotten herself into? How could she marry Thomas? She didn't even know this man he had become, or had kept hidden from her. But her mother—

"Wait, Miss Wright."

She spun about, startled to find the reverend still with her. In two long strides he was by her side.

"You shouldn't be alone while you're ill. Please allow me to escort you home."

His deep voice, calm and quiet, both soothed her jangled nerves and made her want to burst into tears.

She shook her head. "You mustn't leave your children. I—"

"I asked Miss Hall to watch over Joshua and Sally until I return."

Ellen? Watching his children? Inappropriate laughter bubbled up. Her mouth twitched. She bit down on her lip…hard. Her thoughts raced, but she could think of no other reasonable excuse to refuse his polite offer. She took a breath to gain control. Her nerves were taut as bow strings. She had to get home before she came totally undone.

She nodded and turned onto the path leading to town, with Matthew Calvert's presence beside her unreasonably comforting. She had neither the strength nor the will to figure out why.

The sounds of the late afternoon settled like a blanket around them. She blocked out all thought and concentrated on the whisper of her long skirts and the soft thump of his boots against the ground, timed her breathing to match them. The tension in her body eased.

"You make a habit o' poaching on 'nother man's property, Reverend?"

Thomas! She jolted to a stop, jerked her head up. He stood in the center of the path, his eyes glassy from drink, narrow with anger. Her stomach contracted and bile surged into her throat.

"You have the advantage of me…sir."

She flicked her gaze to Matthew Calvert. His voice was calm and controlled, but there was nothing of the tranquil gentleness she had come to associate with him in his face. A tiny muscle along his jaw twitched; his brown eyes were dark, wary.

"Thomas Hunter. I'm Willa's b—betrothed."

No. Oh, please no. Tears stung her eyes.

Matthew Calvert's jaw tightened, the tiny muscle leaped. "I see." His gaze shifted, bored down into hers. "Is that true, Miss Wright?"

Words clogged in her throat.

Thomas fisted his hands, took a step toward them. "'s true all right. You qu-questionin' my—"

"Yes." Thomas's belligerence pushed the answer from her. *Please, please understand that I don't want it to be so.* She closed her eyes and clamped her lips together lest she blurt the truth.

Silence descended, scraped along her strained nerves. She held her breath. *Please, Reverend Calvert, please go before—*

"You have no reason for anger, Mr. Hunter. There is no impropriety here. I was escorting Miss Wright home because she felt unwell. I leave her in your hands."

His voice was different, controlled and cold. Dismay gripped her. Matthew Calvert's footsteps trailed away. She heard movement and opened her eyes. Thomas pushed his face close to hers, his hand gripped her wrist.

"Don't e'er do that again, Willa. Don't e'er go walkin' out with the reverend or any other man, 'cause if you do, the gossip that flies 'round this town won't be 'bout your pa desertin' your ma an' you." He smiled. The pressure on her wrist increased. "You're mine. See you remember it."

She stared into the eyes mere inches from her own. A ruffian's eyes. Thomas was no different from the occasional bully she had dealt with among the children. Strength flowed into her. She lifted her chin, forced every ounce of "teacher" authority she possessed into her voice. "Unhand me."

Shock flashed into his eyes. His grip slackened.

She pulled her hand from his grasp before he had the chance to recover. Her wrist throbbed. She refused to rub it, or to step back. To do so would encourage his bullying. "What do you want, Thomas?" She held her voice steady, allowed no trace of fear to color it. "And do not insult me with your answer. It's obvious you have no regard for me."

He studied her a long moment, then shrugged. "Jack and I lost our stake in a game of chance, so we come back to get more. I figure about six months of your teacher's pay should be enough to stake me again. Meanwhile, I'll live cozy and warm with you in that cabin of your ma." His eyes flashed. "That is, lest you want gossip about your loose virtue spread around town."

What a vile man! How had she ever thought him handsome or charming? She clenched her hands until they hurt to stop a shudder then drew back her shoulders and adjusted her hood. He had unwittingly given her the answer she had been searching for. "You have made a serious error in your plans, Mr. Hunter."

His face darkened, his eyes clouded with suspicion. "What's that?"

"Were you to marry me, I would lose my position. There would be no pay. Married women are not permitted to teach school."

Chapter Twelve

Willa's steps lagged. She might be free of Thomas, but she was quite certain he would take revenge and start the gossip he threatened. How was she to tell her mother? How was she to face her friends and neighbors?

She took a deep breath and opened the door to the cabin.

"Willa!" Her mother stopped sewing. A frown drew a small, vertical line between her arched brows. "Why aren't you at the stump burning?"

"I decided to come home and help you with the mending. You have a lot to do tonight." She hung her cloak on a peg and crossed to the table by the window, sat so that the lamplight would not fall on her face.

"How are Ellen and Agnes?" Her mother had not gone back to her sewing, and the look in her eyes made her want to fidget the way she had as a child.

"Ellen is fine. She's going to be teaching a Sunday school class for the young children." She lifted a shirt off the pile at her mother's side and examined the rent in the sleeve. "I didn't see Agnes. I left before—"

She sighed, let the shirt sleeve fall into her lap. "I saw Thomas, Mama. He was with Arnold Dixon and Johnny Taylor. They were imbibing."

Her mother stilled, fixed a look on her. "Those two are no good, Willa, but what has it do with you if Thomas—" The look in her mother's eyes sharpened. "Dora said Thomas walked you home from church last Sunday. And that he had waited for you and spoken with you after school a few times, but— Oh, Willa! You haven't accepted his court again?"

She shook her head. "Not really, Mama. It was only for a few days until I could think of what to do about—"

"About what?"

She blew out a breath and folded her hands in her lap. "He threatened to tell everyone the truth about his running off and deserting me. And he hinted that he would resurrect the gossip about Papa abandoning us. I couldn't face that. I couldn't put you through that again, Mama, so—"

"So you let Thomas court you to protect me from *gossip?*" Her mother's voice was hushed, horrified. "Oh, Willa…" Tears slid down her mother's cheeks.

She pushed out of the chair, went to her knees and grasped her mother's hands. "Not you alone, Mama. I *hate* gossip. That's why I pretended I told Thomas to go west before. I don't want people's scorn, or their pity. And I don't want them to hurt you again. But—" her mother squeezed her hands "—there's no way—" another squeeze "—to avoid it now." She stopped her rush of words. "What, Mama?"

"Willa, I have done you a disservice." Her mother,

her eyes bright with tears, gazed down at her. "You were so young when your papa left I didn't realize you even noticed the talk about the village." Her mother's hands squeezed hers again, gave them a little shake. "*Talk,* Willa, not gossip. The people in this village are our friends. They care about us—about you. They were angry and concerned when your papa deserted us, and so they talked about it."

"Yes. And they hurt you, Mama." She rose and went back to her chair. "I heard you crying at night. And I hated Papa for leaving and them for gossiping about us and hurting you."

"You're *wrong,* Willa. I didn't cry because of gossip. I cried because I didn't know how I was going to care for you. We were about to lose our home and I had nowhere to go, no way to earn a living. It was our friends, talking together, who came up with the idea of my doing laundry in exchange for living in our cabin. I will be eternally grateful to them for that."

"I didn't know… I thought you were the one…"

Her mother shook her head and wiped moisture from her cheeks. "No. I was too devastated when your papa walked out on us to think clearly. All I could see was the trouble and want ahead. It was the women of the village who figured out the answer. Now… What did you mean by 'there's no way to avoid it now'?"

She studied her mother's face, took a deep breath and let the words flow. "When I saw Thomas tonight, I hurried away. I was shocked by his drinking and did not want him to approach me. Reverend Calvert, who was chatting with Ellen, thought I was ill. He followed and offered to escort me home."

The memory of his concern for her stole the strength from her voice. She leaned down and picked up the shirt that had fallen to the floor earlier and smoothed it out on her lap. "Thomas stopped us on the path and accused Reverend Calvert of 'poaching on his property.' He told him we were betrothed." *The look on his face! What must he think of her...* She blinked, swallowed back a rush of tears. "When the reverend left, Thomas reminded me I was 'his,' and warned me not to 'walk out' with another man again. He said if I did, he would spread gossip about my 'loose virtue.'"

Her mother jerked erect. "I wish David Dibble *had* beaten him!"

She'd never seen her mother so angry. She grabbed hold of her nearest fisted, work-roughened hand. "It's all right. Sit down, Mama."

"It certainly is *not* all right!" Her mother pulled her hand away and paced around the room, stopped by the door. "I've a good mind to go and speak to David right now."

"David?" She stared at her mother, shocked by her use of the given name, even more by the color that climbed into her mother's cheeks.

"I mean, *Mr. Dibble,* of course. I misspoke in my anger."

She nodded, watched her mother rub her hands on her skirt, smooth back her hair, then come back and take her seat. She was *nervous!*

"Why do you say it's all right, Willa?"

The question brought the memory of her confrontation with Thomas flooding back. "Because the strangest thing happened. I was frightened of the way

Thomas was acting, and then I suddenly realized he was a bully, like some children are, and I was no longer frightened." She folded the shirt and set it aside. "I demanded to know what he wanted as it was obvious he had no regard for me. And he told me." She stopped, still amazed at the way things had changed.

"What did he say?"

"That he had lost his stake to go west in a game of chance and come back to Pinewood to get another. That he figured about six months of my teaching pay would be enough."

His note! *Willa, I'm sorry I haven't time to wait and talk to you, but I must hasten to meet Jack. He sent word he has funds for us to head west, and I am going after my dream*. It all made sense now.

"Willa..."

She jerked her thoughts back. "I just realized he *never* wanted me, Mama, not even before when he wooed me. He only wanted to marry me for my pay, and this time, when I refused, he threatened me to make me agree."

"But, Willa, if—"

"Yes." She looked at her mother and nodded. "I told him his plan was flawed, that married women were not allowed to teach and, therefore, there would be no pay if he wed me." Laughter surged. She shook her head. "Isn't it *odd*, Mama, that the very thing that made Thomas pursue me is the thing that set me free of him!"

The urge to laugh died. Her breath caught. "I could be *married* to him, Mama. Thank goodness he left that first time."

"Yes, thank goodness!" Her mother leaned forward and gripped her hands. "I'm so glad you're rid of him, Willa."

"Yes, but he was very angry, and I'm certain he will seek revenge. I'm afraid the gossip will start tomorrow, and that I might be dismissed from my teaching position because of it. A teacher must have no hint of a taint on her reputation." Her throat constricted, tears stung her eyes. "I'm sorry, Mama. I don't know what we'll do without my earnings."

Her mother rose and came to her. "Hush, Willa." She yielded to her mother's comforting arms, rested her head against her breast. "There's no reason to cry. Trust our friends, dear. No one in this village will believe such a vicious tale about you." Her mother cupped her chin and tilted her head up to meet her gaze. "I promise you, Willa Jean, if Thomas Hunter spreads that rumor, all he will do is make it impossible for him to stay in Pinewood."

Moonlight flowed from the sky, endowed the landscape with silver splendor and created shadows and dimensions that played tricks on the eye. Cold from off the small window panes touched Matthew's face. He frowned, wished for something pressing to do. He had heard Joshua and Sally's bedtime prayers, and now there was nothing but the empty night stretching out before him.

Willa was betrothed. The knowledge brought an inner emptiness, a hollowness. He would no longer be able to seek her out, to try to win her...favor. He yanked his hands from his pockets, scrubbed the back of his neck and paced to the other side of his study. He sat at his desk, closed his eyes to pray, saw an image of Willa's face, the stricken look in her eyes as she had acknowledged her betrothal, and opened them again.

Something was wrong. She had seemed…what? He couldn't put a name to it. It was simply something he'd sensed. Or was it something he wished? How could she marry a man like that? There was something about Thomas Hunter, something beyond the drinking and the belligerence, something in his eyes…

The muscles in his face drew taut. It had taken all of his inner strength to walk away and leave Willa standing there alone on the path to town with that two-bit drunk. And then he'd had to go back and pretend to enjoy the stump burning for Joshua's and Sally's sakes. It had been a miserable afternoon.

It was time for some coffee. He yanked his thoughts from the memory and headed for the kitchen. It would give him something to do. He raised the wick on the oil lamp to give more light, quietly fitted it into the slot on the stove plate and set it aside even though his hands itched to slam it down. He'd wanted to slam and bang things ever since he'd refrained from punching Thomas Hunter's sneering face. If only the man had thrown a punch with those fisted hands and given him a reason, he would have put all that sparring he and Robert had done when they were young to good use.

He curved his lips in a grim smile, cleared away the ashes, placed wood on the smoldering embers, then replaced the plate and opened the draft. The lingering smell of the beef stew Bertha had cooked for dinner made his stomach turn over. It was good, and Bertha was an excellent cook, but he'd only been able to choke down a few bites for the children's sakes.

Being a parent was more difficult than he'd expected. He shook his head and ladled water into the coffeepot. He hadn't thought about all the little ordinary things you had to do, like smiling and pretending you were having a good time, or eating when your stomach was tied in knots. But Joshua and Sally were worth it.

He snatched up the bag of "Old Java" and grabbed a spoon. He'd always wanted a family, a wife and children of his own, and lately he'd been thinking—

A knock jolted him out of his thoughts. He spun around and hurried to the door. People coming at this time of night meant an emergency. He paused and closed his eyes. "Give me grace to answer the need, Lord. Amen." He opened the door, peered out into the night. "Yes?"

Thomas Hunter stepped out of the shadows into the moonlight and looked up at him. "C'mon outside, Reverend. You an' me got to talk."

Something decidedly unspiritual rushed through him. *I'll handle this one on my own, Lord.*

The thought went winging on its way before he had even closed the door. His second thought, as he crossed the porch, was that he'd have to repent for the first one later. He found he didn't mind. He walked down the steps and stopped. "You have something to say to me, Mr. Hunter?"

"I want money."

Was the man asking alms of the church? That was

doubtful, judging from the look on his face. "Would you care to explain that request?"

"I need money to head west. See, I planned to marry Willa, figured about six months or so of her teacher's pay would stake me, and meanwhile, I'd have it nice and cozy living with her in her ma's cabin."

He sucked in a breath, stepped forward. *Wait, let him strike the first blow.* He stopped, took another breath.

"Don't like that idea, do you, Reverend?"

What he would like was to wipe the sneering smile right off Thomas Hunter's face.

"Well, don't fret about it. I found out tonight married women can't teach school, an' if I married Willa she wouldn't have any pay."

Thank You, Lord!

"That's why I come here."

The *gall* of the man! "To ask alms of the church?"

Thomas stepped closer, narrowed his eyes. "I ain't askin' nothin' of any church." His lips curled into that contemptuous smile again. "I seen the way you looked at Willa today, an' your bein' a preacher an' all, I figure you wouldn't want any sort of gossip 'bout that gettin' round."

Let him strike the first blow. He flexed his hands, left them open. "And you want me to give you money to keep those rumors from starting. That, Mr. Hunter, is blackmail."

"I don't care what you call it, just give me the money. I figure a hundred dollars will do."

He shook his head. "I'm afraid not. I'm not frightened by your threatened rumors, Mr. Hunter, and I do not pay blackmail. 'Treasures of wickedness profit nothing, but righteousness delivereth from death.' I suggest you give up your scheme, repent and go to work to earn your money."

"I ain't interested in your suggestions, Preacher!" Thomas's eyes darkened, glittered. Moonlight outlined his jutted chin. "Maybe you don't care if rumors 'bout you travel 'round town, but how 'bout Willa? How would you feel if rumors of Willa's loose virtue—"

His left fist jabbed forward in a blur, connected with Thomas's jaw with a satisfying thud, his right followed in an uppercut to that perfectly outlined jutting jaw that landed with all the force of his shoulder behind it. Thomas Hunter's head snapped back and he dropped like a stone at his feet.

"'Violence covereth the mouth of the wicked.' But you sure took your sweet time about it, Reverend."

He pivoted. Bertha stood in the dark shadow on the porch. He frowned. "How long have you been there, Bertha?"

"I followed you out the door."

"Then you heard—"

"Not a thing worth repeating." She stepped to the edge of the porch and looked down at him. "You needn't fear of anything that plug-ugly said going any further than us, Reverend. I love Willa, too."

Too. His heart jolted. Were his feelings for Willa that plain to see? Probably so because he'd just knocked a man unconscious for threatening to besmirch her reputation. He grinned and rubbed his stinging knuckles. "I trust that information also will go no further than the two of us."

Bertha grinned right back. "I let a man do his own courting, Reverend. Now, you'd best stop feeling proud of yourself and think about what comes next." She dipped her head toward Thomas, who was beginning to stir. "What're you going to do with him?"

"Why, I'm going to give him his heart's desire and help him on his way west." His grin died. "Thankfully, no one will pay any attention to my leaving in my buggy this time of night. Pastors get emergency calls at all hours." He leaned down, grabbed hold of the back of Thomas Hunter's jacket collar and started dragging him toward the stable. "But I have to say, this one is going to befuddle those who see my buggy and try to figure out what the emergency was and who came for me."

"For sure it'll give people something to talk about." Bertha chuckled and turned to go inside. "I'll get your coat."

The buggy jolted and swayed. Thomas Hunter gave a groan and lifted his head. "What happened?"

Matthew watched as the trussed man slumped in the corner tried to shove himself erect by placing his shoulder against the roof frame. "A wheel hit a deep rut. Go back to sleep."

Hunter swore and gave up the struggle. "Whyn't you untie my hands now? My jaw hurts an' I want to rub it."

"I'll untie you when we get to the depot and it's time for you to board the stage, not before." An animal broke from the woods and dashed across the road in front of them. He tightened his grip on the reins as the mare snorted and tossed her head. "Easy, girl, easy. It's only a fox."

"I can always come back you know."

He glanced at Hunter. Must be the alcohol and the fogginess from being knocked unconscious had worn off—the man's belligerent attitude was back. "I wouldn't advise it. You're not the only one who can start gossip, and if you ever show up in Pinewood again I will personally see to it that you are not welcomed by anyone. Including your drinking pals. How will Johnny Taylor…excuse me…I mean, *Jack,* feel when he finds out you had money for the stage ride and headed west without him? He did share his stake with you the last time, did he not?"

"How did you find out about that?"

He turned his head and gave the two-bit bully a wide smile. "You talk in your sleep. It's very enlightening."

Hunter glared. "I ain't afraid of your threats. You're a preacher an' preachers don't do things like startin' rumors."

"I'll bet you didn't think preachers knew how to throw a knockout punch, either." He gave him another smile.

A surly growl was his only answer. A few minutes later snores came from the other corner. He drove on, thankful for the bright moonlight.

Matthew glanced up at the sky. Dawn was but a lighter gray promise in the east. It was a long trip to the depot in Dunkirk, especially through the night, but worth the time. He didn't want anyone to find out about this. Thankfully, he had Bertha to care for Joshua and Sally until he got home. He frowned, glanced at the sky again. He ought to reach home by dusk, he'd make better time in the daylight.

He tightened his grip on Hunter's arm and hurried him to the stage. "I've paid your fare to Buffalo." He stepped behind him and untied the rope that bound his hands. "This time, when you get to Buffalo, you will have to get a job on a boat and work your way west from there."

Hunter scowled and rubbed his wrists. "I'll need some money for food and such, 'til I get that job."

He coiled the rope and shook his head. "Sorry, but paying your stage fare is as much as I will do."

"Then I'll have to take the money!"

Hunter's fist punched through the air toward him. He jerked his head to the side, rammed his fist into the bully's exposed gut, then caught his chin with an uppercut when he bent over.

"Ugh!" Hunter's eyes widened, then closed. He collapsed in a heap beside the stage.

He opened the door, picked Hunter up by the collar and the seat of the pants, heaved him inside and closed the door. He handed a half eagle up to the driver. "That's for putting him on a boat headed west."

The driver nodded, tucked the coin in his leather vest and grinned down at him. "That's quite an uppercut you've got there."

He rubbed his swollen knuckles and returned the grin. "Thanks. I learned it from my brother."

"You a boxer or somethin'?"

His grin widened. "No, I'm a preacher."

Chapter Thirteen

"Very good, Eli." Willa took the stick of chalk the boy handed her and turned to the class. "Chloe, please come and work the next problem."

Someone coughed. She sighed. It was that time of year. There would be coughs and sniffles among the children all winter. She made a mental note to bring in camphor and keep thyme and peppermint tea on hand and gave Chloe the chalk.

The sun's golden rays streamed through the small glass panes from a blue, cloudless sky. It was a welcome break after the cold weather they had been experiencing. But there was a dark cloud hanging over her. This afternoon it would be two days since Thomas had made his threats. Nothing had happened yesterday. When would the gossip start? Would she have to face it when she left school today? Her already-sour stomach roiled. She dreaded having her name besmirched, even if, as her mother said, no one in the village would believe the lies.

"I'm done, Miss Wright."

"Oh. Yes. Very good, Chloe. You may take your

seat." She focused her thoughts and moved over to stand by the slate board. "Now that the examples are completed, I want you first graders to copy the last four problems on your slates and write the answers. Be sure to keep your numbers in a straight line and make your plus signs clear."

She raised the piece of chalk and wrote the five vowels in upper and lower cases. "Kindergartners, write these letters on your slates, and form them carefully. I shall come around to check them and to help you. Second graders—" She brushed the chalk dust from her fingers and lifted her gaze to the last bench where the oldest children in her class were seated. Mary Burton was bent forward, her forehead resting on her crossed arms on the bench desk. That did not bode well. Mary was a very painstaking scholar.

"Mary?" She hurried to the young girl, placed her hand on her small back and leaned over her. "What's wrong, Mary?"

"I don't f-feel good." The muffled words ended with a cough.

"Look at me, Mary."

The eight-year-old lifted her head and looked up at her through squinted eyes.

"Have you a headache?" She noted Mary's glassy eyes and red cheeks and placed her hand on her forehead. Too warm.

"Yes, Miss Wright." Mary coughed and winced. "My stomach feels sick, too."

"All right. You rest, dear."

Mary's friend and seatmate raised her hand.

"Yes, Susan?"

"Mary didn't eat her potato at dinnertime, Miss Wright. And she's been coughing all day."

"Thank you, Susan." That was true. She'd noticed the cough, but only as a distraction. One or the other of the children were always coughing and, given the cold weather they'd been having until a few days ago, she'd placed little importance on it. Now, with the headache, fever and stomach upset taken in conjunction with the cough…

She shifted her gaze to the second row. "Jeffery…" The boy stood and turned to face her. "I want you to run home and tell your mother that I said Mary is ill and she should bring the wagon to take her home."

"Ma's not home, Miss Wright. Pa took the wagon to Olville to get some supplies, and Ma went along to see Aunt Beth's new baby. Cissy's the only one at home."

"I see. All right, Jeffery. Take your seat." She looked down at Mary, brushed a lock of hair off the child's hot, dry temple. Now what? She could keep her here until her parents came home, but that might not be until late tonight. That wouldn't do.

She lifted her head and scanned the class. The children had twisted around on the benches to watch. "Continue your assigned work, please."

There was a rustle as the young scholars turned back to face the front, then silence, broken only by the ticking of the pendulum clock on the wall. She glanced up at its round face. It was almost time for dismissal. Perhaps she could walk Mary home. No, that wouldn't do, either. Mary was too ill to walk that distance.

She sighed and drew her gaze back. It snared on

Joshua's golden-blond curls. She straightened, stared at the boy as he bent over his slate working the problems, fought a battle with herself and won. "Joshua, come here please."

The boy stood and hurried to her. "Yes, Miss Wright?"

"I have a very important task for you, so listen carefully." She held his gaze with hers. "I want you to go home, and if your uncle is there I want you to tell him Miss Wright says Mary Burton is ill and asks if he will please take her home in his buggy. Then I want you to come back and tell me what he says. Do you understand?"

"Yes, Miss Wright."

"All right, then. Go, and please hurry."

She moved to the front of the room as Joshua rushed out the door. "Children, it's time to go home. Leave your work. We will continue it tomorrow. For now, quietly gather your things and leave. Sally and Jeffery, you wait here until Joshua returns."

She opened a desk drawer, lifted the top rag off the pile she kept there to wipe the slate board clean, crossed to the short bench, doused the rag in the bucket and squeezed out the excess water. She turned, glanced at the children silently filing out the door, then looked at the two still seated and smiled reassurance. "Joshua will be back soon, Sally. Jeffery, you may gather your things now—and Mary's also. I want you to be ready to go if the pastor comes."

The boy scurried to obey.

The clock ticked. Her long skirts whispered across the plank floor as she hurried back to her sick scholar.

"I have a cold cloth, Mary. It should help you feel better. Lift your head a bit." She folded the rag to fit Mary's small forehead, slipped it in place, then sat on the bench beside her and rubbed her back to comfort her and ease her coughing. She looked up at the sound of tiptoeing footsteps. Sally climbed onto her knees on the bench.

"I'll hold your hand, Mary. It made me feel better when Mama held my hand." Sally's small hand clasped Mary's larger one.

Willa blinked and swallowed past the lump Sally's concern for her schoolmate brought to her throat. She couldn't resist touching Sally's cheek, then smiling her approval when Sally glanced at her. The little girl's face lit with a return smile so sweet it made her catch her breath.

"He's coming!" Joshua burst into the schoolroom, bent over, grasped his knees and gasped for air. "Uncle Matt is…hitching up the buggy. He says to tell you… he'll be…right along."

"That's wonderful. Thank you, Joshua. You've been very helpful." *The poor boy, he must have run the entire way.* She rose, placed her hand on his shoulder and led him to the bench. "Sit down and catch your breath, then gather your things and take Sally home."

She touched the rag on Mary's forehead. It was already warm. The little girl coughed again, a raspy, dry cough. Worry squiggled through her. She removed the rag, carried it to the bucket, squeezed it out in the cold water and hurried back.

Joshua and Sally were going out the door. She waved goodbye, replaced the rag then sat on the bench, rubbed Mary's back and tried to recall the signs of the various childhood illnesses the children in previous classes had suffered. It didn't work. The embarrassment crept in. How was she to face Matthew Calvert after the insulting accusations Thomas had hurled at him? She had hoped at least a few days would pass before—

She jolted at the click of the door opening. Her stomach knotted.

"I understand there is a sick young lady here who needs a ride home."

She rose, watched Matthew Calvert close the distance between them in two long strides and lifted her chin. "Yes, and her brother also. Thank you for coming, Reverend Calvert. I wouldn't have sent for you, but Mary's mother and father are in Olville, and I could not think of any other way." She took a deep breath, pressed her lips together to stop her nervous prattling and bent over Mary. It was easier not to look at him.

"I'm happy to be of service, Miss Wright."

His deep voice was calm and pleasant, without a trace of accusation or disgust. She glanced sideways, watched him bend down and scoop the young girl into his arms. Her tension eased. He would be gone in a few moments.

"We'll have you home soon, Mary. Come along, son." He stepped to the door. Jeffery, his hands full of his and Mary's things, walked at his side. The reverend stopped at the door and turned his head. The expectant look in his eyes brought the word he'd used crashing into her consciousness.

We'll. She opened her mouth to explain she would not be going with them, then closed it. Mary needed her to hold her to protect her from the buggy's jouncing. Avoiding embarrassment was a petty and selfish aim in the face of the child's misery. And the fear that someone might see her riding in the buggy with the pastor and add that tidbit to the gossip that must by now be circulating throughout the village was not to be considered. She hurried to open the door.

The buggy dipped and swayed over the rutted, weed-covered wagon path that stretched from the Burton farmhouse. Willa gripped the hold strap and held herself erect as Matthew Calvert reined the horse back out onto the road.

"Mary seemed relieved to get home. She looked quite ill to me, Miss Wright—and you look concerned. Is there something seriously wrong with the girl?"

She turned her head and met his troubled gaze, noted the frown that creased his forehead. "I don't know, Reverend. I've seen these symptoms before, and I think she may be coming down with measles or, perhaps, chicken pox or whooping cough." She let her breath out in a long sigh. "If I'm right, it's likely that, whatever the disease, it will spread through the entire class."

His frown deepened. "Then Joshua and Sally could become ill?"

There was worry in his voice. For the children or himself? "We'll know in a few days. Whatever is wrong with Mary will be apparent by then." She stared ahead at the horse's rump, wished for more speed. Being alone with Matthew Calvert was disquieting.

The reins snapped. The horse picked up its pace.

A wry smile touched her lips. Perhaps he was as eager to be out of her company.

"Whenever I think I have this parenting thing figured out, something else comes along." Frustration laced through his ordinarily calm tone. "There's only one thing I know for sure."

She couldn't resist. "And that is?"

"Raising children is no easy task."

"Indeed." She glanced over at him. He sounded so sincere. But where was his concern and worry over the children's welfare the night of the Halls' dinner when he had put them abed early as punishment for needing to be with him? It seemed as if—like her father's—Matthew Calvert's concern for his children rose only when their welfare did not interfere with his own pleasures. It would no doubt give out quickly in the face of the time and attention demanded of a parent by a sick child. She turned her head back to face forward, dipped it when wagons passed and wished for her cloak to hide behind.

The buggy wheels whispered a gritty accompaniment to the thud of the horse's hooves as they rolled along the hardpacked dirt road. The silence grew tense. She cast a sidelong look at Matthew Calvert, caught his gaze on her and clenched her jaw. Why was he looking at her like that? She smoothed a fold from the skirt of her red wool dress and frowned. It was such a plain, serviceable gown. Certainly nothing like the satin confections Ellen wore.

Something tickled her cheek. She reached up to brush the irritation away and froze. Hair! No wonder he'd been staring. She stole another glance at him. He was looking at her hand. Warmth rushed along her cheekbones. "Forgive my appearance, Reverend Calvert. I didn't realize, in the hustle of getting Mary out to the buggy, I'd forgotten my bonnet." *More fodder for gossip if they were seen.* She would warn him when she apologized.

"The Bible says a woman's hair is her glory, Miss Wright. I find nothing wrong with your appearance. It is both modest and pleasing."

Her pulse skittered and sped. She whipped her head back around, stared into his warm, quiet gaze and irritation surged. The man was doing it again. He always managed to undermine her strongest intentions to stay aloof.

The buggy jolted, jarred her back to her senses. She jerked her gaze forward, tucked the errant wisp of hair behind her ear, tugged the rolled hem of her dress sleeve down in place and clasped her hands in her lap. The buggy swayed around the corner onto Oak Street. Relief relaxed her grip. The school was just ahead.

"Shall I stop at the schoolhouse so you can fetch your bonnet and other things?"

Stop so— Surely he didn't think she expected that he would take her home? "Yes. Please stop."

He pulled back on the reins, the horse stopped and the buggy swayed to a halt.

She burst into speech before he could climb down to assist her. "Before I leave you, I want to, again, thank you for taking Mary home. It was very kind of you."

"Leave?" He draped the reins over the dashboard and turned on the seat to face her.

She ignored the measuring look he fixed on her and rushed on. "And also, I wish to apologize for Thomas Hunter's uncivil behavior the other day."

His eyes darkened. "There's no need for you to apologize, Miss Wright. You did nothing wrong."

"Yes, Mr. Calvert, I did." She looked into his frowning face and lifted her chin. "Were I not so cowardly, you would not have been placed in such an embarrassing position. You see, Thomas and I were betrothed a few months ago, but then he…left town. When he returned recently, he wanted to continue with our plans to wed. I refused him, but he did not accept my answer." She took a breath and looked down. "He was angry when he confronted us, and, well, I was frightened, and so did not deny his false statement." Why was he rubbing his knuckles? They looked bruised. His hands stilled.

She lifted her gaze, found it ensnared by his. Everything in her went quiet. His eyes darkened, amber flames burned in their depths.

"I would never have allowed him to harm you, Miss Wright."

His soft, quiet words settled over her like a warm blanket.

"Willa! *There* you are."

She snapped her gaze to the road. Ellen was coming down the path toward the buggy. *Ellen.* She gathered her wits and looked back at Matthew. He was looking at Ellen—of course. What a weak-willed fool she was. She rose, grabbed hold of the roof brace and turned to back out of the buggy. "Thank you again for your help, Reverend Calvert."

"Wait, I'll help—"

"No, I'll manage." Satisfaction shot through her. Her voice was as cool as the metal brace she clutched— he would never guess these last minutes had brought her to the brink of tears. She lowered herself to the ground, stiffened her spine and headed down the path to meet Ellen.

Chapter Fourteen

The last person she wanted to see at the moment was Ellen. But Ellen was also the person she most needed to see—fancy gown and all. Willa squared her shoulders.

The clop of a horse's hooves sounded behind her. Wheels started to roll. She clenched her hands. Would he stop? She couldn't bear the thought of Matthew Calvert flirting with Ellen. Not after…what? The caring she had felt from him. Or had she misread him? Was he only being polite in saying he would have protected her from Thomas? She could have misunderstood that. But his eyes…

She thrust the image of Matthew Calvert's dark, intent gaze from her mind and pasted a smile on her face. "You were looking for me, Ellen?" The hooves sounded beside her. *Please don't stop. Please go home.*

"Yes, I wanted to tell you—" Ellen stopped, turned toward the street and smiled.

She clenched her hands tighter and held her breath. From the corner of her eye she saw Matthew Calvert smile and doff his hat in greeting. Her breath escaped in a gust when he drove on. She braced herself and studied Ellen's face. Had the gossip about her started? Is that what she was going to tell her?

Ellen frowned and stared after the buggy. "I guess Matthew is in a hurry."

Matthew. Ellen's use of his given name stabbed deep. She'd forgotten they were on a first-name basis in private. Should she warn Ellen that he was a Lothario? No. She could be wrong. "What did you want, Ellen?"

Her friend turned back, gasped, her eyes widened. "Willa, for goodness' sakes! Where is your bonnet?" Her eyes narrowed. "And why were you riding in Matthew's carriage?"

"Mary Burton is ill, and Reverend Calvert was kind enough to help me take her home. In the rush, I forgot my bonnet." *That's all it was. He was being kind. It was a mistake to read anything more into those last few minutes.* "Now tell me what you wanted, so I can get my things and go home."

"Well, you needn't be huffish! What's wrong with you?"

What indeed? "I'm sorry, Ellen. I'm concerned about Mary and her illness. I suspect it is either measles or chicken pox or—"

"Chicken pox!" Ellen gasped the word and stepped back. "You know I haven't had chicken pox, Willa. I was visiting Grandma Stanton when you all caught them."

She frowned and hurried to cover her slip of the tongue. If she weren't so upset she never would have mentioned the disease. "I don't *know* if Mary has chicken pox. It will be a few days before we will find out what is causing her illness. Now—"

"Nonetheless, you know how I feel about being around illness."

Memory rose and overcame her irritation. "Yes, I do." Her voice softened. "I remember when Walker died. He was my friend."

"And he was my only brother. And the measles took him from me. I suppose it's well that I've been warned, but I don't want to talk about it." Ellen tossed her head. "I chanced to meet Mrs. Sheffield at *Evans's Millinery,* and she requested that I ask you to stop and see her on your way home."

Ellen's head toss, and her emphasis on the store's name, drew her attention to the bonnet that framed Ellen's beautiful face. A dark blue chip cottage bonnet with flowers adorning the quilted brim. "Your new bonnet is lovely."

Her friend smiled, lifted her hand and touched the bow of wide satin ribbon beneath her chin. "Mrs. Evans finished it today." Ellen glanced in the direction Matthew's buggy had gone and her lower lip pouted out. "I so wanted Matthew to see it. He's so attentive and—" She gasped. Her hand pressed against her chest. "Oh, Willa! You don't think Matthew will get ill? I couldn't bear to lose him."

Horror whispered through Ellen's voice. Guilt shook her. "I'm sure he will be fine, Ellen. And it may well be that Mary only has a very bad cold." She smiled reassurance and changed the subject. The less she thought about Matthew Calvert the better. "Do you want to come with me while I fetch my things?"

Ellen's gaze darted to the schoolhouse. A shudder shook her. "I'll not step foot in that building again until we know it's safe."

She stood and watched her friend hurry away. Ellen *was* afraid. She wasn't gliding now. She was walking the way she had before her vanity had taken over. She sighed and started up the stone walk to the schoolhouse. There was nothing she could do to relieve Ellen's fear. Only time could do that.

She climbed the steps, crossed the small porch to the door and stopped. Ellen hadn't mentioned any gossip. And Ellen had been to town. She would surely know. But then, there was Sophia's request that she come to see her....

She sighed and entered the schoolhouse to gather her things.

Willa skirted the settle, stepped to the door and knocked. Her fingers tightened on her basket's handle. Why had Sophia asked her to come by?

"Come in!"

Sophia's voice, not Rose's. She took a deep breath, put her worries aside and opened the door. If anyone in the village would reject tales of her having "loose morals" it would be Sophia. The smell of stewing chicken permeated the air. She stepped inside, set her basket on the table and sniffed. "Mmm, I remember that smell. Your guests will enjoy their supper tonight."

"Some of them will."

"What do you mean, 'some of them'?" She crossed to the long work table, picked up a piece of diced carrot and popped it in her mouth.

Sophia looked up. "Gracious, that's like old times, except that Callie is not here begging for a piece of chicken." A smile warmed the older woman's violet eyes. "I'd give you a hug, Willa, dear, but my hands are a mess." She wiggled her fingers in the air, then went back to pulling chicken meat off the bones. "I meant that two of my guests are feeling poorly. I'm making chicken soup for them, but I'm not sure Mr. Arthur will be able to eat."

"Have you given him some of your red pepper and sumac leaf tea?" She pulled a face and gave an exaggerated shudder.

Sophia laughed and picked up the platter of chicken pieces. "I have. And it has helped Mr. Wingate. But I fear Mr. Arthur's illness is too advanced to benefit from it." She headed for the fireplace. "Bring along those carrots and onions please, Willa."

She grabbed the large, crockery bowl and followed. Chicken broth, with ripples of clear, rich fat floating on top, simmered in two large iron pots hanging from the crane. Her mouth watered at the delicious smell. "It reminds me of when I was a child to see you cooking. Is Rose still suffering with her back?"

"Yes, poor dear. If she's not better soon, I'll have to find a new cook. It's most inconvenient being without one." Sophia divided the pieces of meat between the pots, set the platter down and turned to her. "Hold on tight." She scooped her hands into the bowl, cupped them and added the captured diced carrots and onions to one of the pots, then reached for more. "I had a letter from Carrie this week."

The vegetables plopped into the broth, sank beneath

the liquid, then floated to the top. Another double handful followed them.

"I hope she's well."

"Yes, but she seems unhappy. She mentions lots of beaus, but she seems to have little regard for the lot of them. I'm getting a mite concerned. I don't suppose she's told you anything?"

Don't tell Aunt Sophie. She shook her head. "Only the same. That she doesn't really care for any of her suitors." *And that her parents keep insisting she choose the wealthiest and most prominent socially among them.*

"Well, I don't like what I'm feeling when I read her letters. I'm going to write and insist she come for a visit soon." The older woman frowned and picked up the empty platter. "Dump the rest of those vegetables into the other pot, Willa. And mind your skirts with the fire. Have you time for tea?"

"I'm afraid not today." She added the carrots and onions to the soup broth and carried the bowl back to the work table. "Mary Burton took sick just before school let out, and I'm already late getting home."

Sophia slipped the platter into the dishpan and reached for the bowl. "Mary's mother and father went to Olville this morning. How did you get the poor child home?" The bowl joined the platter in the dishpan.

"Reverend Calvert was good enough to take her home in his buggy." She held her breath. The mention of Matthew Calvert would give Sophia the opportunity to bring up any gossip Thomas may have started.

Sophia nodded, scooped the chicken and vegetable leavings into the waste bucket, scrubbed her hands together in the dishwater and wiped them on her apron. "I would expect that of him. From what I've seen and heard of the reverend, he has a kind heart."

"Yes." *Though a wayward one.*

"Did you know he leaves a lamp burning all night? Bertha says he does it so people won't feel bad if they have to call on him for an emergency. And he always answers a call for help, no matter the hour. Like the other night." A frown creased Sophia's lovely face. "No, *two* nights ago, it was. I was straightening up a bit in the sitting room after the guests had retired, and I saw him heading toward Olville in his buggy." Her frown deepened. "No one seems to know where he went or what the emergency was."

And I don't want to gossip. Especially about Matthew Calvert and his pursuits. "No. I didn't know." She forced a smile. "I don't mean to press you, but if you could tell me why you wanted me to call? Mama will be wondering where I am."

"Mercy! I forgot all about that in the pleasure of your company. Wait here."

"Of course." She walked to the table and picked up her basket.

Sophia hurried to the door that led to her private quarters. Her voice floated back out the door. "I saw your mother when I was buying groceries at Barley's this morning, and she mentioned she needed to buy some fabric to make new aprons." The older woman emerged carrying a small bundle of cloth. "I told her I had some pieces left from the last time I had bed and table linens made that I thought would suit, and that I would send them home with you."

"Oh, how kind and thoughtful of you." She took the bundle into her arms, leaned forward and kissed Sophia's cheek. "I'm sure Mama will be most appreciative of these. Thank you. Now, I must get home."

"Of course, dear. And I must go check on my guests." Sophia patted her cheek and stepped in front of her. "Let me get the door for you."

Dusk had fallen. Willa hurried off the porch and around Sheffield House to Main Street. Oil lamps on the storefronts lit her way to the bridge over Stony Creek. She shifted the bundle in her arms to a more comfortable position and quickened her steps onto Brook Street.

Ahead, a shadow detached from a tree trunk, morphed into a man. *Thomas?* It was too dark to tell. She lifted her chin and, heart pounding, walked forward. No, not Thomas. The man was too short. He stepped out onto the path in front of her.

"Evening, Miss Wright."

Arnold Dixon. The smell of alcohol wafted toward her. Apprehension tingled along her nerves. He'd always been flirtatious, but he'd never been this bold before. She stopped, took a breath to steady her voice. "Let me pass, Mr. Dixon."

"Not yet." Johnny Taylor stepped from behind the tree and came over to them. "We want to talk to you."

Her mouth went dry. A tremor started in her knees and spread into her legs. She hiked her chin a notch higher. "I'm not interested in anything you have to say. Now, let me pass." She started around them.

They moved to block her.

Her heart lurched. She inched the bundle upward in front of her chest, took comfort in the barrier it presented between her and the men.

"Where's Thomas?"

"Thomas?" She stared at Johnny Taylor, confused by his tone. "I don't know where he is. I haven't seen him."

"Neither have we. Not since the stump burning. We thought maybe you two had gone off and got married."

"Certainly not." She itched to slap the leer off Arnold Dixon's face, but dared not make a move toward him. She shifted her gaze to Johnny Taylor and pushed authority into her voice. "I refused Thomas's suit that evening. We will not be wed. And it is certain he will no longer call on me. I would think he would come and see you, however. You *are* his friends, are you not?" *Where was Thomas?* She took a breath and tried again. "Now, please step out of my way."

"He figured to get the money from you to stake our trip west. Did you give him the money?"

Our trip? Johnny Taylor's tone sent shivers slithering up and down her spine, anger stiffened it. "I did not. I have no money to give anyone, Mr. Taylor. Now, good evening." She stepped straight ahead and looked up at him.

He scowled, nodded at Arnold Dixon and stepped aside.

She walked between the two men, fastened her gaze on her cabin and kept her shaking legs moving. *We haven't seen him since the stump burning.* Had Thomas left town again? Is that why there had been no gossip thus far? If only it could be so!

Two terse sentences and a scripture reference. Not much to show for two hours of work—or rather nonwork.

Matthew shoved back from his desk, scrubbed his hand over the nape of his neck and frowned. He needed a haircut. Come to think of it, so did Joshua. The boy's hair was getting so long his blond curls flopped into his eyes. He would take him with him to Rizzo's barbershop tomorrow.

Why had she turned cool and aloof?

The thought hovered in his head. He rose and paced the room. No matter what he thought about, no matter what he did, or more accurately, *tried* to do, his thoughts circled back to Willa, to the way she had looked at him in the carriage this afternoon. There had been such warmth, such softness, such…trust… in her eyes in those last moments. And then, in an instant, it was gone. What had he done to make her withdraw like that?

His frown deepened, drew his brows down and creased his forehead. He'd never felt like this in his life. The woman had him completely flummoxed. He was elated and hopeful one moment, deflated and despairing the next. A wry smile tugged at his lips. Was this love? Was this what Robert and Judith had shared that had made them so blissfully happy? It was making him miserable.

He turned, grabbed his suit coat off the back of his

chair and snuffed the lamp. He climbed the stairs by the dim light of the lamp in the entrance hall.

All was quiet. He opened the door and peeked in at Sally. She was sound asleep, the kitten curled on the cover beside her small hand. Her empty hand. She had put Judith's glove in the drawer of her nightstand a few days after she got the kitten, and there it had stayed. But she still wanted the lamp burning.

He stepped inside and lowered the wick. The kitten opened its eyes, yawned and closed them again. He stared down at the curled-up ball of fur. The day they had gone to pick out the kitten had been the first time he suspected his feelings for Willa Wright were growing beyond a strong attraction. He *had* wanted to kiss her that day. And that want was getting stronger every time he saw her. This afternoon, in the buggy, he'd had all he could do to keep from taking her in his arms.

He closed Sally's door, moved down the hall and peeked in at Joshua. The boy was sprawled out on his stomach, one arm hanging down over the side of the bed, the dog's head resting on his other shoulder. He grinned. That dog purely wore the boy out.

A feeling of lack spread through him, a hunger to share these quiet, private moments with a wife. And the wife he wanted to share them with was Willa.

He picked up the lamp from the hall table and walked to his bedroom. Light moved in a golden circle over the carpet as he crossed the room. He set the lamp on his nightstand, threw back the covers, slipped out of his shirt, shoes and pants and flopped down against the pillows.

He'd begun seriously praying about a wife and family of his own about a year ago, but he'd met no woman who had drawn his heart. And then Robert and Judith had died and he'd brought their children here to Pinewood to heal and met Willa.

Nothing in his life had ever prepared him for the immediate, strong attraction he'd felt the moment he looked into Willa's eyes. Nor for the way that attraction continued to grow, to deepen every time he saw her. He snuffed the lamp, pulled the covers up to his chest and laced his hands behind his head. Was she the mate God had for him?

He let out a frustrated growl, flopped onto his side and yanked his pillow into place. "The woman has me going in circles, Lord. My head can't figure out what is going on, and I don't dare trust my heart. Make Your will clear to me, oh, Lord. Tell me, what is Your will?"

Willa bolted upright and stared into the darkness. Something kept taunting her—floating just out of reach at the edge of her dream. What *was* it?

She frowned and propped her pillow against the headboard. Whatever nagged at her, she would get no sleep until she figured it out. Her day had certainly been an unsettling one. Beginning with Mary's illness and that unnerving buggy ride alone with Matthew Calvert on the way back to the schoolhouse. What was wrong with her, responding to him that way? Ellen loved him, and believed that he cared for her. That they would be wed.

She tugged the quilt up around her shoulders and thought about those last few minutes. He had seemed

so sincere, so…caring, sitting there rubbing his
knuckles and listening to her apology. And the way
he had looked at her when he'd said "I would never
have let him hurt you, Miss Wright" had stolen her
breath. The thing gnawing at her slipped closer. She
grasped for the thought, and it skittered away.

Was that it? Had it to do with her apology? She
had been honest. Perhaps not precise, but honest.
Nothing came to her. She sighed and skimmed over her
conversation with Ellen, found nothing enlightening
there, and moved on to her call on Sophia. There was
nothing of note there, either. She had helped with the
soup…they had spoken about Callie and about Mary's
illness and Matthew Calvert taking her home. Sophia
had commented on Matthew's kindness, and shared
a bit about how she had seen him driving his buggy
toward Olville two nights ago to—

She stiffened, went still. There it was again! She
tried to capture the thought, but it disappeared like a
wisp of smoke. Was it the gossip? How could it be?
What had Matthew Calvert's driving his buggy to
Olville to do with her?

Two nights ago.

She gasped, jerked forward and clasped her hands
over her mouth. *We haven't seen him since the stump
burning.* That was two nights ago. And Matthew
Calvert's knuckles were bruised. Had he… Oh, that
was ridiculous! Why would he fight with Thomas and
then take him out of town? The man was a *preacher.* It
was all a mere coincidence. Still…where was Thomas?

I would never have let him hurt you, Miss Wright.

She frowned, lowered her pillow, slipped beneath

the quilt and closed her eyes. Matthew Calvert was courting Ellen—or soon would be. And he was a gentleman. What he had said meant nothing beyond mere politeness. A gentleman was expected to protect a lady, and of course, he would profess to do that. Yet, his remembered words enfolded her like a warm, soft blanket.

Chapter Fifteen

"I'm home, Mama." Willa set her basket on the lamp table, shoved off her hood, unfastened her cloak and hung it on a peg beside the door. "Mama?"

Silence.

She frowned and walked into the kitchen, skirted around the table and glanced into the lean-to wash shed. Water steamed in the large iron pots hanging from the crane in the fireplace. Clothes soaked in the wash and rinse tubs.

She crossed to the back door and stepped outside into the chill November air. "Mama?"

The yard was empty. An uneasy feeling hit the pit of her stomach. Her mother was always home. She whirled and went back inside, headed for her mother's bedroom.

"Oh!"

"Mama!" She jolted to a stop, pressed her hand to her chest and stared at her mother who had jerked to a halt in the kitchen doorway.

"Gracious!" Her mother huffed out a breath. "You startled me, Willa."

"And you, me." She laughed and patted her chest. "I was looking for you."

"Are you ill?" Her mother's long skirts swished as she hurried toward her with a purposeful stride.

"No, Mama. I'm fine."

"Then why are you home this time of day?"

Her mother stopped in front of her and scanned her face, touched her cheek with the backs of her fingers. How often that touch had soothed her as a child, especially when she was ill. There would likely be a lot of such concerned, yet comforting, touches going on around the village soon.

"I'm home because school is closed. Mary broke out with chicken pox last night. And so did Jeffery. I'm sorry if I worried you." She leaned forward and kissed her mother's cheek. It was smooth and soft, unlike the dry, work-roughened hand that had pressed against her face. "Mr. Townsend came by early this morning and told me the board had decided to close the school in hope that it will stop the spread of the disease. When the children arrived, I sent them home."

"That's different. It sounds like a good idea."

"Perhaps, but I fear it is already too late. Mary was very sick the other day, and Jeffery was coughing a bit, too. In my experience—from past years—it's likely that some of the other children may have already caught chicken pox from them."

"I suppose. Seems like it doesn't take much."

She followed her mother into the lean-to and watched her remove her old, threadbare wool cape and hang it by the back door. A frown wrinkled her brow. She'd been saving every penny she could to buy fabric and sew her mother a new cloak. One with a collar. And Mrs. Hall had promised to help her make a matching bonnet. Now, with the school closed, and no pay… She shook off the gloomy thought. "Anyway, until school opens again, I will have more time to help you."

She lifted an apron off a peg on the wall, slipped it on, grabbed the ties and made a bow at the small of her back. "I don't recall your mentioning going to town. I would have been happy to pick up whatever you needed on my way home."

"I didn't go to town. I was next door at Dora's." Her mother lifted a shirt out of the water, soaped it, then bunched it in her hands and rubbed it up and down on the washboard. "I went out to hang— Oh, I forgot about the clothes! They're still outside in the basket. When I saw Dora looking so sick, I left them and went to help her." Her mother dropped the shirt back in the water and rinsed her hands free of clinging soapsuds.

"I'll go hang the clothes, Mama." She took the old cape down and swirled it around her shoulders. "What's wrong with Mrs. Braynard?"

"She thinks she's got the grippe. Ina and Paul were sick with it when they came home from their visit to Luke, and Dora helped nurse them. I guess they told her the grippe is rife in Syracuse. It's awful when your children are sick." Her mother shook her head and went back to scrubbing the shirt. "It took Dora awful fast. I saw her carrying water to the hogs when I carried the laundry outside. By the time I hung a couple of shirts up to dry, she was leaning against the fence and holding her head in her hands. I hustled over to see if she was all right and ended up helping her to the cabin and putting her to bed. She's some fevered. I told her I'd look in on her this afternoon."

"I could make her some chicken soup. It might make her feel better." Memory flashed. She frowned and absently fastened the ties down the front of the cape. "There were two men staying at Sheffield House the other day when I went to pick up the apron fabric. Mrs. Sheffield said they were quite ill—so much so she thought one of them would not be able to eat the soup she was making for them. Perhaps the men were from Syracuse."

She shrugged off the speculation and pulled her attention back to the work at hand. One way or the other, those men had nothing to do with her. Unless Sophia Sheffield took sick. The thought was unsettling. She was very fond of Callie's aunt. "Where are the clothes pegs, Mama?"

"In the basket. On top of the clothes."

She nodded and opened the door. "As soon as I finish hanging the clothes, I'm going to town and call on Mrs. Sheffield. I'll stop by Brody's and get a chicken, then come home and start the soup."

She closed the door and walked through the dead leaves and dying grasses to the wicker basket holding the laundry. The chill in the air was more pronounced. She glanced up at the overcast sky and sighed. It looked and felt like snow was on the way. She shook out a pair of pants, folded the edge of the waist over the thin rope loggers that stretched from tree to tree around the yard, then slipped a peg over the fabric, moved a few inches along the waist and slipped on another.

A sudden, sharp gust of wind set the pant legs flapping. She shivered, the threadbare wool of the cape little protection. Her determination firmed. She would find a way to earn money to buy the fabric for a cloak. Her mother was not going to suffer another winter shivering from the cold.

She bent down and picked up a shirt, snapped it through the air to shake out some of the wrinkles and cast another look at the sky. Hopefully, the snow would hold off until the clothes were dry.

Matthew climbed the stairs to the second floor of Sheffield House, the doctor's words weighting his steps. *There's no hope. His heart's weakened. At best, he won't last more than an hour or so.*

No hope. A fallacy. There was always hope in God. He squared his shoulders and walked down the hall, grateful for these few minutes he would have alone with Mr. Arthur before the doctor returned. He glanced at the numbers on the doors he passed. Number eight. The fourth door on the left. That was it.

He stopped before the paneled portal, bowed his head and closed his eyes. "Almighty God, I humbly beseech Thee to give unto me the right words to speak that this man's need of comfort may be met, and he will peacefully enter into Your rest. Amen."

He lifted his hand and gently rapped his knuckles against the polished wood. No summons to enter came. He took a breath and opened the door, crossed the room.

Raspy, shallow and uneven breaths issued from the man in the bed. He gazed down at the gaunt, pale, yet fever-flushed features and released another silent prayer for guidance. "Mr. Arthur…"

The man's eyelids fluttered, opened.

He looked into watery, glassy blue eyes filled with fear. His heart swelled with compassion. He rested his hand on the covers over the man's shoulder and hoped Mr. Arthur would sense God's love flowing through him. "I'm Reverend Calvert, Mr. Arthur. You asked to speak with me?"

The man gasped, struggled to form words. "Need… pray…for me."

He nodded, leaned closer to better hear the man's weak, halting voice. "Do you enjoy salvation, Mr. Arthur? Are you assured in your relationship with the Lord?"

The man's eyes flooded with dread. "Never…seen much…need…" He gasped, struggled for air.

"It's never too late for God's salvation, Mr. Arthur." He spoke slowly, deliberately, willing the man to hear him, praying he would accept the truth and live long enough to proclaim it. "Do you believe Jesus is the Son of God?"

"Yes…" The word wheezed out. Mr. Arthur's eyes closed.

He jerked the covers aside, grabbed the man's hand and squeezed. The closed eyelids fluttered. "Mr. Arthur!" He squeezed harder.

The man sucked in a ragged breath, opened his eyes and fixed his gaze on him.

Thank You, Lord. "Mr. Arthur, do you ask Jesus

into your heart and proclaim Him to be Your Lord and Savior?"

"Yes…" The man stared at him. He watched, rejoicing, as the fear drained from Mr. Arthur's eyes and peace washed over the gaunt face. "Thank… you…"

Joy flooded him. He smiled. "You are now a child of God, Mr. Arthur. Welcome to His Kingdom, where you shall abide forever more."

The man's trembling lips parted to struggle for air, relaxed, then lifted in a small smile. The fingers on the thin hand gripped in his tightened slightly, then released. A soft sigh escaped the previously straining lungs and Mr. Arthur closed his eyes.

He stood for a moment, his head bowed and his heart lifted in prayer, then gently drew the covers back over Mr. Arthur's arm and shoulder.

The door opened. The doctor entered and strode to the bedside, looked a question at him.

He shook his head and left the room to find Sophia Sheffield and inquire if Mr. Arthur had left any requests or instructions to be carried out on his demise.

Willa shifted the large, paper-wrapped bundle of cotton sheeting she'd picked up for Mrs. Braynard to one arm, lifted her free hand and knocked.

"Come in."

She opened Sophia's door, stepped inside and bumped the door shut with her hip, turned to put her burden on the table and looked straight at Matthew Calvert. "Oh."

Shock streaked through her, slackened her grip

and her jaw. The bundle slid. She snapped her gaping mouth closed and grabbed for it, caught the edge of the basket dangling from her arm instead. The package slipped to the floor. She dropped to a stoop to pick it up, saw Matthew Calvert rise from his chair, and bowed her head to hide her face. What was *he* doing here?

"Slippery paper, Willa, dear?"

She glanced up and met Sophia's knowing, amused gaze. If Sophia had guessed her reaction was due to Matthew Calvert's being there, then perhaps he had also. Heat rushed to her cheeks. "The package is awkward to carry."

"Hmm."

Black boots appeared at the edge of her vision. *No!* She grabbed the package and rose before Matthew Calvert could offer her his hand and she came completely undone. She certainly didn't need *that* happening with Sophia watching. The older woman was obviously misreading her surprise at seeing Matthew Calvert seated at the table in her kitchen for something else entirely.

He stepped closer. "Allow me to relieve you of your burden, Miss Wright."

His presence, so near to her, set her already-taut nerves atingle. She shook her head. "Thank you, but no, Reverend. I can't stay." *Not with you here.*

"Are you sure, Willa, dear? It must be getting colder out—your cheeks are quite rosy."

She shot a stop-teasing-me look at Sophia.

The older woman's violet eyes twinkled, her lips

curved in a sweet smile. "Surely, you can stay long enough to join us for a nice warming cup of tea?"

She swept her gaze to the tea set on the tray in front of Sophia, slid her gaze to the half-empty cup across the table in front of a pushed-back chair. "No, truly." She turned slightly, used the movement to gain a little space between herself and Matthew Calvert. "I have to get home. Mrs. Braynard has taken ill, and I'm going to make her some chicken soup."

The amused look in Sophia's eyes died. "What's wrong with Dora?"

She relaxed and launched into the safe subject. "She has the grippe. Ina and Paul took sick with it when they were visiting Luke in Syracuse. They said it has spread all through the city." She stepped closer to Sophia. "That's why I came. I remembered about the two men you said were so ill and I wondered if they were from Syracuse. I wanted to make certain you were all right."

Sophia reached up and patted her arm. "I'm fine, Willa."

"I'm so glad." She smiled and took a firmer hold on the bundle. "I really must go. I have to stop at Brody's and get a chicken."

"Nonsense. Dora is my friend, too. And I ordered a stewing chicken this morning that I…no longer need." Sophia took a swallow of tea and rose. "Bring your basket and come with me to the buttery."

Sophia's tone left no room for discussion on the matter. She placed her bundle on a chair and followed her out the door to the small, stone building a few feet from the porch.

Hams and thick slabs of bacon hung from hooks

in the ceiling. Crocks of various sizes, some with lids, some covered with cloth, sat on the floor or on a bench along the wall. Eggs were piled in a bowl. Her lips curved. She and Callie and Sadie used to come in here and sneak cream from the top of the milk.

"Here we are." Sophia pulled a piece of cheesecloth off a deep bowl, lifted out a plucked chicken, wrapped it in the piece of cheesecloth and put it in her basket. "Now, let's get back to my nice warm kitchen."

She followed her outside and stopped. Matthew Calvert, wearing his hat and holding her bundle tucked under his arm, stood at the bottom of the porch steps. He smiled and doffed his hat at Sophia. "Thank you for the tea and the pleasure of your company, Mrs. Sheffield." His gaze shifted to her. "Are you ready to go, Miss Wright?"

"Yes, but—"

"Then let me carry that." He stepped forward and took hold of the basket.

She stood frozen in place and stared at her things in his hands, unsure of whether to be grateful for his gentlemanly kindness, or offended at his high-handed tactics.

Sophia turned and, eyes twinkling, kissed her cheek. "Goodbye, Willa, dear." She leaned closer. "Oh, yes, a much, *much* better catch than Thomas Hunter."

She stiffened at the whispered words, darted a glance at Matthew Calvert. Had he heard Sophia? It didn't appear so.

"Goodbye, Reverend. Come and have tea with me

again sometime—under better circumstances." Sophia climbed the steps and entered the house.

They were alone. Something close to panic gripped her. Why did this man so unnerve her? How could he both attract and repel her? She knew him for the flirt he was, and he was not to be trusted.

"Shall we go?"

She nodded, reached up and pulled her hood forward, squared her shoulders and started down the path to the gravel carriageway that led out to Main Street.

Matthew glanced at Willa's set face and frowned. She had changed the minute Sophia Sheffield had left them. Why? *Lord, if she is the one you have for me, please help me reach her heart.*

They stopped where the Sheffield House carriageway met Main Street and waited for a wagon loaded with cabbages to pass. "Mind the ruts, they've gotten deeper with the recent rains." He shifted the basket into his other hand and took her elbow to cross, felt her stiffen and let go immediately when they reached the other side. "Until you mentioned it, I didn't know Mrs. Sheffield had two ill guests. Dr. Palmer did not mention a second man."

"Dr. Palmer?"

Ah, he had gotten her to break her silence. "Yes. He summoned me to the hotel at Mr. Arthur's request." He stopped as she paused and looked up at him, worry clouding her beautiful blue-green eyes.

"I wasn't aware Mr. Arthur's illness was severe enough to require a doctor's attendance." She sighed, and started walking again. "I hope he improves quickly and leaves the hotel. And the other man as well. I'm concerned about Mrs. Sheffield's health."

He hated to tell her, but there was no help for it. "Mr. Arthur passed away this morning, Miss Wright. Mrs. Sheffield and I were discussing his last wishes when you came."

She stopped and stared at him. The cloud of worry in her eyes darkened. "What was Mr. Arthur's illness? Was it the grippe?"

He shook his head, wished he could tell her no and take the worry from her. "I don't know. I was called at the last to pray with Mr. Arthur."

"Clearly, prayer didn't help."

Such bitterness in her voice! He looked down and shifted the package he carried to hide his shock, then took a breath and addressed her comment. "But it did, Miss Wright. The prayer of salvation alleviated Mr. Arthur's fear, and he entered into God's rest peacefully."

"It was kind of you to comfort him in his last moments."

She thought he prayed only as a means to comfort Mr. Arthur? The thought chilled his heart, settled like a rock in his gut and raised a question he didn't want to face. But he must. "You do not believe in prayer, Miss Wright?"

She stopped and looked up at him. "As a source of comfort for those who believe in it, yes."

Lord, please... "But *you* do not believe in prayer?" Hurt flashed in her eyes, hovered there like a shadow.

It was all he could do not to drop her things and take her in his arms right there on Main Street.

"If you are asking if I believe that God hears our pleas and answers them, then my answer, sir, in truth, is no, I do not." Her chin lifted. "I'm sure that is disturbing to a man of faith, such as yourself, but I learned very early in my childhood not to depend on a benevolent, loving God who watches over us. He has never bothered to demonstrate any such care toward me or my mother. I do, however, as behooves a teacher, keep such thoughts to myself." She turned and headed down the walkway toward the Stony Creek bridge, the heels of her shoes clicking against the planks.

He fell into step at her side, his thoughts churning, his heart sick with fear. He *did* believe in prayer. Was this God's answer to his cry to show him His will? Was the one woman he had ever been attracted to, the woman he was in love with, to be denied him?

"I wish I knew if Mr. Arthur was from Syracuse."

He dragged his attention from the sickening fear in his heart to address hers. "Because of the grippe your sick friend said is prevalent there?"

"Yes. If Mr. Arthur brought the grippe from there… And if he died of it, then Mrs. Sheffield and Mrs. Braynard are both in danger."

"There is no need to be concerned about that, Miss Wright."

She lifted her chin. Her pained gaze fastened on his. "Because of prayer, Reverend Calvert?"

He set his personal need aside and let her challenge pass. He was her pastor, and it was too soon to confront her hurt. He needed first to seek God's wisdom. "Because Mrs. Sheffield told me Mr. Arthur was from Schenectady. It was his wish that she write his family there."

Chapter Sixteen

Matthew scowled, pushed back from his desk and headed for the kitchen. It was hard to separate his personal feelings from his pastoral ones where Willa was concerned, but one way or the other, he needed information. He couldn't help her find her way to God if he didn't know the problem. And whether he ever held her as his wife, he wanted her safe in God's arms.

He stepped into the kitchen, caught a flash of Joshua going outside, heard his footsteps pound across the porch and an anguished plea from Sally for Joshua to hurry before the door slammed shut. "What's that about?"

Bertha looked up from the dough she was kneading. "Cat's up the tree again." She grinned and punched the dough. "Sally calls Joshua now. *He* scales that tree like a country boy—doesn't hurt himself grabbing on to dead branches."

Matthew snorted, lifted the coffeepot Bertha kept filled for him off the stove and poured some of the steaming brew into a cup.

Bertha's brow furrowed. "What're you looking so sour about?"

"I didn't know I was." He blew across the surface of the coffee and took a tentative sip, followed it with a bigger swallow. "Bertha, you've lived in Pinewood a long time, haven't you?"

"Since it was only a lumbering camp with a few cabins amongst all the trees. It didn't even have a name back then." She stopped kneading and glanced up at him. "I've been around you long enough now to know you don't ask questions for no reason. What's on your mind?"

"Do you remember Willa as a child?" He took another swallow of his coffee and indulged himself thinking about how good her name felt on his tongue. So did not having to hide his love for her. He'd been honest about that with Bertha ever since the night he'd escorted Thomas Hunter out of town.

"'Course, I do." Her gaze sharpened. "Why?"

He looked down into his cup, swirled the coffee up close to the rim and chose his words. Bertha was not one to take part in idle gossip. "She said something a few days ago that made me think someone had hurt her badly when she was small."

"Seven years old, she was."

He swallowed, lowered the cup from his mouth and looked at her.

"Her papa up and walked away." Anger glinted in Bertha's hazel eyes. "Left Helen alone with little Willa and nowhere to live and no way to provide for her."

Willa had been only a little older than Joshua. The muscles in his jaw twitched. He set his cup on the table, leaned against the wall and crossed his arms over his chest. "What happened to them?"

"The women in the camp took a hand." Bertha shoved the heels of her hands against the pile of dough, turned it and shoved again. "The cabins on Brook Street belong to Manning Townsend. If you don't work for Manning, you can't live in the cabins. So, when George Wright left, it meant Helen had to get out—and she had no folks to go to. We women got together and reasoned out if Helen worked for Manning, she and Willa could still have the use of the cabin. We lit on the idea of her doing wash for the bachelor loggers."

"And Mr. Townsend agreed?"

Bertha's lips twitched. "Willa and Sadie Spencer— she's the Townsends' granddaughter—were best friends, and Rachel Townsend wouldn't have any part of putting Willa and Helen out of that cabin. Manning wasn't given a choice."

An image of sweet-natured, plump and gray-haired Rachel Townsend popped into his head. The woman must have more starch to her spine than it appeared. He'd never heard of their granddaughter. And he didn't know Mrs. Wright. "I've never met Willa's mother. She doesn't come to church." He frowned, stared at the floor and searched his memory. "I don't believe I've ever seen her about town. Of course, I can't put a name to everyone I've seen."

"It's not likely you've laid eyes on her. Helen works at doing wash from break of day to full dark, and pretty much keeps to herself otherwise. Doesn't come into town very often. Willa picks up what they need at the store."

He nodded, thought about how hard it all must have been, especially for a young child. "What happened to Willa's father?"

"Never heard and don't care to." Bertha clamped her lips closed, flopped the kneaded dough into a bowl, greased the top and covered it with a cloth. "You'd best check on those youngsters. I've work enough to do without having to care for a broken leg or something."

He summoned a grin. "I thought you said Joshua scaled that tree like a real country boy."

She looked at him.

"I'm going." He pushed away from the wall, picked up his cup, refilled it and headed for the kitchen door. Whatever happened to a man being the king of his castle? He smiled and shook his head. One thing was sure, whoever that king was, he didn't have a woman like Bertha Franklin for his housekeeper. And was the poorer for it.

A knock on the front door interrupted his musings. He reversed directions, set the cup down on the table and hurried to the entrance hall to open the front door. "Why, hello, Billy." He glanced through lazily drifting snowflakes at the barebacked horse tied to the hitching post by a halter. "Did you want Joshua?"

The boy shook his head and sent the lock of black hair on his forehead flopping from side to side. "No, sir. Ma sent me to fetch you." The boy's eyes teared up, he swallowed hard. "Grandma's took sick and is doing poorly. Doc Palmer said you best come."

"As soon as I hitch up the buggy." He rested a comforting hand on the boy's shoulder. "We'll tether your horse to the back, and you can ride home in the buggy with me. Meanwhile, Joshua is in the side yard. Why don't you go see him while I'm in the stable? He's rescuing Sally's cat from the tree."

The boy nodded and trotted down the steps.

He stepped back to shut the door, paused as a buggy stopped out front. A young man climbed from the carriage, tethered his horse and hurried toward the house.

He studied the man's face, tried to place him and failed. "May I help you, sir?"

The man stopped at the base of the steps and looked up at him. Fear shadowed his blue eyes. "I was told Bertha Franklin is here. May I speak to her please?"

"Of course, come in Mr...."

"Danvers. Charles Danvers." The man trotted up the stairs and across the porch, stepped into the entrance hall. "I'm Bertha's son-in-law. If you'll—"

"You'll find Bertha in the kitchen. It's through that door." He gestured toward the kitchen, frowned as the man spun on his heel and hurried that direction. Should he follow? No, Bertha was quite capable of handling Mr. Danvers and whatever was upsetting him on her own. He slapped his hat on his head, grabbed his coat and headed for the stables.

"Billy, it's time to go. Take your horse around to the stables and tie him to the back of the buggy. I'll be right along."

"Yes, sir." Billy ran for his horse.

Matthew smiled at Joshua, safe now on the ground, and Sally holding her beloved kitten. "It's getting colder. You two had best come inside for a while." He gestured the two of them up the porch steps ahead of him and grinned down at the dog who stood looking up at him, his tail wagging furiously. "You, too."

The dog raced up the steps ahead of him. "Mind you wipe your feet." Too late. Children and animals were already through the door. He lunged, caught the door before it slammed closed, and stepped inside. "Bertha, I'm leav— What's wrong?"

"Take these to the buggy. I'll come in a minute."

He glanced at the tied bundle of clothes Bertha handed her son-in-law, then raised his gaze to her face, drew in a sharp breath at her grim expression.

"My daughter and her baby are dreadful sick with the grippe, Reverend. I have to go tend them. I'm sorry to leave you with no supper prepared, but—" Her eyes narrowed, clouded. "You going somewhere?"

"Yes, Billy Karcher came for me. His grandmother is ill and not doing well." He stepped toward her. "I'm sorry about your daughter and her baby, Bertha. If I can help in any way, please let me know."

She nodded, then looked up at him, her brow furrowed. "The youngsters—"

"Will be all right, Bertha. I'll find someone to—"

"Isobel!" Bertha grabbed her cloak off a chair, threw it around her thin shoulders and headed for the door. "You go comfort Grandma Karcher, Reverend. I'll run across the street and get the Halls' maid to come stay with the children 'til you come home."

Willa stomped the snow from her boots and opened the door of the apothecary shop. The bells on the door tinkled merrily when she closed it again. She blinked and walked into the warm interior.

"Hello, Willa. Looks like winter has arrived."

"Yes, and with a vengeance." She smiled at Steven Roberts and set her basket on the counter. "There is already three inches of snow on the ground, and it shows no sign of stopping."

"At that rate, we'll have six inches or more by closing time." The proprietor's lips lifted into a wry grin. "I guess I'd better hunt up my shovel. Meantime, what can I do for you?"

She opened her basket and consulted the list she'd tucked inside. "I'd like one pint of medicinal spirits, one-half ounce each of snakeroot, golden seal and wormwood please. Oh, and some ginger root."

"This for you?" The store owner turned and began lifting containers down from a shelf.

"Only the ginger root. The rest goes on Mrs. Braynard's account."

"Mrs. Braynard is still not feeling well?" Steven Roberts started measuring out the requested amounts of the dried herbs.

She shook her head, pulled off her gloves and warmed her hands over the round heating stove. "She still has a cough and is very easily fatigued."

"It's good of you and your mother to care for her, Willa." He placed her order in her basket, drew his account book toward him and dipped his pen in the inkwell.

"She would do the same for us." She tugged her gloves on, grasped the basket and headed for the door.

"Be careful, Willa. The grippe is spreading, and it seems to hang on for a good long while."

"That's what the ginger root is for. Mama won't let me tend to anyone unless I keep a piece of it in my mouth." She smiled, opened the door to the accompaniment of the tinkling bells, and hurried out so she didn't chill off the store.

"Willa! Wait!"

She turned and squinted through the rapidly falling snow in the direction of the call.

Ellen waved at her from the other side of the street, then lifted her hems and started across.

She stopped and waited, waved as Mr. Totten drove his trolley past, the horses' heads bobbing in time to the thud of their hooves against the snow-covered road.

"I'm so glad I saw you, Willa." Ellen stepped up onto the wood walkway and shook her cloak of blue wool into place over her long skirts. "I'm so excited to tell you what has happened!"

She looked into Ellen's shining blue eyes and smiled. "It must be good news."

"Oh, it is." Ellen tucked her hands into her fur muff and stepped closer. "Bertha Franklin's son-in-law came for her late this morning. Her daughter is very ill with the grippe, and other members of her family are sick as well. Bertha has gone to Bentford to care for them."

She stared through the falling snow at Ellen's sparkling blue eyes. "Forgive me, but I do not see how that is cause for elation."

Ellen leaned close. "Oh, but it is! You see, Matthew was gone out on a call, and, of course, Bertha's son-in-law was worried about leaving his wife alone and wanted to start the trip back to Bentford immediately. Bertha came to ask if Isobel could stay with Matthew's wards until he came home, and I immediately realized that with Bertha gone Matthew would be without anyone to watch over his wards when he is called away, or to act as his housekeeper. I asked Mother and Father if I could do so, and they agreed it would be proper as long as Matthew's wards are there."

She gaped. "But Ellen…you don't like children."

"What has *that* to do with it? I love Matthew." Ellen tugged her hand from her muff and gripped her forearm. "Don't you see, Willa? Matthew has been increasingly warm to me since I began teaching the Sunday school class, and he was most grateful to find me watching over his wards when he came home a short while ago. I am certain that when he sees me caring for them and his home every day, during Bertha's absence, he will ask for my hand in marriage."

"Oh, Ellen…"

"What?" Her friend's lower lip pouted. "I thought you would be happy for me, Willa."

She gazed at her lifelong friend's lovely, crestfallen face and forced a smile to her lips and conviction into her voice. "I am, Ellen. I simply think it's a little premature for celebrating your betrothal." The possibility of that truly happening struck her with unexpected dismaying force. She firmly closed her mind to the thoughts being conjured, ignored the sudden, sick feeling in the pit of her stomach and widened her smile. "That usually comes after your beau asks you to be his bride."

"Is that what concerns you?" Ellen laughed and tucked her hand back into her muff. "Don't fret yourself, Willa. That shall happen very soon. And I am going to have Mother make me a new gown for when we make the announcement." Ellen's eyes widened and her lovely lips parted in a small gasp. "I just thought—I shall have Matthew make the announcement in church! Oh, how exciting! That will be perfect. I have to go tell Mother. But first, I have to pick up some buttons for her at Cargrave's. Bye, Willa."

She stood and watched Ellen glide down the street, her long skirts brushing a wide swath through the snow. *I am certain that when he sees me caring for his wards and his home he will ask for my hand in marriage.* She pressed her free hand against her stomach and took a deep breath. The queasy feeling stayed. And why wouldn't it? She was concerned for Sally and Joshua. That's all it was. She was concerned for the children. Ellen didn't even call them by name.

Matthew prowled through the house, his hands stuffed in his pockets and his brows drawn into a deep scowl. Nothing was working out as he had hoped.

He'd been too long paying his comfort visit to Mrs. Karcher to have time to speak to Willa today. And Bertha had left to care for her ill family members. And Ellen Hall was going to come and spend the days so he would have someone to watch over Joshua and Sally when he was called away.

He flopped onto the settee in the sitting room and stared up at the ceiling. He should be grateful for Miss Hall's thoughtfulness in realizing his need and offering her services, but the truth was, the woman made him uncomfortable with her constant flirting. And Joshua and Sally were not happy that Miss Hall was coming.

He yanked his hands from his pockets and laced them behind his head. It wasn't as if he had a choice. Dr. Palmer had told him the grippe was spreading rapidly, and so was chicken pox. Little Trudy Hoffman had come down with the pox today, and the Brody boy had them, also. He frowned and blew out a long breath. As the sicknesses spread there would be an increased demand for him to make comfort calls and pray for the sick. When would he find time to speak with Willa? Was he being selfish? No. If she should become ill before—

He shoved the thought away, lunged to his feet and crossed to look out the window. Snow was piled in the corners of the grids that held the small panes and more was falling. If this weather kept up, he would have to start using the cutter to get around.

What if Joshua or Sally got sick? The thought set him hurrying up the stairs to check on them.

The other thought, the one hovering in the deep recesses of his mind, he wasn't ready to face. But it would not be denied. *Was God using these obstacles that kept him from being with Willa to show him His will?*

Chapter Seventeen

There! The last piece for her mother's new hood was cut out. Willa added it to the pile of other pieces on her bed and picked up the remnants of green wool. She would quilt some of the linen material Sophia had given her mother for a lining.

She sighed, folded the pieces, wrapped them in half of a worn-out blanket she'd saved to make a rag rug and hid them under her bed. She had so wanted to make her mother a new cloak, but it would have to wait until school opened again and she could save more money from her earnings. And the hood would be warmer than her mother's old bonnet. And lovely.

A shiver shook her. She rubbed her cold hands together and pictured just how she would make the hood. She would gather it at the nape, to ensure enough fullness to fit easily over her mother's pulled-back hair, and she'd buy some of that dark gold satin ribbon she'd seen at Cargrave's for ties. And flowers. Yes! She smiled, the image clear in her mind. She would have Mrs. Hall make two flowers out of the wide ribbon, and then she would attach the ties with them. Oh, her mother would look so pretty with her green eyes shining above the gold satin bow!

Another shiver shook her. She whirled around, picked up the scissors and hurried out to the sitting room to put them back in the mending basket before her mother returned from next door.

The flames in the fireplace beckoned. The wood crackled a welcome. She stepped close and held out her hands to warm them. Another shiver passed through her. How was she ever going to keep the hood a secret until it was finished? It was too cold to sew in her bedroom, and— Thread! She had forgotten to buy thread. She couldn't use her mother's; she would know it was missing. She would have to pick some up at Cargrave's later, when she went to Brody's to buy meat for supper.

The door creaked open. A draft of cold air hit her back, made the flames of the fire leap and dance.

"Mercy, it's getting cold out there!"

She turned, stepped to the side and smiled. "The fire's nice and warm, Mama. Come join me."

"For a minute." Her mother hung her cape on a peg and came to stand beside her. "Edda stopped to visit with Dora. She said the grippe has spread into the logging camps now. As sick as Dora's been, she's some worried about Daniel."

An image of Daniel's grinning face popped into her head. "I hope he's spared. I hate to think of him being sick out in the camp with no one to care for him." She lifted a piece of wood out of the woodbox beside the hearth and added it to the fire. "Who will care for the loggers who become seriously ill, Mama? Dr. Palmer is already overburdened caring for the villagers."

"That's true, 'specially with chicken pox spreading around on top of the grippe. But, I'm thinking, he'll hold up to the load well enough now he's got Reverend Calvert helping him." Her mother pulled a chair close to the hearth, picked up a shirt she was mending, drew the needle out of the fabric and resumed stitching a torn sleeve.

He's got Reverend Calvert helping him. Her mind seized on the thought. Would Matthew know about chewing on a piece of ginger root to keep the grippe from taking hold of you? Did he know he should carry spirits of alcohol and clean his hands with it when he left a sick person's bedside? What if he didn't wear a wool scarf to keep his chest warm? Or drink birch bark and cherry stone tea when he came home?

Silence.

She looked down. Her mother was staring at her. "I'm sorry, Mama. You were saying…"

"The Karcher boy and Susan Lund are down with chicken pox now." Her mother's head tilted, her eyes narrowed. "Is something troubling you, Willa?"

She shook her head and turned toward the fire, away from her mother's penetrating gaze. Why? What was she afraid her mother would see? She had nothing to hide. "No. It's only… There's so much sickness…" Did Ellen know all of those things? Would she think to tell him?

A deep breath helped calm her. "I think I'll go to town now, Mama. I have to go to Brody's and get stew meat. And we're out of molasses and saleratus, and I want to make a pudding for supper."

Her long skirt whispered against the rug as she hurried to the door. She swirled her cloak around her shoulders and pulled the hood up in place. "I may call on Ellen to see how she's faring, so don't worry if I'm not home directly."

She opened the door and stepped outside.

"You forgot your basket."

There was a speculative look in her mother's eyes. She stepped back inside, grabbed her shopping basket off the lamp table and hurried out the door.

"How lovely that you are home in time for dinner, Reverend Calvert. You must be hungry and tired after your long morning."

Matthew ignored the way Ellen Hall was looking up at him through her long lashes and shook his head. "Thank you for your concern, Miss Hall. But I haven't time to wait for dinner. I merely stopped to see how you were getting on with…things." Why was the house so quiet? "I am very appreciative of your generous offer to watch over Joshua and Sally, and I don't want you to be overburdened by their care."

"Not at all, Reverend. But please, can't you spare time from your calls to eat? Everything is in readiness for you."

For *him?* What about Joshua and Sally? Had they already eaten? Where were they? And why didn't Happy come to greet him? He held back a frown and placed his hat on the tree in the corner beside the door.

He wasn't leaving until he found out what was going on. "Very well. It's most kind of you to think of me."

He shrugged out of his chesterfield, hung the coat on a peg and followed her down the entrance hall.

"If you will be seated, Reverend, I will bring in the stew."

Matthew paused in the dining room doorway and looked at the table. A vase of colored tissue paper flowers sat in the center of a linen cloth with two place settings of good china on either end. His thoughts flashed back to the night of the Halls' dinner party. He took a breath. "Where are Joshua's and Sally's places, Miss Hall?"

Ellen turned at the kitchen door and her lips lifted in a winsome smile. "Your wards will be eating at the table here in the kitchen. I'm sure you agree they are too young to be included at an adults' meal. At their tender ages, their manners are still unformed and their minds are not equal to educated conversation."

"Nor will they ever be if they are not exposed to it, Miss Hall." He kept his voice pleasant and his expression bland. "The table looks lovely, and I thank you for your consideration in preparing it, but I will be eating in the kitchen with my children."

Annoyance flashed in Ellen Hall's blue eyes, but was quickly erased by another smile. "Of course, Reverend, if that is your wish. I'll set places at the table immediately. Perhaps you would be so kind as to call your wards from their rooms." The long skirts of her fancy gown billowed out as she whirled into the kitchen.

He strode to the stairs and trotted up them. Muffled

voices came from Joshua's room. He opened the door and looked in. Sally was sitting on the bed beside her brother, her kitten in her arms. Josh was holding a picture book. They looked…resigned.

The dog jumped from his sprawled position across Joshua's extended legs and ran to greet him. Sally's face lit. Joshua grinned. "Uncle Matt!" They chorused his name, scrambled off the bed and rushed toward him.

"What are you two doing here in your room, Joshua? Why aren't you downstairs playing checkers, or drawing pictures or something?"

"We'd rather stay up here with Happy and Tickles."

Sally gave an emphatic nod. "We don't want them to have to stay outside. Tickles might go up the tree and get gone!"

"I see." Indeed he did. "I'm sorry I didn't tell Miss Hall your pets are to be allowed to stay in the house. Let's all go down to dinner, and I'll explain it to her."

Joshua grinned and rubbed his stomach. "Good, I'm hungry! I haven't had any cookies or *anything* since breakfast!"

"Me neither!" Sally tucked Tickles under her arm and slipped her free hand into his. "When is Bertha coming back, Uncle Matt?"

"I don't know, Sally. And I'm sorry I have to be gone so often, but the people who are sick need my help. We'll all just have to do the best we can meanwhile." He smiled and guided the whole entourage toward the kitchen. "I saw Billy today, Joshua."

"Is his grandma better?"

"She's still ill." He glossed over the subject. The

elderly woman was not doing well, and he didn't want to discuss her with them unless needed. "And Billy has chicken pox. Susan Lund has them, too."

Joshua's shoulders slumped. "I guess we won't be going back to school, then."

"Not for a while."

Sally's lower lip quivered. "I want to see Miss Wright."

So do I. "Hopefully, the chicken pox won't spread any further and school will be open again soon." He smiled and tweaked her little nose. "Now, let's have dinner. I know there are some of Bertha's molasses cookies left that we can have for dessert."

Willa hurried down Main Street, her head ducked against the wind-blown snow, the toes of her boots flashing in and out from beneath the hems of her long skirts. Dread dogged her steps.

Please don't let him be there. Her face tightened. Who was she talking to? *God*—who cared nothing about her? She set her jaw. It didn't really matter anyway. She would have to get used to seeing Ellen with Matthew and the children in his home. That sick feeling hit her stomach again. She took a deep breath, broke into a coughing fit when the cold air hit her lungs.

"Willa, are you ill?"

She lifted her head and looked toward Cargrave's entrance, blinked as snow blew against her face. The tension in her stomach eased. She wouldn't have to go to the parsonage after all. "What are you doing here, Ellen? Aren't you supposed to be watching over Joshua and Sally?"

"Isobel is with them." Ellen's narrow nose wrinkled. "Those animals are smelly creatures, and all their running around has given me a headache. I came outside for some fresh air."

"Are you speaking of Happy and Tickles?"

Ellen's face went blank.

"The children's pets."

"Oh. Yes."

It didn't sound as if things were going well for the children. She held back a frown and followed Ellen into the warmth of the store's interior.

"Good day, ladies."

"Good day, Mr. Cargrave."

She smiled at the proprietor and stepped closer to Ellen to better hear her lowered voice.

"...told his wards they must confine them to their rooms, but when Matthew came home, he insisted the dirty beasts run free throughout the house."

"He's home?" Thank goodness she hadn't had to go there. She moved over to the dry goods section and picked up the dark gold satin ribbon.

"Of course not, or I would be there. Oh, that's a pretty color, Willa." Ellen pulled her hand from her muff and touched the ribbon, moved on and ran her hand over a bolt of plaid foulard on the shelf. "I asked him to stay at home for a while this afternoon, but he insisted he had to make more calls."

She looked at the perplexed expression on Ellen's face. It seemed dangerously close to becoming a pout. "He's comforting the sick, Ellen. It's part of his calling."

"I suppose. Still, I thought once I was in his home, he would devote more of his time to me."

"I'm sure he will once the grippe and chicken pox have passed, and he's not so busy making calls and helping Dr. Palmer." The sick feeling in her stomach struck again. Perhaps, despite her precautions, she was coming down with the grippe. She moved to the notions shelf and picked up the thread she needed. "Do you know if he carries ginger root to chew on? Or spirits of alcohol to cleanse his hands once he leaves the sick?"

Ellen dropped a packet back into the button basket and stared at her. "I hadn't thought… He might bring the grippe or chicken pox home, and I— Oh dear! I have to go to the apothecary and get those things immediately."

"Ellen, wait, he may already—"

"No, I must protect myself!"

Herself—not Matthew. She watched Ellen rush out the door to the accompaniment of the tinkling bells, sighed and carried her selections to the counter. She would think no more about it. She had done the best she could.

Matthew scrubbed a towel over his still-damp hair, then tossed it over the side of the emptied bathtub and eyed the growing pile of dirty clothes in the corner. What should he do with them? Bertha had taken care of their laundry, but somehow, he couldn't picture Ellen Hall washing clothes. He'd have to think of something. He would soon be out of clean socks, shirts and cravats. Perhaps he could hire Isobel to do the wash.

He fastened the waist on his long underwear, pulled his clean undershirt over his head, tucked it in and buttoned it. Weariness weighted his movements. He lifted the oil lamp from the washstand, trudged up the stairs, threw back the covers, snuffed the lamp and flopped into bed.

The dark silence enveloped him. He yawned and closed his eyes, yielded to its caressing arms. At last. It had seemed as if Ellen Hall would never stop her flirting and go home. Sleep fled with the thought.

He scowled and jammed his fist beneath his pillow to better support his head. This situation could not go on. Her actions today had made it clear Ellen Hall had matrimony on her mind, and that was not going to be. So what was he to do? He had no wish to encourage the woman's hopes by allowing her to come and care for his children and his home. But how was he to get out of the situation? He didn't want to hurt Miss Hall, and he needed someone to stay with Joshua and Sally. And with so many sick or tending to the ill in their families, choice was limited.

He struggled to find a solution, but his tired mind refused to cope with the problem. He yawned and yielded to the weariness enticing him to close his eyes and let sleep come.

"Almighty God, I don't know…what to do. Please have…Your way…"

* * *

Willa carried her writing materials through the dark silence of the sitting room to the kitchen table, removed a front stove plate, touched a spill to the smoldering coals and lit the oil lamp. She added a few pieces of wood to the fire, opened the draft to make them burn and scooted a chair closer to the warmth. If she wrote down some of her churning thoughts, perhaps she would be able to sleep. She pursed her lips and unstopped the inkwell. How much should she tell?

Dearest Sadie,
It has been long since my last letter and much has happened. I hope this finds you well.

There has been a serious outbreak of illness here in Pinewood. Chicken pox came to the village when Mary and Jeffery Burton's cousin came for a visit. Ina and Paul Johnson brought the grippe home to the village from Syracuse, and two of the guests at Sheffield House were ill with the grippe when they arrived. The disease strikes fast and seems to be of long duration.

I write you of the presence of the grippe in our area lest you should hear from another source and it causes you to worry. I hasten to assure you your grandparents remain healthy. As does Sophia Sheffield. Mama and I are well also.

The new preacher, Reverend Calvert (I wrote you of him in my last letter), is helping Dr.

Palmer tend the sick as the disease has spread even to the logging camps. Ellen is watching over his children.

She stopped and frowned down at what she had written. Matthew Calvert kept doing things that surprised and unsettled her. He could have taken the children home to Albany until the diseases had run their courses. Instead, he had stayed to care for his flock and help Dr. Palmer.

She braced her elbow on the table, rested her chin in her palm and stared off into the distance. Her father and Thomas would never have done that. Thomas. She hadn't thought of him in days. Matthew was so different from Thomas. He was unselfish and dependable and—

She jerked erect. And he was Ellen's intended. She had no business thinking about him. She set her jaw, dipped her pen in the ink and leaned over the paper.

I must tell you, in closing, that Ellen is smitten with Reverend Calvert. She feels he is the perfect mate for her and plans to marry him. Perhaps they will be wed this summer. I know you will not attend their wedding, Sadie, and, of course, I understand why. But, oh, how I wish you would. I miss you, my dear friend.
My fondest love always,
Willa

That sick feeling had returned to her stomach. She blotted the letter, folded and sealed it, put her writing materials back in the basket and took a deep breath. Perhaps some ginger tea…

She rose and pulled the teapot to the front of the stove over the fire. Maybe after a soothing cup of tea, she would be able to sleep. If she could quiet her thoughts.

Chapter Eighteen

"Willa!"

The back door of the house slammed. She stopped and looked over her shoulder, frowned at the sight of her mother hurrying across the yard toward her. "What is it, Mama?"

"Ellen says she needs you. She's sent her father to fetch you. He's waiting out front in his sleigh."

Matthew or the children? Her stomach flopped, coiled into a hard knot. Her mind spun out dire scenarios.

"Give me the slop bucket, dear—I'll feed the pigs." Her mother took hold of the bucket's handle and shoved the basket she held in her other hand toward her. "I put everything in here I thought you might need."

She closed her fingers over the braided wicker handle. "Thank you, Mama."

Her mother touched her cheek. "It will be all right, Willa."

She nodded, blinked back a rush of tears and ran for the street.

"Don't forget to chew the ginger, Willa!"

"I won't, Mama!" She rounded the corner of the cabin and hurried to the sleigh sitting in the road at the end of their plank walk.

"Good afternoon, Willa." Mr. Hall stepped forward, took her basket, handed her in, then returned it to her and walked around the horse to climb in. He slapped the reins against the horse's rump and the sleigh slipped forward.

Willa gripped the basket handle with both hands and glanced over at Ellen's father. "Do you know why Ellen has sent for me, Mr. Hall?"

"No, I don't, Willa. All I know is she came to the house, told me she needed you and asked me to come and fetch you right away, then hurried back to the parsonage."

She nodded, faced forward and reassured herself she was being foolish to imagine dire things. With Ellen, it could be anything. Perhaps she was having trouble getting along with the children and simply wanted her advice.

She held on to that thought as they turned the corner, glided over the Stony Creek bridge and traveled down Main Street toward the parsonage at a brisk pace. But it was not enough to keep her in her seat when the sleigh halted.

"Thank you, Mr. Hall."

"Wait, Willa, I'll help you—"

"There's no need. I can manage." She gripped the edge of the frame with her free hand, kicked the hems of her long skirts out of the way and climbed down. She took the basket Mr. Hall handed down to her and turned to start up the walkway to the parsonage.

"Ellen!" She broke into a run toward where Ellen stood on the stoop. "What's wrong?"

"I don't know, Willa. The girl was crying when I went to the stairs to call them for dinner." Ellen shuddered, wrapped her arms about herself. "I sent Father for you right away. I think the girl may be sick."

"Oh, *Ellen!* You haven't left her *alone* all this time, have you? She may be hurt!" She brushed past Ellen and yanked open the door.

"The boy is with her. I couldn't—"

She let the door slam shut on Ellen's words and ran up the stairs, followed the sound of muted voices to a room on the right and opened the door. Joshua was sitting on the edge of the bed leaning over his sister with a cup in his hand.

"C'mon, try to drink some water, Sally. It might make you feel better."

The poor boy sounded frightened to death. And well he might. Sally's face was flushed with fever. She pasted a smile on her face and swept into the room. "Well, what is going on in here?"

Joshua leaped from the bed and spun toward the door, his young face dark with anger. The water in the cup sloshed over the brim onto the floor.

"Miss Wright!"

Relief swept the anger from Joshua's face. He took a step toward her, stopped, looked at his sister, then back at her and squared his shoulders. "I think Sally's sick, and I couldn't find Miss Hall. I— I didn't know what to do." His voice wavered.

How brave he was, trying to care for his sister.

Her heart ached to comfort him. "Why don't I have a look?"

He swallowed hard and nodded.

She moved forward, allowed herself to touch his blond curls, then brush his smooth cheek with her fingertips as she withdrew her hand and took his place on the side of the bed.

She set her basket on the floor and placed the backs of her fingers against Sally's flushed cheek, just as her mother had touched her so many times.

Sally's eyes opened—glassy and watery with fever and tears. Her lip quivered.

"I don't…f-feel good."

"I know, sweetie." She placed her palm against Sally's fevered forehead, brushed back a clinging curl. "Does your head hurt?"

"Yes…" Tears overflowed Sally's eyes, rolled down her temples onto her pillow. "And my throat…and… and…"

"Your stomach?"

"Y-yes…" Sally sobbed the word, pushed up from the bed and threw herself into her arms. "I w-want Uncle M-Matt."

"Shh, sweetie, shh. I'm sure he'll be here soon." She held the little girl close, pressed her cheek against the damp blond curls and rubbed her small back. "Try not to cry, Sally, it will make your head feel worse. Can you do that?"

Sally's head nodded against her shoulder. The sobbing lessened, stopped.

"That's better." She kissed Sally's cheek and eased her back down onto her bed. "Now, I want you to close your eyes and rest while I go downstairs and fix you a cup of tea that will make your stomach and throat feel better."

"Can I have my k-kitty?" Tears flooded Sally's eyes.

Her heart sank. Where was the kitten? If Ellen had put it outside— She cast a tentative look at Joshua.

"He's in my room with Happy. I didn't want—"

The boy pressed his lips together and set his jaw, obviously holding back the words he'd been about to speak. She nodded and rose. "Would you please bring Tickles to Sally, Joshua? And then I think it would be good if you took Happy outside for a romp in the snow."

She saw the protective look flash in Joshua's eyes and spoke before he could voice a protest. The boy needed to go outside and play with his dog the way little boys were supposed to do. "It only need be for a short time. I'll be here to watch over Sally. Dress warmly, Joshua. It's cold outside."

He nodded and ran from the room.

She leaned over the bed and tucked Sally's small too-warm hand beneath the covers. "Try to sleep, Sally. I'll be back as soon as I've made your tea."

Willa hurried down the stairs and peeked out the front door. There was no sign of Ellen. Had she gone home? Well, she would have to worry about Ellen later. Right now she had tea to make—as soon as she found the kitchen.

She turned and looked down the length of the entrance hall. The door on her right opened into the sitting room. A memory of that rainy day when

Matthew had asked her to come to the house flashed into her head. She pushed it away and peeked into the door on her left, swept her gaze over a desk and bookshelf, a suit coat hanging over the back of the desk chair.

Her gaze fell on his open Bible and the notes written in a strong, bold script that rested beside it. Matthew's personal things. A flush crawled into her cheeks. She hurried past the stairs and peered into a second door on her left. The dining room. Colored tissue paper flowers filled a vase on the table. Her stomach tensed. Ellen made flowers like those.

She spun from the doorway and hurried to a door straight ahead, stepped into a large, well-appointed kitchen. She set her basket on the work table, lifted out the spirits of alcohol her mother had included, poured a bit into her cupped palm and then scrubbed her hands together. There was no heat radiating from the stove. She touched the edge of the cooking surface with her fingertips. It was barely warm. She lifted the cold lid of an iron pot and peered inside. Stew.

Footsteps and the padding of paws drew her gaze to the door. Joshua stood there in his coat and hat, Happy beside him. "Have you eaten dinner, Joshua?"

He shook his head.

"Well the stew is cold and the fire in the stove is out." She looked around the kitchen. "Do you know where Bertha keeps the bread and jam?"

"In there." Joshua pointed to a large cupboard.

She opened the tin-paneled doors, peeked into various small covered crocks, found butter and jam and set it on the table along with a cloth-covered loaf of bread.

"The knife's in there."

She opened the drawer of the step-back cupboard Joshua indicated, pulled out the knife, stepped to the table and cut a thick slice of bread, then spread it liberally with butter and jam. "This will have to do for now, Joshua."

She took a plate off the open shelves of the cupboard, put the bread on it, set it on the table and smiled. "Come here and hold out your hands."

Joshua gave her a suspicious look but did as she bid.

She poured some of the spirits into her palm, rubbed her hands together and scrubbed them over his small ones.

"What's that for?"

She laughed at his wrinkled nose. "It helps to keep sickness from spreading. Now, sit down and eat, while I get the fire going."

He sat, removed his hat and bowed his head. "Thank You, Lord, for this food. Thank you that Miss Wright has come to help us. And please make Sally better. Amen."

The prayer spoken in his sincere young voice brought a lump to her throat. She turned to put the bread away.

Woof!

She looked down. Happy stood at her feet, looking up at her.

A smile tugged at her lips. "So you're hungry, too. Is that it?"

Woof! The dog's tail swept back and forth.

Joshua slipped off his chair, reached behind the stove and pulled out a chipped bowl. He gave her a hesitant look. "Bertha let me feed him here by the stove, if that's all right?"

What had Ellen done to make him look so worried? She smiled reassurance. "Of course it is. Hold on tight." She tore a piece of bread into the bowl and ladled some cold stew onto it. His smile melted her heart.

Joshua put the bowl down for Happy, slipped back onto his chair and took a bite out of his bread. Jam clung to the corners of his mouth.

She grinned, opened the door of the firebox on the stove, grabbed the handle and shook off the gray ashes. A few small, live coals remained. She opened the draft and added small pieces of kindling to coax the fire. Tongues of flame flickered, then licked hungrily at the new fuel. She added larger pieces of kindling, and finally, a few small chunks of firewood and closed the door.

A cast-iron teakettle sat on the back of the stove. She checked it for water, then pulled it forward to the front stove plate, turned to the work table and lifted the lid from the wicker basket. A blend of pungent and sweet scents rose.

"What's that?" Joshua came to her side and stretched up to try and look in the basket.

Her heart warmed at his exhibition of a boy's curiosity. "Herbs and spices that help people get better when they're sick."

"Oh." He grabbed his hat off the table, tugged it

on and opened the door to the back porch. "C'mon, Happy."

She grinned as boy and dog trotted out onto the porch and down the steps. The door slammed shut behind them.

The stove pipe crackled. She turned and closed down the draft for a slow, steady burn, checked the teakettle, then hurried to the bottom of the stairs. There was no crying coming from above. Hopefully, Sally had fallen asleep.

A knock on the door made her jump. She hurried to open it before the knocking woke Sally. "Ellen!" She gathered her startled wits and stepped back. "Come in."

"No. I only stopped to leave a message for Matthew."

Stopped? She looked beyond Ellen to the sleigh at the end of the stone walk.

"Please tell him, as he has little time to spend with me at present, I am going to Buffalo to stay with Aunt Berdena. I will return when the chicken pox and grippe are gone from Pinewood."

"You're leaving town?" She took a breath to control the spurt of anger that rushed through her. "And what of your promise to take care of his children?"

Ellen shook her head. "You know I can't care for anyone who is ill, Willa. The school is closed—you do it. Now, I must hurry. Goodbye, Willa."

Shock held her mute.

Ellen swept down the steps and hurried to her father's sleigh.

"*Will* you take care of us, Miss Wright?"

She jerked her gaze sideways. Joshua stood at the base of a tree looking at her, fear and defiance in his brown eyes. Had he heard the whole exchange? How she longed to reassure him.

"I can't say, Joshua. That will be up to your uncle Matthew to decide. He will do what he feels is best for you and Sally." She smiled at him. "If he does decide he wants me to care for you, then I shall be happy to do so."

Joshua nodded and grinned. A slow, lopsided grin like his uncle's that went straight to her heart. "That's all right, then. Uncle Matt likes you. I can tell. C'mon, Happy! C'mon, boy." He slapped his legs and took off at a dead run for the back of the house, Happy chasing after him.

She watched the pair out of sight. She knew Joshua meant Matthew Calvert trusted her as a teacher, but for a moment she'd thought—

She shook her head at her foolishness, closed the door and hurried to the kitchen to make Sally's tea.

Chapter Nineteen

Only three pieces of wood remained in the box. She would have to go out and get more soon. Willa placed another log on the fire, then went back to the chair she'd pulled close to Sally's bed and took the girl's small hand in hers. It seemed to quiet her.

Joshua left the chair by the hearth and came to stand beside her, an open book held in his hands. "Look at this bear, Miss Wright. He's a great big one."

His whisper tickled her ear. She glanced at the picture and nodded. "That's a polar bear. They live where it's very cold."

Joshua's eyes widened. "It's getting colder outside. Maybe I'll see one."

"I'm afraid not. Polar bears don't live around here. They live in the Arctic so they can eat the fish and smaller animals that live in the Arctic Ocean."

"Oh."

He looked crestfallen. She hastened to restore his hope. "We do have black bears that live in the forests on the hills. But they don't like the cold weather. When winter comes they go to sleep in caves and sheltered spots and don't wake up until spring."

His eyes darkened as he pondered that. "Don't they get hungry?"

The teacher in her tweaked his curiosity. "How would they know? Do you know you're hungry if you're sleeping?"

He frowned and shook his head. "I don't know anything when I'm sleeping. But I know I'm hungry when I wake up." He grinned at her.

Gracious! She was going to have to be careful. The boy was charming his way right into her heart.

Woof! Woof!

She jerked her head around at the soft bark, saw a streak of black-and-white fur race out the bedroom door.

"Uncle Matt's home! Wait until I tell him what's happened!"

"What? Joshua, wait!" She bolted erect.

The book he had dropped in her lap thudded against the floor.

Sally burst into tears.

Joshua's footfalls faded away.

A door opened and closed downstairs.

Oh dear. She turned and leaned over the bed to calm Sally.

"And Sally got sick. And I couldn't find Miss Hall and—"

"Sally's *sick?* And you're alone?"

Matthew whipped around and pounded up the

stairs, rushed into Sally's bedroom and stopped dead in his tracks. "Willa!"

She jerked around toward the door, rose from her position on the side of the bed. "Good even—"

"Uncle Matt!"

Sally sobbed out his name and burst into tears.

He rushed to the bed and kissed her flushed cheek, brushed her damp hair back with his hand. His anger surged at the feel of her hot skin. He took a tight hold on his choler and smiled down at her. "Josh told me you were sick, princess. I'm so sorry I wasn't here to take care of you." He looked up at Willa. "Will it hurt her if I pick her up?"

She stepped back and shook her head. "It will do her nothing but good, Reverend. She's been waiting for you to come home."

He nodded, threw back the covers, scooped Sally into his arms and cuddled her close. "Shh, don't cry, Sally. Don't cry."

"She'll stop in a moment, Reverend." Willa's hand appeared before his eyes, touched Sally's curls. "She's crying because you're here and she finally feels safe."

He glanced up and their gazes met. "Thank you. I didn't realize…"

"Fathers never do." She smiled—the saddest smile he'd ever seen—then turned, lifted a blanket from the bed and draped it around Sally. "She needs to stay warm." Her gaze touched his again, skittered away. "I'm no longer needed here. I'll just go downstairs and set the stew over the fire to warm for your supper." She turned toward the door.

Would she leave? No. Not as long as Sally needed

her. "I'll be down in a few minutes to talk with you about Sally."

She paused, then nodded and walked from the room.

Joshua rushed over and stood in front of him. "You're gonna ask her to stay and take care of us, aren't you, Uncle Matt? She said she would, and Sally and me want her to and—"

"Whoa, Josh." He studied his nephew's face. The boy looked worried. He smiled and touched his shoulder. "Let me talk to Miss Wright. I'm not sure what's going on here and—" He stopped, looked at the tears flooding the boy's eyes. "What is it, Josh?"

"I *told* you, Uncle Matt. Sally got sick and Miss Hall went outside and left Sally and me alone."

"Yes, I know, but—"

"And then Miss Wright come upstairs and hugged Sally and she made Sally tea to make her feel better and she made me dinner and she fed Happy, too!" Josh sniffed, swiped his sleeve across his eyes and gulped in air.

He kept quiet, waited.

"And then Miss Hall come back and said she was going away 'cause she doesn't like to be around sick people, and Miss Wright scolded her for not taking care of us, and she told Miss Wright to take care of us, and then I asked her would she and she said she would if you said so." He stopped, gulped and wiped tears from his cheeks with the heels of his hands. "So will you? Please?"

He blinked, shot out his arm and pulled Josh close,

cleared the lump from his throat. "I sure will, Josh. You don't have to worry about it anymore."

The anger simmered, felt like it was bubbling beneath his skin. Matthew flexed his hands and rotated his shoulders, took a deep breath and stepped into the kitchen. Willa was at the work table, doing something with a wicker basket.

"I am in your debt, Miss Wright…again."

She lifted her head. Light from the overhead oil lamp cast a golden glow on her dark auburn hair, shadowed her eyes. "There is no debt, Reverend. I am only thankful I was able to help."

"As am I. *Very* thankful." The muscle along his jaw twitched. He took a breath and moved toward her. "I don't know how anyone could leave a sick child alone like that. And to put the burden for that child's care on a six-year-old!" He took another breath. "Forgive my anger, Miss Wright—I know you are Miss Hall's friend. But when I think— What if you hadn't been able to come?"

"But I did come." She lifted her chin. "And had I not, I'm certain Ellen would have seen to Sally's care."

"From the front porch?"

She sucked in a breath. "How much did Joshua tell you?"

He stepped closer so he could see her eyes. "I think most everything." The muscle in his jaw twitched again. "Once he started talking, the words poured out of him like water over a dam. The boy was terrified."

"Yes, I know. I tried—" She shook her head and turned away, took something out of the basket. "Ellen had an older brother. Walker died of the measles when Ellen was Sally's age. Ellen's been terrified of becoming ill ever since. She cannot bring herself to enter a sick room."

"You're very loyal to defend your friend, Miss Wright. But there is no acceptable reason to leave a sick five-year-old without care or comfort."

She turned back to face him, her shoulders squared, her chin lifted. "Ellen did the best she could. She ran home to send her father for me and then came back here to wait on the porch where she would be close by until I arrived. She knew I would come and care for Sally and Joshua."

"And then she told you to continue to care for Joshua and Sally and left town!"

"I— Yes."

At last he could see her eyes. He looked into their beautiful blue-green depths and the words he'd been about to utter died. His breath caught. Had he been letting his anger blind him to what could become the biggest blessing of his and the children's lives? *Forgive me, Lord.* His anger drained away.

He rested back against the work table and looked at her.

She dropped her gaze, lifted her hand to brush back a tendril of hair, wiped her palms on her apron.

"And will you continue to care for Sally and Joshua, Miss Wright?"

She took a breath. "If that is your wish."

"It is." He locked his gaze on hers. "I will, of course, compensate you."

She shook her head. "In Pinewood we help each

other. You are caring for the sick in the village. The least I can do is to help you until Bertha returns. I will accept no pay."

"But—"

"Those are my terms." She spun toward the stove, stirred whatever was cooking. "The stew is hot. If you will take your seat, I'll— No. Wait."

She turned back and grabbed the bottle she'd taken from the basket. "Hold out your hands."

He looked at the bottle, straightened and held his hands out in front of him. "What's this?"

"Spirits of alcohol. Turn your palms up please."

His fingers brushed against her hand. He looked into her eyes, dropped his gaze to her mouth. So close…

Pink spread across her cheekbones. She took a quick little breath, splashed a bit of the liquid into his cupped palms.

He looked down. The bottle was shaking.

She stepped back. "Now scrub your hands together. The alcohol will help prevent the spread of illness. You should carry some with you and use it each time you leave a sick person. And ginger. You should carry slices of ginger root with you and chew on it while you make your calls. It helps to keep you from taking the disease."

Her words were a little rushed, her voice a bit breathless. He glanced up. She was nibbling at the corner of her lower lip. He gripped his hands together to keep from reaching for her.

Her gaze rose and met his. She whipped around and put the bottle back in the basket.

His brows lifted. Was the prim and proper, cool and collected Miss Willa Wright nervous because of him? A grin started way down at his toes. He stifled it before it reached his lips and stepped to the table and took a seat before he betrayed himself.

"Here is some bread. The butter is in the crock on the table. And here is your stew. *Ellen* made it this morning."

He glanced up, but she turned away.

"I hope you don't mind, but I fed Joshua and Sally earlier. Joshua had little for dinner and was hungry. And Sally needs nourishment."

"The number of those taken sick is growing. There may be many days when I return too late for their supper." He rose and pulled out a chair. "Won't you join me, Miss Wright?"

She shook her head and took a step toward the door. "I need to get home. Mama will be wondering where I am."

He stepped to her side. "You can't walk home by yourself. It's full dark outside. I'll—" He stopped, stared at her.

"You cannot leave the children, Reverend Calvert. Please don't trouble yourself over the matter. I am accustomed to walking home alone."

"I don't like it." He sounded surly, even to himself.

"You have no choice." She glanced around the room. "I think that's all. Oh! Sally's tea." Her gaze came back to meet his. "The china teapot is full of ginger tea. If Sally wakes, it would be good if she took some tea through the night. Sweeten it with a bit of honey. It will help her throat and her stomach. And keep her warm. I believe she is coming down with chicken pox and it would not do for her to become chilled."

He lifted her cloak off the peg and held it for her. She turned around, and he draped it over her shoulders.

She took a quick step forward and pulled up her hood. "Good evening, Reverend Calvert."

"Good evening, Miss Wright." He opened the door and stepped out onto the porch.

"Your stew will get cold, Rev— Oh dear." She turned back, a look of consternation on her face.

"What's the matter?"

"I forgot to add wood and trim the drafts on the stove."

"I will tend to the stove."

She nodded and started down the walk to the street.

He stood on the porch and watched her out of sight, then turned and went in the house. She was right. He had no choice.

It *was* dark. Willa hurried along Main Street, crossed Church Street and continued on, the click of her heels loud against the wood walkway in the quiet of the night.

She glanced around and quickened her pace. She had never been nervous, but since the night Arnold Dixon and Johnny Taylor had accosted her— "Oh!"

She jerked to a halt, stared at the tall, lean figure that rose from the bench outside of Dibble's Livery and strode toward her. "Gracious, Mr. Dibble, you startled me."

"I'm sorry, Willa. I didn't think about that. I guess the next time I'll have to whistle or something."

"The next time?"

He nodded and gestured her forward, fell into step alongside of her. "Word has it you're going to be caring for the preacher's boy and girl while he's out making calls on the sick. So I figured I'd just keep a watch and walk you home at night."

Something warm slipped into her heart. Her mother was right. The news that flew from mouth to mouth about town was not meant to harm but to benefit one another. She stopped and tilted her head back to look up at him. "Why?"

He shook his head and took her arm. "Mind your step. The edge of the bridge gets icy on cold nights." He released her arm and shortened his long strides. "You know what's wrong with schoolmarms, Willa?"

Where did *that* come from? She gave him a sidelong glance. "I didn't know there was anything wrong with schoolmarms."

"Well, I might be speaking too general there. But the one I know is too curious by half. She's always wanting to know the whats and whys of something instead of just taking a thing for what it is."

His words took her aback. She looked from the kindness in his eyes to the surrounding darkness, listened to the comforting sound of his boots thudding on the bridge planks in concert with her own softer steps. "I think you may be right, Mr. Dibble." He switched sides when they turned onto Brook Street, placing himself between her and Turner's Wagon Shop where Arnold Dixon worked. The warmth in her heart grew. "I'll simply relax and enjoy our evening stroll." She smiled up at him. "And look forward to those promised."

He returned her smile, guided her around an icy spot on the path and stopped at the end of her walk.

She paused and looked at him. "It's a cold night, Mr. Dibble. Won't you come in for a cup of tea?"

He glanced at the cabin, looked back at her and shook his head. "It's a kind offer, but no thank you, Willa. Remember me to your mama."

He sounded…sad. She opened her mouth to speak— *She's always wanting to know the whats and whys of something instead of just taking a thing for what it is*—then closed it again. "I will, Mr. Dibble. Good evening." She walked up the path and opened the door, heard him start back up the path and waved.

"Well, you've had quite a day."

She stepped inside and closed the door. "I have, Mama. I think Sally Calvert is coming down with chicken pox, but she's very sick. I'm concerned about her." She shoved off her hood and unfastened her cloak.

"How's the boy?"

"Joshua is fine." A smile curved her lips. "He's a delightful little boy, Mama. Perhaps someday you'll meet him."

"Perhaps."

What did that tone mean? She studied her mother a moment, then shrugged and hung her cloak on a peg and smoothed back her hair. "Have you had supper?"

"No. There's potatoes baking in the oven." Her

mother set aside the sock she was darning, rose and started for the kitchen.

"Take a small pouch of oatmeal along in the morning. If it's the pox she'll likely break out sometime tomorrow. When she commences itching, steep the bag in hot water a few minutes, squeeze it so it don't drip and dab the pox with it. That should help. Saleratus water helps, too."

She nodded, grabbed a towel and took the potatoes from the oven. "You heard about Ellen leaving, then?"

"I heard." Her mother put plates, flatware and a crock of butter on the table.

"Have you also heard that she's going to marry Reverend Calvert?"

"Wishing don't put food on the table, Willa."

"What does that mean?" She frowned, cut her potato and spread it with butter. She must be hungrier than she knew, her stomach had that sick feeling again.

"It means...we'll see."

There was that odd tone again. She stopped with a bite of potato halfway to her mouth and looked across the table. Her mother smiled, looked down and shook salt over her plate. She stared at that small smile, then shrugged and ate the bite of potato.

"I almost forgot, Mama. Mr. Dibble asked to be remembered to you. He waited for me at the livery and walked me home. He said he'll walk me home every night." She took another bite of potato, glanced at her mother and straightened. "Are you crying, Mama?"

"Don't be foolish. I bit into a big piece of black pepper. It stings my tongue." Her mother blinked and took a swallow of water.

"Why do you think Mr. Dibble would do that, Mama?"

"I don't know, Willa. I suppose because he's a kind man."

She lifted her head and stared. Her mother never spoke with that sharp edge in her voice.

Her mother looked down, stabbed her fork into her potato, broke off a piece of the buttered flesh, then lifted her head and gestured across the table toward her. "You'd best eat before your potato gets cold."

Everything was ready. The pieces of the hood she'd cut out were tucked into her basket and covered with an apron she'd been hemming. She would take it along to work tomorrow.

Tomorrow.

Willa snuffed the lamp and climbed into bed, curled into a ball to get warm. It would be all right. The uneasiness she'd experienced around Matthew today was because everything had been so unexpected. Tomorrow she would be prepared.

He certainly loved those children. She couldn't deny it now. The look on his face when he'd seen Sally had removed all doubt. And the way he had held and comforted the child… Her papa had held her like that once. *Please don't let Matthew ever turn away from those children.*

She swallowed and blinked away the sting of tears, turned onto her side and burrowed deeper beneath the covers. He had been very angry with Ellen. How strange it was to defend Ellen's behavior to her intended. But she had succeeded. Matthew had stopped being angry and then...

Why had he looked at her that way? It was... unsettling to the point of her trembling. But when she had spoken of Ellen making the stew, the queer quivering in her stomach had stopped.

She sighed, pulled the quilt close around her face and closed her eyes. Yes, tomorrow everything would be all right. She had only to remember Ellen.

And to forget the way Matthew had looked when he rushed into Sally's room and saw her sitting there and the way his voice had sounded when he called out her name.

Chapter Twenty

Big, fluffy snowflakes fell so thickly, so rapidly that they blocked out the sky. Willa fisted her gloved hand and knocked on the door, tipped her head back and smiled.

She put her basket down and scooped up a handful of the white flakes, pressed them between her cupped hands and nodded. Yes, it was good packing snow. Perhaps Joshua would make a snowman this afternoon, or snowballs for Happy to chase after—like the perfectly good one in her hand.

Her lips twitched. She'd had quite good aim once. Of course that was years ago....

A quick glance showed no one was around. She shoved her hood back out of her way with her free hand, eyed the trunk of the tree in the side yard, imagined Daniel hiding behind it and let the snowball fly. It hit with a satisfying splat. She looked at the white blotch on the rough bark and grinned, slapped and brushed her hands together to rid her gloves of the snow.

The door opened.

She blinked the clinging snowflakes from her lashes and stared at a disheveled-looking Matthew Calvert. Something in his eyes sent heat rushing into her cold cheeks. "I'm not too early?"

"Not at all." He huffed out a cloud of warm air, grabbed her basket, brushed the snow from its cover and stepped back. "Come in, Miss Wright."

The invitation brought an odd nervousness. She stared at him, suddenly uncertain of the wisdom of being there. And how foolish was that? Sally and Joshua needed her. She brushed off the strange feeling, shook the clinging snow from her cloak and skirt hem, walked through the door he held open for her and stopped to remove her cloak. He put down the basket and stepped behind her.

"If you'll permit me— You don't want this melting."

His hands moved across the roll of hair at her nape. His warm fingertips brushed against her cold skin, sent a shiver down her spine and froze the breath in her lungs.

"That's better." He threw a handful of snow outside and closed the door.

They were shut away from the world. Her nerves tingled. It was too…*close* in the small entrance hall, though it hadn't seemed so before. What was wrong with her this morning? The memory of yesterday?

She averted her gaze from Matthew's broad shoulders and the open vest over his white shirt, removed her gloves and unfastened her cloak.

He glanced down, gave her a rueful smile and buttoned his vest. "Please forgive my appearance. I've been trying to ready myself to make morning calls, but Sally's still restless. She's been asking for you." His gaze lifted, fastened on hers.

She dropped her gaze to the floor. "I'll go to her right away." She reached up to remove her cloak, went still when he stepped close. He lifted the cloak from her shoulders, turned and hung it on a peg.

She snatched up her basket and hurried to the stairs, lifted the hems of her long skirts to begin her climb and paused. The basket was heavy, and she had no free hand with which to grip the banister. His footsteps sounded behind her.

"Allow me."

His hand brushed against hers on the basket handle. She jerked hers away, willed her quivering knees to support her and climbed, trying not to hear his footfalls on the stairs behind her. What was *wrong* with her, allowing this situation to so unnerve her? Was she so lacking in willpower that she would fall apart because of being alone with a man? *Not a man—Matthew.* Her face went taut. That was pure foolishness! Matthew was all but betrothed to Ellen.

The thought steadied her, but the idea of them wed brought the sick feeling in her stomach again. Well, why wouldn't she sicken at the thought of Ellen and Matthew married? What would happen to these children? She took a breath and wished for some ginger to chew on.

Her skirts whispered against the hall floor, blended with the soft tap of her boots. She entered Sally's bedroom and tiptoed to the bed.

The little girl's eyes opened.

She smiled and touched the child's cheeks with

the backs of her fingers. Still hot. "Did you want me, Sally?"

The girl's fever-bright brown eyes filled with tears. "I don't feel good. Will you h-hold my hand?"

I'll hold your hand, Mary. It made me feel better when Mama held my hand.

Her heart squeezed. She cleared her throat. "Of course I will." She brushed back the blond curls clinging to Sally's fevered brow. There was no sign of chicken pox. Was she wrong? Was this sickness something else? She clasped Sally's small hand in hers and sat in the chair beside the bed.

Matthew left his place by the door, came and set the basket on the floor beside the chair.

She glanced up and their gazes met. Her pulse leaped at the look in his eyes. She jerked her gaze back to Sally, chided herself for her failing.

"I have to finish preparing for the day. I'll be in my bedroom down the hall should you need me."

His deep, rich voice, so vibrant and resonant in church, was little more than a whisper. She nodded, settled her mind on practical matters and glanced up at him. "Have you and Joshua had breakfast? Did Sally eat?"

He shook his head, ran his fingers through his already-tousled hair. "We've had nothing yet. I've been here with Sally, and Joshua is in his bedroom still. I think yesterday wore him out." He leaned down and kissed Sally's forehead. "I'll be back in a few minutes, princess."

He left the room and she drew her first easy breath since coming in the house. She looked at Sally. Her eyes were closed and she was resting more quietly. "Are you hungry, Sally?"

"I don't w-want to eat. My throat hurts."

"I know, but you have to take nourishment to get better. Will you try and go to sleep while I go downstairs and fix you a nice gruel that won't hurt your throat?"

The fever-bright eyes opened. "Will you come b-back and hold my h-hand?"

"Yes, I will. I promise."

Sally's little lips trembled into a smile. "I promise, too." She sighed and closed her eyes.

It took only a moment to coax the coals in the stove into a hot fire. Willa trimmed the dampers, lifted the top off the coffeepot and wrinkled her nose. That explained the abundant coals and the sour odor that hovered in the air. Matthew had made coffee sometime during the night and forgotten to set the pot back off the fire.

She carried it to the sink cupboard, gripped the pump handle and splashed water into it, then left it there to soften the burned-on grounds while she hunted for oatmeal. The small amount in the pouch she'd brought was not sufficient.

She rooted through the tin cupboard, found coffee, oatmeal and maple syrup, set them and the crock of butter and a crust of bread on the work table and went searching for pans. She located them in the bottom of the step-back cupboard and carried one to the pump.

How lovely to have water right in the kitchen! She filled the pan and set it on the stove, scrubbed the coffeepot, dumped the rinse water into the slop bucket on the bottom shelf of the sink cupboard, tossed a palmful of the ground coffee in the clean pot and pumped in water.

"Do I smell coffee?"

She jerked and the pot slipped. She tightened her grip and turned.

"I'm sorry, I didn't mean to startle you."

"I thought you were upstairs." She almost dropped the pot again at the sight of Matthew with his suit coat on and his hair freshly combed. The man was too handsome by half.

"Sally is asleep. And Josh and Happy are awake and stirring about."

She managed to return his smile. "I'm only just putting the coffee on to boil. I made it strong, but I can add more water if you like."

"Strong and black is perfect."

She nodded, marched to the stove and set the pot down then turned to the work table. Matthew was standing in front of the step-back cupboard watching her. Her taut nerves stretched a bit tighter. "It will take a few minutes for the coffee to brew properly. I'm sure you have work to do, Reverend Calvert. I can call you when the coffee is ready."

"I'll wait." He smiled, rested back against the cupboard and crossed one ankle over the other.

"Very well." She dropped a small lump of butter into the boiling water, then ladled a small amount of the water into a bowl of oatmeal and stirred the thickened mixture into the water on the stove.

He hadn't moved. She blew out a breath, rubbed

her hands down the front of her apron and turned to face him across the table. "Do you have a buttery for keeping perishables?"

"Yes indeed. It's through that door." He nodded toward a narrow door to the left of the stove.

She escaped into a large stone closet lit by the dim light filtering in through the snow-flecked glass of a small window. Cold air chilled the exposed flesh of her face and hands.

"Did you find what you need?"

Matthew's deep voice filled the buttery, made the chill bumps on her flesh tingle. "Yes." She whipped the cover off a crock, grabbed a tin cup and scooped it full of milk, then snatched up a bowl of eggs and turned. He was in the doorway. Her breath snagged in her lungs.

"Excuse me." She took a step, and he moved aside.

She put the eggs on the work table, picked up the spoon and stirred the cup of milk into the thickening gruel, wished he would go sit down at the table.

"The coffee smells good."

"It will be ready soon." She moved the boiling brew to the back of the stove to let the grounds settle, wiped her hands down her apron and turned to dice the crust of bread.

He moved past her to the window on the other side of the stove. "All of this snow reminds me of my fondest wish as a child—a toboggan my brother, Robert, and I could fly down the hills on." He glanced her way and smiled. "I prayed long and fervently for that toboggan. I finally got it for Christmas when I was eight years old. It was that answered prayer that set me on the path to becoming a minister." He leaned a shoulder against the window frame and fastened his gaze on her. "What was your most fervent childhood prayer, Miss Wright?"

"That my father, who had abandoned us, would return. He never did." The hurt of all those years of unanswered prayers brought a bitter taste to her mouth. She scooped the diced crust into her hands and dropped it into the gruel, set her jaw to keep from saying more, but the anger she'd carried so long drove the words from her. "However, all of those prayers I prayed were not wasted. They taught me a valuable lesson."

"And that is?"

She stirred the softening bread into the gruel and threw a quick glance his direction. "Forgive me, Reverend, but the lesson I learned was that the God preachers, such as yourself, speak of as a 'loving father' who cares for us and watches over us does not exist. And, as I told you before, I learned it was a waste of time to pray."

He straightened and stepped toward her. "God gave man a free will, Miss Wright. He allows man to choose his own path." His voice, warm with compassion, flowed over her. "God would never *force* your father to do something against his will—that would go against His Word. But that does not negate the fact that God truly is a loving Father who cares for us and watches over us. And He does hear and answer prayer."

Woof!

She started and glanced over her shoulder. Happy trotted into the kitchen. Joshua, dressed in his hat and coat and holding the kitten in his arms, trailed behind. His brown eyes were overbright. Her heart sank.

"If you give me a moment to get my coat, Joshua, I'll go out with you to help keep Tickles corralled and out of that tree." Matthew started toward the kitchen door.

"I think you will have to take the animals out by yourself, Reverend." She shoved the pot of gruel back off the fire, hurried to Joshua and sank to her knees to touch his flushed cheek. "Joshua has a fever."

"I'll stop by again tomorrow to see your grandmother, Miss Karcher. Good afternoon." Matthew stepped outside, slapped his winter felt on his head, tugged the collar of his chesterfield up around the nape of his neck and strode through the snow toward his cutter.

He frowned and slowed his steps before he caused the mid-calf-high snow to fly over the top of his boots and dampen his pants. He always felt as if he were escaping when he left the Karcher home. Agnes was clearly not giving up on her matrimonial ambitions, and these daily visits to her grandmother were encouraging her pursuit.

He shot a glance toward the sky—or where the sky would be if it could be seen through the thick snowfall—pulled the small flask from his coat pocket, splashed alcohol onto his palm, then held the flask against his body with his elbow and scrubbed his hands together. He still had two calls to make for Dr. Palmer before he could go home and ease his worry. "Lord, please watch over Sally and Joshua. Please touch Sally with Your healing power, and make her well. And please touch Willa's heart, oh, God. Please make her aware of Your love and care for her, and draw her heart to You. I ask it in Your holy name, Lord. Amen."

Clover whickered and tossed her head, pulled his thoughts back to his present problem. "I know, girl. If this snow doesn't stop it's going to be hard going for you." He pulled on his gloves and shoved the flask back into his pocket. "I'll bet you wish you were back in the stable, don't you?"

He shook the mare's mane free of snow, then swiped his arm over her back to clear the piled flakes off her protective winter blanket. The bells attached to the blanket's hem tinkled merrily as his body brushed against them.

He paused at the sound, looked again at the falling snow and imagined trotting down the country road with Willa close beside him in the small cutter, snowflakes clinging to her long lashes, and her blue-green eyes glowing with fun while a smile of pure pleasure curved her soft, full lips. The way she'd looked this morning when he opened the door.

Glory, but he'd wanted to take her in his arms and feel her cold lips warm beneath his, to taste of their sweetness…

He huffed a cloud of warm air, leaned into the cutter and scooped the snow off the floor, lifted the lap robe he'd used to cover the seat and dumped off the snow, then paused and eyed the narrow space. There would be room enough for all of them to take a ride, Willa beside him on the seat holding Sally on her lap, and

Josh sitting on his and learning to handle the horse. And Happy and Tickles on the floor.

If God granted his prayer, next year he'd have to buy a sleigh to accommodate a growing family. But he'd keep the cutter for special rides alone with his bride. "Grant it, Lord! Grant it, I pray."

He tossed the lap robe back over the passenger side of the tufted leather seat, put his foot on the metal step, climbed in and picked up the reins. "Let's go, Clover. Let's get these calls made so I can go home and see if I can help make that prayer come true."

There were at least seventeen or eighteen inches of snow on the church roof. If it didn't stop snowing soon they would have close to two feet by morning.

Willa moved to the top of the porch steps and clapped her hands. "Come here, Happy. Let's go see Joshua."

The dog spun around toward her and came bounding through the deep snow. He raced up the all-but-invisible steps, stopped beside her and shook, sending snow flying in every direction.

"Oh, Happy! Now see what you've done." She laughed, swiped the snow from her apron and opened the door. The dog dashed through the kitchen and thundered up the stairs.

She gave the potato soup she was keeping warm on the back of the stove a quick stir to make sure it wasn't sticking to the bottom of the pan and followed him.

The dog had curled up on the floor with his head resting on the pallet Matthew had made for Joshua in

Sally's room, his soulful black eyes fastened on his sleeping master.

"Good boy, Happy." She leaned down and placed her hand on Joshua's forehead. He was still flushed and fevered the same as earlier, but his skin wasn't hot like Sally's.

She sighed and brushed a curl back off his forehead, touched a tiny bump with her fingertip. She pulled the oil lamp on the nightstand closer, went to her knees and used both hands to brush back all of his curls. There were small, pink bumps scattered along his hairline.

His eyes blinked, opened. He stared up at her. "Whatcha doing?"

There was no sense in evading the truth. He would know soon enough. She sat back on her heels and smiled. "I was looking at your chicken pox."

His eyes widened. "I got *chicken pox?* Really?"

"Really."

"I'm gonna have Uncle Matt tell Billy!"

She laughed and brushed his hair back into place. "It isn't a contest, Joshua."

"I know, but still—" He stopped, and that slow, lopsided grin so like his uncle's slanted his rosy lips. "I guess that smelly stuff doesn't work after all."

"I guess not, Joshua."

There wasn't enough willpower in the world to stop her—not with him looking at her with that mischievous grin on his adorable face. She leaned forward and pulled him into her arms for a big hug.

"You need to drink some water, Sally."

The little girl's eyelids fluttered, stilled.

Willa slipped her arm beneath the child's small shoulders, lifted her to a sitting position and gave her a little shake. "Wake up, sweetie!"

Sally's eyes opened.

"Good girl. Now drink the water." She lifted her a little straighter and touched the cup to her fevered lips, coaxed a few swallows into her before she lowered her back to her pillow and let her sleep again.

A log on the fire hissed and snapped. She checked to make sure no cinder had popped out into the room, then wandered over to the window. It was getting late. Where was Matthew? Did he have lamps on his cutter? And what was she doing worrying about Ellen's intended? Though it was probably natural enough under the circumstances. And she should stop thinking of him as Matthew. It wasn't decent.

She frowned and returned to the bedside chair, sat and picked up her sewing. Her mother's hood had come together quickly. Quilting the lining had been painstaking work, but with so much idle time spent watching the children sleep, she'd finished it by suppertime. As soon as she finished the front edging on the hood she would be ready to add the ties.

Sally whimpered, turned onto her side and curled into a tight ball.

She studied the little girl's flushed face a moment, then resumed her sewing. She had done all she knew to do—all her mother had suggested. Why didn't Sally get better? Why hadn't she broken out with chicken pox as Joshua had? Was her sickness something else?

She thrust her sewing into the basket and rose to

touch Sally's cheek. It was so hot! If only she could *help* her.

He truly is a loving Father.... He does hear and answer prayer....

Matthew's words slipped into her thoughts. She closed her mind to them. God didn't hear *her* prayers. *Please, God in heaven. Please make my papa come home so Mama will stop crying.* Over and over she had prayed that prayer. And her father had never returned.

But her mother had stopped crying.

She froze, astounded by the thought. Her mother had stopped crying. Why had she never thought of that before?

I cried because I didn't know how I was going to care for you. We were about to lose our home and I had nowhere to go, no way to earn a living.

The memory of her mother's words brought a new understanding. She had not known why her mother was crying, but God had. And He had answered her prayer. The certainty of that settled deep into her heart and spirit. Somehow, in a way she couldn't explain, she knew it was true.

And what Matthew had said about God not forcing a man to do something against that man's own will—was that true also? Had she been wrong all these years in blaming God for what her father chose to do? And for what Thomas did?

She walked to the window and stared out into the darkness. She was a teacher. She had trained herself to look for solutions to problems, and she had absorbed enough biblical knowledge sitting in church to know that God had given man a free will. Preachers preached on it all the time. Choose! Choose! Choose!

Her heartbeat sped, yet everything inside her felt still…poised and waiting.

She wrapped her arms about her torso, closed her eyes and let the truth come. It wasn't only about choosing salvation. Freedom of will, of choice, applied to a person's every action. And her father had *chosen* to walk away.

"Forgive me, Almighty God. I've been wrong to blame You for what my papa chose to do of his own free will. Please forgive me. And thank You, Almighty God, for answering my prayer."

How clean, how *light* she felt after her whispered words. She smiled, walked to Sally's bed, sank to her knees, folded her hands and closed her eyes.

Chapter Twenty-One

Willa swirled her cloak around her shoulders and hurried toward the lean-to washroom, came to a dead halt at the sight of her mother sitting at the kitchen table. Dread squeezed her heart. "Are you taking sick, Mama?"

Her mother jerked up her head and rose from her chair. "No, I'm fine, Willa. I have something to tell you."

Something that would stop her mother from starting the laundry first thing in the morning? She couldn't imagine... She stopped fastening her cloak and stepped closer. "What is it?"

"I went to Cargrave's for laundry supplies yesterday and Mr. Hubble gave me a letter."

"A letter? For you, Mama?" Her mother never got letters. She stared at the folded sheet of paper her mother had drawn out of her apron pocket. *For any member of George Wright's family.* The boldly slanted words carried a sense of foreboding.

She took the offered missive in her hands and unfolded it, scanned the brief message.

I hereby testify that George Wright died of
pneumonia caused by the grippe on October
eighteenth, in the year of our lord, 1840. By
my hand, Doctor Harold Tremont, Binghamton,
New York.

Her papa was never coming home.

The finality of it crushed the little girl's hope she
hadn't realized was still a part of her—a hope that had
been buried under years of anger. She pushed away
the sorrow for all that would never be, squared her
shoulders and handed the letter back to her mother.
"Well, now we know what has happened to Papa." She
lifted her hands and fastened her cloak.

"Yes…" Her mother's hands covered hers. "Are you
all right, Willa?"

She forced a smile. "I'm fine, Mama. Are you?"
She studied her mother's face, found a sort of relieved
peace in her green eyes.

"Yes, Willa. I am."

"I'm glad." She leaned forward and kissed her
mother's cheek. "I have to hurry, Mama. I'm worried
about Sally." She yanked up her hood and headed for
the door.

"I've been praying for the little girl. The Lord will
undertake."

She whipped around, stared agape. "You *pray,*
Mama?"

"Well, of course, Willa. God is the only reason I've
managed all of these years."

"My face itches."

"Mine, too."

What beautiful words. And what a beautiful sight. Willa looked from the small bumps and blisters on Joshua's forehead to the pink bumps on Sally's face and clenched her hands, fought to keep from turning into Matthew's arms and crying out her relief against his strong shoulder.

Joshua lifted his hands and scratched at his scalp.

"Oh, no! You mustn't scratch at the itch, Joshua. It will make it worse, and perhaps leave a scar."

A chuckle rumbled from Matthew.

She lifted her gaze up, met his. The look in his eyes mesmerized her. She stood immobile as he clasped his hands behind his back and leaned toward her.

"That is no way to stop Joshua from scratching, Miss Wright. Little boys look on scars as badges of honor. They wear them proudly."

His whispered words filled her mind. Everything in her wanted to be in his arms. She closed her eyes lest her emotion show in them. When had she fallen in love with Matthew Calvert?

She leaned down and snatched the small pouch of oatmeal. "I'll go downstairs and make you a poultice that will help the itching, Joshua. I'll make you one also, Sally. Please don't scratch. I'll be right back."

She sailed out the door and hurried down the stairs, tears stinging her eyes. Stop feeling sorry for yourself! You knew Matthew and Ellen are about to announce their betrothal. How could you be so disloyal to your friend as to fall in love with her intended!

She marched into the buttery, snatched up a piece of cheesecloth and hurried back to the work table.

The clack of bootheels against the hall floor warned her Matthew was headed for the kitchen.

She grabbed the oatmeal out of the tin cupboard and rushed to make the poultice. She did *not* want a repeat of the time they had spent alone in the kitchen yesterday. She folded the cheesecloth double, spooned oatmeal onto it then twisted the edges of the cheesecloth closed and wound the twine around the narrow neck. Her trembling fingers botched the tie. The twist loosened.

"Having trouble?"

Please don't help—

"You twist it tight and hold it. I'll tie it for you."

Don't tremble! She glared at her hands, held her breath as his fingers touched hers.

"I was relieved to learn Mr. Dibble is escorting you home at night." He crossed the ends of twine one over the other, pulled them taut. "I was concerned about your walking home alone."

She felt his gaze on her as if it were a touch. *Don't look at him.*

"Did you want a bow?"

She swallowed to ease the tightness in her throat. "A knot is fine."

"Mr. Dibble is a wonderful example of how God ministers to his children by using us as His hands and feet. As are you, by caring for my children."

She had to stop him—to make him leave before she broke down. "And you, Reverend? Did God use your hands to save me from Thomas?" It had the desired effect. His hands stilled, dropped away. She took a relieved breath.

"How did you know?"

"Sophia Sheffield mentioned that she saw you driving your buggy toward Olville the night Thomas disappeared and that no one could discover where you went, or what emergency had called you out that time of night. And when we took Mary home from school, I noticed your knuckles were bruised."

"I see."

She dropped the two pouches into a bowl, grabbed the teakettle from the back of the stove, poured warm water over them and put the teakettle back.

"I told you I would never let him hurt you."

His voice! So quiet. So...*caring.* And why wouldn't it be? He was a pastor. It was his job to care. She blinked the tears from her eyes and lifted her chin. "Yes, you did, but I didn't understand then. Thank you for...whatever you did that convinced Thomas to leave Pinewood."

She gathered her courage and looked at him. "And thank you for what you said yesterday. I realized later that you were right. God *had* answered my childhood prayer—my mother had stopped crying." She took a deep breath. "And you were also right about God giving man free will. All these years I've blamed God for my father abandoning us—until yesterday. I know now I was wrong. It was my father who *chose* to forsake us. And today I learned he will never return."

The tears came back, pooled in her eyes and overflowed. She wiped them from her cheeks. "Mama got a letter. My father is dead."

His eyes darkened and tiny gold flames sprang to

life in their depths. "Willa…" He started around the table.

Her heart lurched, yearned to go into his arms. Foolish heart, wanting his pastoral desire to comfort her to be something more, longing for a man beloved by a friend. She shook her head.

Someone banged on the front door.

He stopped, his chest heaved as he drew in and blew out a breath. The person banged again—louder. He clenched his hands, turned and strode out of the kitchen.

She sagged against the table and swallowed hard to keep the tears from flowing.

Matthew's footsteps thudded against the hall floor. She straightened and faced the door.

He stepped back into the kitchen wearing his hat and coat, his face taut, unreadable. His gaze sought and held hers. "Grandmother Karcher has taken a turn for the worse. I have to go."

She nodded. "I'll tell Joshua and Sally. Please give my sympathies to the Karchers."

His mouth parted as if to speak, then closed. He nodded and left the room.

She listened to his footsteps fade, squeezed the excess water from the pouches and carried them upstairs.

"I'm home, Mama!"

Willa set down the basket, removed her cloak, hung it on its peg and turned. "Mr. Dibble!" Shock colored her voice.

She shifted her gaze to her mother. Gracious! What

had happened to her mother? Her hair was in soft waves around her face instead of pulled straight back into a bun, and she was wearing her best dress with no apron. And Mr. Dibble's large, callused hands were resting on her narrow shoulders! "Mama..."

"I have news, Willa." Her mother fixed her gaze on her. "Mr. Dibble and I just returned from Olville. We're married."

"Mama!" She closed her gaping mouth, tried to make sense of her mother's words. "You're *married?*"

"I know it seems quick-like, Willa, but it's not."

"I've loved your mama since we were young."

David Dibble's words brought color rushing into her mother's cheeks. She'd never seen her mother blush.

"It's my fault we weren't married way back then, Willa. We planned to. Then David had to go help his granny settle up on the farm and all when his grandpa died, and your papa came to town." Her mother took a deep breath. "He favored me over the other girls and that turned me proud and wrongheaded and I married him."

Her mother held out her hands and stepped toward her. "I'll never be sorry 'cause I got you, Willa. And you're the best thing that ever happened to me. But my foolishness cost David and me all these years of being alone." Her mother's chin raised. "He's stayed faithful to his promise to me all these years, Willa. So I went this morning and told him about the letter and that I wasn't a married woman anymore. And he..." The color swept back into her mother's cheeks—she looked young and beautiful. Willa blinked away the tears that sprang to her eyes. "Well, after a bit, he said,

'I'll get the buggy hitched' and we drove to Olville and got married."

She rushed forward, hugged her mother and finally found her voice. "I'm happy for you, Mama, truly happy." She looked up at the man she'd known as a friend all of her life and smiled. "I guess I know now why you've been escorting me home, Mr. Dibble."

He grinned down at her. "Just take a thing for what it is, Willa."

She laughed and shook her head. "I shall, as soon as I get used to all of this news."

Her mother stepped back and looked up at her. "I been so full of my news, I didn't think to ask…why are you home early, Willa? Is the little girl better?"

"Yes, she is, Mama." She forced a brightness she was far from feeling into her voice. "And Bertha is back. I won't be tending Reverend Calvert's children any longer."

"I see." Her mother fixed a look on her, then nodded. "Well, we need to start gathering up things. I told Mr. Townsend I won't be doing laundry for the loggers and we'll be taking our things to David's house tonight."

Her whole life had turned upside down. Willa sat on the edge of the stripped bed, looked around the room she had called her own all of her years, and tried to think of what to do. She did not want to intrude on her mother's newfound happiness with Mr. Dibble. And how could she bear to watch Matthew and Ellen marry? How could she bear to teach Joshua and Sally when—

She got to her feet, went to the bedside table and opened her wooden box. Mr. Dibble would take care of her mother now. She could use the money she had been saving to make her mother a new cloak to go away. It would pay her stage fare to Buffalo, and once there she would get a job and build a new life.

She took the money from the box, placed it in her reticule, then checked to make sure she hadn't missed any coins. There was a folded piece of paper in the bottom of the box. *Thomas's note.*

Tears filmed her eyes and blurred the words. How could she ever have thought Thomas and Matthew were the same? How had she let her anger at her father's abandonment blind her to the truth of Matthew's goodness? Not that it would have mattered. Matthew loved Ellen.

She blinked, laid the note on the nightstand, snatched the curtain tie off the window and tied it around the large wicker basket that held her other dress and personal grooming items to hold the top on. She was ready.

She snatched up Thomas's note, looked around the empty room, grabbed the basket handle and walked into the sitting room.

"All done, Willa?"

"Yes. There's nothing left." She threw Thomas's note in the fire, watched it burst into flame, turn black and curl, then turn into ash. "But I'm not going to Mr. Dibble's with you tonight, Mama. Bertha is back, school is still closed and I'm free now. I'm going to Buffalo to see Callie. She's been asking me to come for a visit."

"But Willa—"

"I haven't time to talk about it, Mama." She leaned forward and kissed her mother's cheek. "If I hurry I can catch the trolley to Olville."

Chapter Twenty-Two

Matthew trudged up the stairs, weary to his bones. He'd spent a long day conducting Grandmother Karcher's funeral and interment, then sitting with Simon Pritchard who remained seriously ill.

He frowned and walked down the hall. The weariness came not from any physical exertion, but rather from the frustration and heaviness in his heart. Still, Dr. Palmer no longer needed his help, and the comfort calls to pray with the sick were coming to an end. The people living in Pinewood were hardy, it seemed. And those who were going to catch the grippe already had. The spread of the disease through the village had halted. He would soon be able to put an end to the frustration one way or the other.

He opened the door and stepped to Sally's bedside, gazed down at the small pock mark at her temple and felt again the rush of thankfulness for her healing and for Willa's loving care of his children.

Willa. His frustration. Her presence lingered in the house, and the need to go after her, to find out what had gone wrong and to make amends gnawed at him.

Every time he entered Sally's bedroom or the kitchen, memories of her assailed him and made his heart ache. He would never forget the way she had looked standing right here beside him the day Sally's chicken pox had erupted and her high fever had broken. They had shared the thankfulness, the joy of that moment when their gazes met, and he'd had to clasp his hands behind his back to keep from taking her in his arms.

How he wished he'd had the right, and that she were here with him now as his wife. "'Hope deferred maketh the heart sick: but *when* the desire cometh, *it is* a tree of life.' That's Your Word, Lord, and I stand on that promise. You have drawn Willa into Your arms, now draw her into mine, I pray."

Tickles's ears twitched his way at his whisper, one eye slitted open. He soothed the curled-up cat with a few strokes of its yellow fur, stepped to the fireplace, added wood and left the room.

The hall echoed with the tap of Willa's shoes and the brush of her long skirts against the floor. He frowned and stepped to Joshua's door. He'd been so certain that day that she returned his love. He'd seen it in her eyes and felt it in the tremble of her hands at his touch. And he *knew* she loved Joshua and Sally. So what had gone wrong? Why had she left town?

He stepped into Joshua's room. Happy jumped off the bed and came to him, tail wagging. He petted the dog and glanced at the fireplace. Red coals shimmered against the darkness. Tiny flames flickered around a blackened chunk of wood. He went to the woodbox, picked up an oak log with a thick burl that would burn until morning and added it to the fire.

The bed rustled. He turned, smiled at Joshua. "I thought you were asleep."

"I been praying." The boy's earnest gaze met his. "When will Miss Wright come back, Uncle Matt? Sally and me like Bertha an' all, but…well, Miss Wright sorta felt like a mama. Could she be our mama, Uncle Matt?"

He'd never known how a child's hurt could rend your heart in pieces, but he was learning fast. He sat on the edge of the bed. "I don't know, Josh. But God knows." He brushed his hand over the boy's curls and touched his cheek. "You keep praying. And I promise you, with God's help, I will do my very best to bring Miss Wright back."

Willa brushed snow from her cloak, opened the door of the Connors' brick home and stepped into the spacious entrance hall.

"Oh!" She glanced at Callie and the gentleman dressed in a gray double-breasted coat and holding a black felt top hat. He looked familiar, but Callie had so many beaus seeking to court her that it was hard to remember them. "Forgive me, I didn't mean to intrude."

"Not at all, Willa." Callie shot her a look. "I'm sure you remember Mr. Washington? He was just leaving."

She returned the man's polite nod and turned her back to give them privacy while she removed her cloak. She fussed and fumbled with the fastenings and ignored the words murmured in the man's low voice— the look Callie had given her meant Callie did not want her to leave them alone. At last the door opened and closed. She turned around at the click of the latch.

"Thank you, Willa." Callie sighed and led the way into the family sitting room. "I thought he would *never* leave."

"And who could blame him?" She smiled at her friend. "You are simply stunning with those black curls and violet eyes, Callie Connor. I've known you all of my life, and I still find your beauty arresting."

"Please don't say such things, Willa. I get weary of hearing them." Callie slapped at the rows of flounces on her long silk skirt. "*And* of wearing these ridiculous fancy gowns. What I wouldn't give to wear a simple wool dress, don an apron and make some molasses ginger cookies. The kind Aunt Sophie makes."

"I'll loan you mine if you give me one of the cookies."

Callie laughed. "I would accept your kind offer if your gown would fit. But, alas, you're more slender than I."

"A bit, perhaps." She shook out her own plain skirt and sat on the settee in front of the fire, smiled as Callie floated onto the seat beside her—an accurate description given the amount of yardage in all those flounces.

"I'm so glad you came to visit, Willa. It's like having a bit of Pinewood here."

Callie's wistful tone sparked a longing in her for home. She closed off the thoughts before they could reach her hurting heart. She dare not think of Matthew and Joshua and Sally.

"Tell me what happened at your meeting with the

school board." Callie's beautiful eyes were alight with interest.

She drew her thoughts from Pinewood to her new life.

"I believe it went well." She brushed a piece of lint off her wool skirt, fingered a spot that was thinning. She had best find gainful employment soon. "The board members seemed satisfied with the answers I gave to their questions. And—" she looked at Callie and smiled "—I have an interview with the principal of the Swan Street school on Thursday."

"Willa, that's wonderful! Oh, I wish Mother and Father would let me do something besides parade around for the benefit of wealthy men!"

There was a rustle of sound at the doorway. She rose to leave, paused when Callie stood and gripped her arm.

"Good afternoon, Callie, I— Willa!" Surprise flitted across Ellen's face. "I didn't know you were in Buffalo." She rushed forward.

Ellen looked prettier than ever. Willa's heart sank, her stomach knotted. She wasn't ready to face Ellen, to talk about Matthew.

"What fun to have you here, Willa. It would be like old times if only Sadie were here also." Ellen gave her a quick hug, thrust her lower lip out in a pout. "I'm so sorry I haven't time to visit, but Mr. Boyd is calling on me this evening."

Mr. Boyd? A friend?

Ellen's blue eyes gleamed with excitement. "Callie, I simply had to come and thank you for gaining me an invitation to the Halseys' soiree. I'm so *thrilled* to be attending. I know if you want to be accepted into *the* social circuit, you simply *must* be included." Ellen smiled, glanced in the mirror over the mantel and fluffed her curls. "Mr. Boyd has already asked if he might be my dinner partner. Of course, I delayed answering in hope that Mr. Lodge will ask me." Ellen glanced her way. "Harold Lodge is the heir to the Lodge Shipping Line."

Mr. Boyd? Mr. Lodge? "And what of Reverend Calvert, Ellen?"

"Reverend Calvert?"

"Yes, the man you love." How those words hurt.

"Oh, poof!" Ellen made a pretty little moue. "Matthew is fine for Pinewood, Willa. He holds a position of honor in the village, and he is *exceedingly* handsome, but his calling as a pastor is too demanding. And his wards and those animals—"

"So, because of his *children* and their pets, you are not being faithful to him?" Her disgust leaked into her voice. "What of his love for you?" A band of pain tightened around her chest at the thought.

"The way Matthew loves is not good enough for me." Ellen's lower lip pouted out again. "Why, he wouldn't even stay home with me when I asked him. And after all the trouble I went to cooking his dinner and caring for his wards!"

She stared, caught a ragged breath. "You told me you were to be *betrothed.* That you would soon be *wed.*"

Ellen's face flushed. "Well, I changed my mind. What good is a husband who is so concerned with others?" Ellen's smooth brow creased into a frown.

"What's wrong with you, Willa? Why are you looking at me that way?"

She clenched her hands, lifted her chin, looked straight into Ellen's big, beautiful blue eyes and forced words out of her constricted throat. "Because your vanity and your selfishness have ruined my life."

Ellen's mouth gaped.

She turned her back and walked from the room.

"Whoa, Clover." Matthew draped the reins over the dashboard and climbed from the cutter. He grabbed the top lap robe from the pile on the passenger side of the seat, tossed it over his own place and snatched the tether weight off the floor.

The three men in the yard in front of Dibble's Livery looked his way, stood watching. He waved a hand in recognition, snubbed the tether rope to Clover's bridle and strode up the shoveled path to David Dibble's house, rehearsing the reasons why Willa's mother should tell him where she had gone. There was a horseshoe for a knocker. He banged it against the metal plate embedded in the door, rocked back on his heels and waited.

The men watched.

The door opened.

He gazed down at the slender woman looking up at him with eyes amazingly like Willa's, only green, and whipped off his hat. "Mrs. Dibble?"

"Yes?"

"I'm Reverend Calvert. I've come to inquire about Willa."

Her gaze locked on his, her head tilted and her lips pursed. "About time, I'd say."

He blinked, taken aback by her unexpected remark, then smiled and met her gaze full on.

Her lips curved into an answering smile. "Well, I can see why my daughter fell in love with you."

His breath gusted out in a gray cloud.

She laughed, stepped back and pulled the door open wider. "No need to stand out in the cold, Reverend. Come in where it's warm so we can talk."

"Willa, you have to go back to Pinewood." Callie gave her an earnest look. "It's the only sensible thing to do. If Reverend Calvert is half as wonderful as you say he is, he'll understand."

She shook her head and moved closer to the fire seeking warmth. She hadn't stopped shivering since Ellen's visit, and she was terribly afraid her inner cold was caused by her anger with her friend.

"And what do I say to him, Callie? I'm sorry, Reverend. I abandoned your children and ran like a coward because I'm in love with you?" She caught her breath at her spoken admission.

"It would probably work."

Her lips twitched at Callie's wry tone. She smiled, gulped and burst into tears. "Oh, Callie! He'd probably think me *mad*." She sank into a nearby chair and covered her face with her hands. "I don't know how Matthew feels about me. Just because Ellen lied about his feelings for her doesn't mean he cares for me. I— I thought perhaps— I mean, the way he looked at me and spoke my name was— Oh, I'm being pathetic!"

She lifted her head and wiped the moisture from her cheeks. "What I saw in Matthew Calvert's eyes was most likely nothing more than gratitude for my care of his children. I must stop this foolishness and concentrate on building my new life here in Buffalo."

Matthew took the reins in one hand, lifted the other arm and blew warm air into the cuff of his leather glove to warm his fingers. He wiggled his toes and clacked his feet together beneath the lap robe that covered them, relaxed his hunched shoulders and drew his head into the robe draped around his shoulders to protect his ears from the biting cold.

The tinkle of bells sounded clear on the night air. He glanced over his shoulder at the large sleigh drawing close behind him, turned and snapped the reins to urge Clover to pick up her pace.

It wasn't far now. He'd soon be in Dunkirk where Clover could feast on some grain and have a well-deserved rest in the stables at the hotel while he slept away what remained of the night.

Tomorrow.

The word jolted through him. Tomorrow he was going to see Willa. And, somehow, in spite of Ellen's lies about his intentions, he was going to convince her of his love and bring her home as his bride.

He glanced up at the moonlit sky and sent the prayer winging. *"'Hope deferred maketh the heart sick: but when the desire cometh, it is a tree of life.' Grant this my hope and prayer, oh Lord. Grant it, and turn it into a blessed new life for all of us, I pray. Amen."*

Chapter Twenty-Three

Willa sighed, set aside the book she was pretending to read and rose. She really wasn't in the mood to rescue Callie from another of her gentleman callers, but she would answer her friend's summons and go and intrude on their privacy and stay until the man got disgusted and left. Hopefully, this time it wouldn't take long.

She shook her head and hurried down the hall from the library to the formal sitting room where Callie received her suitors. How ill-mannered these wealthy city men must find Callie's poor country friend. Well, so be it.

She paused outside the door to catch her breath, then pasted a smile on her face and swept into the sitting room. "Callie, dear, I simply must—"

Her heart lurched, stopped. "Matthew!" She stared, her senses reeling. "What—" The blood drained from her face. She pressed her hand to her chest to stop her heart's sudden wild pounding. "Sally..."

"No, Willa! Sally is fine and so is Joshua." He moved toward her. "I'm sorry if I frightened you."

She nodded, closed her eyes and took a calming breath. "I'm only glad—" She stopped, opened her eyes and stared at him. "How did you find me?"

"Your mother told me where you were." He took another step toward her.

"My *mother?*" She slipped behind an upholstered chair. She felt safer with something solid between them. "I don't understand. You don't know Mama. How— I mean, why—" She clamped her lips together, tried to order her jumbled thoughts.

"I heard you had left town and I called on your mother to ask where you were." He took another step, locked his gaze on hers.

His eyes! Her heart started its wild pounding again.

"You see, I wanted to tell you that until the day I walked into the Oak Street schoolhouse with Joshua and Sally, I had never met a woman who drew my heart."

He came around the chair. Her mouth went dry.

"But there you were, so neat and trim and prim and proper. And when I looked into your eyes—"

He lifted his hand, cupped the side of her face and brushed his thumb along her cheekbone. Her knees went weak.

"Your beautiful, blue-green eyes…"

He lowered his head and his breath touched her cheek. She held hers…waited.

"I fell in love with you."

His lips touched hers, soft…gentle…questing… She slipped her arms around his neck, went on tiptoe and pressed her parted lips against his in answer. His arms tightened, his lips parted and he claimed her mouth fully. Time and place fell away.

At last Matthew lifted his head, drew in a ragged breath. She laid her head against his chest, her breathing unsteady, her heart stumbling to find its rhythm. His heart thudded beneath her ear. Joy flooded her eyes with tears.

His finger slid beneath her chin, tilted her head up until their gazes met...held.

"I love you, Willa. I'm not a rich man, but I have wealth enough to ensure you comfort and freedom from want. And I have two adorable children who want you for their mother almost as much as I want you for my wife. Will you marry us?" His voice, rich and deep and warm, flowed over her like a caress, saying the words she'd so longed to hear.

She blinked away the tears, touched his cheek with her hand. "I don't care about wealth, Matthew. All I need to make me secure is your love. I love you. And I love Joshua and Sally." Warmth spread along her cheekbones. "I want very much to be your wife and to be their mother."

He sucked in another ragged breath and claimed her lips in a kiss that promised forever.

"See, Sally. I told you she's our mama now. That's what Papa used to do to Mama."

Joshua?

Joshua! And *Sally.* She stiffened, jerked back as far as Matthew's arms would allow.

"Does that mean we can call you gramma and grampa now?"

"It surely does, Sally."

"Mama!" She twisted around in Matthew's arms, stared at her mother and David Dibble and Joshua and Sally—and Callie beside them, laughing. "What— How—"

Matthew chuckled and drew her back against him. "David brought them along in his sleigh to attend our wedding—" his mouth slanted in that lopsided grin that made her heart stop and her stomach flutter "—just in case you said yes."

Her mother smiled, came to her and touched her cheek. "And after you're wed, David and I will take our new grandchildren home and care for them while you and Matthew spend a few days here in Buffalo."

"And Happy."

"And Tickles."

David Dibble chuckled. "Looks like we're gonna have a lively house for a few days."

Her mother laughed and shook her head. "It does indeed." She walked back, corralled Joshua and Sally with a hand on each of their small backs and started out the door. "Come along now, you two. We need to get your coats and hats on for the ride to the church."

"The church?" She looked at Matthew, got another lopsided, stomach-fluttering grin.

"I wanted everything to be ready—just in case. So I talked with a preacher on my way here. He's waiting to perform the ceremony that will join us forever." He gave her another lingering kiss, then took a deep breath and tucked her hand in his arm. "Let's go get married, Miss Wright."

* * * * *

Dear Reader,

It is always exciting to begin a journey. When I was young, I would get butterflies in my stomach when our family would climb in the car and start on a visit to Grandma's house. *Wooing the Schoolmarm* is the beginning of a different sort of journey, but I still had butterflies in my stomach as I began writing this new Pinewood Weddings series.

There are always challenges to be met when you embark on a new journey, and I pray that with God's help, I met the ones I encountered while writing *Wooing the Schoolmarm* in such a way that you delighted in the triumph of love in Willa and Matthew's story. And I hope you enjoyed getting to know the village of Pinewood and its residents.

Willa's friends will be returning to Pinewood as I write their stories. Desperation has made the stunningly beautiful, sweet-natured Callie Connor request that I write her story next. She simply can no longer abide being pursued by wealthy city men who think they can buy her like some bauble in a jewelry store!

I do enjoy hearing from my readers. If you would care to share your thoughts about Willa and Matthew's story, or about Pinewood village with me, I may be contacted at dorothyjclark@hotmail.com or www.dorothyjclark.com.

Until Callie comes home to Pinewood,

Dorothy Clark

Questions for Discussion

1. Matthew Calvert became the guardian for his young niece and nephew. How did that event affect his search for a wife? Did it alter his qualifications for a mate? In what way? Why?

2. Matthew is a pastor. What difficulty does his calling put in the way of his desire to marry Willa? Why should it matter?

3. Willa's father abandoned her as a child. Did his act have long-lasting consequences in Willa's life? How did it color her opinions as she grew? How did it affect her faith?

4. Do you believe Willa's father's desertion of her uniquely suited her to help Joshua and Sally? In what way?

5. Joshua and Sally were traumatized by the loss of their mother and father in a carriage accident. How did Willa's suggestion of pets for the children help them over their grief? Do you believe pets can help people through traumatic times? Can you give an example?

6. Matthew explained the principle of "free choice" given to man by God. How did his explanation help to bring about Willa's healing and her return to her faith? What changed?

7. Willa's mother explained to Willa that there is a difference between gossip and talk. Do you believe there is a difference? What is it?

8. Matthew prayed for wisdom to help Willa find her way back to God's arms, even if he never held her in his own arms as his wife. How does that prove Matthew's love for Willa is true?

9. The story is set in a rural village in 1840. Would Willa and her mother's circumstances be improved or worsened if the story took place in the present?

10. Did God turn Matthew's sacrifice into a blessing? How? Has God ever used something you fully expected to be a sacrifice to bless you?

11. What strong character trait dictated Willa's treatment of Ellen? Was there more than one? What are they? Was she right or wrong in your opinion?

12. Have you, or someone you know, ever suffered a traumatic event that affected your faith? Was the effect positive or negative? What makes the difference in the outcome?

COMING NEXT MONTH
from Love Inspired® Historical
AVAILABLE AUGUST 7, 2012

CHARITY HOUSE COURTSHIP
Charity House
Renee Ryan

When a misunderstanding puts Laney O'Connor at odds with hotel owner Marc Dupree, the truth endangers Laney's beloved Charity House orphanage—but silence could ruin her chances with Marc forever.

THE SOLDIER'S WIFE
Cheryl Reavis

Bound by a promise, Jack Murphy heads to North Carolina, and war widow Sayer Garth. If only he could be certain that his past won't put them both at risk....

GROOM WANTED
Debra Ullrick

The plan was for best friends Leah Bowen and Jake Lure to select each other's mail-order spouses. As the postings pour in, will they spot happiness waiting close to home?

INSTANT PRAIRIE FAMILY
Bonnie Navarro

Will Hopkins's new housekeeper was supposed to be matronly and middle-aged. Young, beautiful Abby Stewart is determined to win him and his sons over—in spite of Will's best intentions!

Look for these and other Love Inspired books wherever books are sold, including most bookstores, supermarkets, discount stores and drugstores.

LIHCNM0712

REQUEST YOUR FREE BOOKS!

2 FREE INSPIRATIONAL NOVELS
PLUS 2
FREE
MYSTERY GIFTS

Love Inspired.

HISTORICAL
INSPIRATIONAL HISTORICAL ROMANCE

YES! Please send me 2 FREE Love Inspired® Historical novels and my 2 FREE mystery gifts (gifts are worth about $10). After receiving them, if I don't wish to receive any more books, I can return the shipping statement marked "cancel". If I don't cancel, I will receive 4 brand-new novels every month and be billed just $4.49 per book in the U.S. or $4.99 per book in Canada. That's a saving of at least 22% off the cover price. It's quite a bargain! Shipping and handling is just 50¢ per book in the U.S. and 75¢ per book in Canada.* I understand that accepting the 2 free books and gifts places me under no obligation to buy anything. I can always return a shipment and cancel at any time. Even if I never buy another book, the two free books and gifts are mine to keep forever.

102/302 IDN FEHF

Name	(PLEASE PRINT)	
Address		Apt. #
City	State/Prov.	Zip/Postal Code

Signature (if under 18, a parent or guardian must sign)

Mail to the **Reader Service:**
IN U.S.A.: P.O. Box 1867, Buffalo, NY 14240-1867
IN CANADA: P.O. Box 609, Fort Erie, Ontario L2A 5X3

Not valid for current subscribers to Love Inspired Historical books.

Want to try two free books from another series?
Call 1-800-873-8635 or visit www.ReaderService.com.

* Terms and prices subject to change without notice. Prices do not include applicable taxes. Sales tax applicable in N.Y. Canadian residents will be charged applicable taxes. Offer not valid in Quebec. This offer is limited to one order per household. All orders subject to credit approval. Credit or debit balances in a customer's account(s) may be offset by any other outstanding balance owed by or to the customer. Please allow 4 to 6 weeks for delivery. Offer available while quantities last.

Your Privacy—The Reader Service is committed to protecting your privacy. Our Privacy Policy is available online at www.ReaderService.com or upon request from the Reader Service.

We make a portion of our mailing list available to reputable third parties that offer products we believe may interest you. If you prefer that we not exchange your name with third parties, or if you wish to clarify or modify your communication preferences, please visit us at www.ReaderService.com/consumerschoice or write to us at Reader Service Preference Service, P.O. Box 9062, Buffalo, NY 14269. Include your complete name and address.

Love Inspired HISTORICAL

celebrating
15
YEARS

Finding love in unexpected places

Another inspirational tale by

DEBRA ULLRICK

It's the perfect plan—best friends Leah Bowen and Jake Lure will each advertise for mail-order spouses, and then help each other select their future mates. When the responses to the postings pour in, it seems all their dreams will soon come true. But the closer they get to the altar, the less appealing marrying a stranger becomes. Will they both realize that the perfect one has been there the entire time?

Groom Wanted

Available in August wherever books are sold.

www.LoveInspiredBooks.com

LIH82929